THE HAMPTON CONNECTION

G. P. PUTNAM'S SONS/NEW YORK

THE
HAMPTON CONNECTION

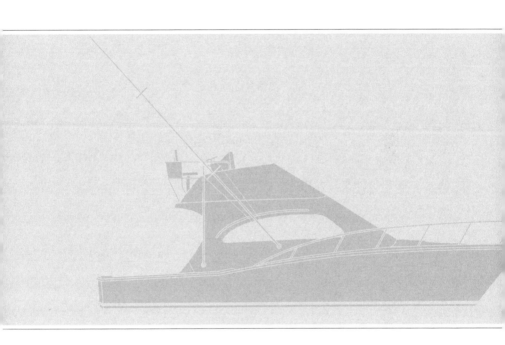

VINCENT LARDO

This is a work of fiction. Names, characters, places, and incidents either
are the product of the author's imagination or are used fictitiously,
and any resemblance to actual persons, living or dead, business
establishments, events, or locales is entirely coincidental.

G. P. PUTNAM'S SONS
Publishers Since 1838
a member of
Penguin Putnam Inc.
375 Hudson Street
New York, NY 10014

Library of Congress Cataloging-in-Publication Data

Lardo, Vincent.
The Hampton connection / Vincent Lardo.
p.   cm.
ISBN 0-399-14631-8
1. Hamptons (N.Y.)—Fiction.   I. Title.
PS3562.A7213 H36   2001   00-051728
813'.54—dc21

Printed in the United States of America

1   3   5   7   9   10   8   6   4   2

This book is printed on acid-free paper. ⊗

Book design by Gretchen Achilles

ACKNOWLEDGMENTS

Besides the haves and have-nots and the famous and the infamous, East Hampton is also home to the Ashwagh Hall Writers' Workshop. Founded and facilitated by Marijane Meaker (writing professionally as M. E. Kerr), the workshop has encouraged, nurtured and provided a shoulder for East End writers for almost two decades. I am grateful for this opportunity to acknowledge the workshop, its director and its staunch supporting cast.

FOR

DR. ALBERT SABATINI

THE HAMPTON CONNECTION

PROLOGUE

The sun was just setting when the fishing boat pulled out of its pier on Lake Montauk and veered north. Night fishing is a popular sport in Montauk, the easternmost village on Long Island's south fork, but the craft carried only the boat's captain and one crew member. The pilot was well into his fifth decade, the boy not yet done with his second.

The boat headed for the inlet that would take it into Long Island Sound, passing Gosman's Dock, a sprawling enterprise named after its founders. The original Gosman family offered the summer residents of East Hampton a popular seafood restaurant, a clam bar, refreshment stalls, fish markets and several gift shops. On this chilly March evening Gosman's was dark and hushed as if holding its breath in anticipation of spring and the annual invasion of paying customers.

Man and boy wore pea coats and navy blue watch caps for protection against the damp March night. The prow of the boat cut through a dense fog as it entered Long Island Sound, setting a northwesterly course toward glorious Block Island, linked to Montauk by a pleasant ferry ride of just under two hours.

Block Island, a popular excursion for day-trippers, a part of Rhode Island, is as quaint a parcel of New England real estate as its neighbors, Martha's Vineyard and Nantucket. Its official location is Rhode Island

Sound, but only a seaman with professional nautical instruments could say where Long Island Sound ends and Rhode Island Sound begins.

Several hours later, in either of these sounds, the fishing boat turned off its engine and bobbed in the choppy sea beneath a sky as pitch black as the surrounding water. The man and the boy waited patiently, speaking not a word, until they heard the powerful engine of another vessel in the immediate vicinity. The latecomer switched on its fog lights as it approached, emerging from the mist like a sea monster to expertly align itself with the fishing boat. The trawler's name, *Billy Budd*, was clearly visible on its hull.

"Now that's a good omen," the captain whispered to his young mate, "same name as you."

The boy was certain the man did not know the origin of the name *Billy Budd*, or how the story ended. He decided not to offer a crash course in American literature but, fingering his throat, prayed that the name was anything but an omen.

Only one man was visible on the deck of the *Billy Budd*. He wore black jeans and a black turtleneck sweater. The boy avoided looking directly at the man and the man hardly glanced back at either the boy or his companion. Then the man in black tossed a package across the few feet of sea that separated the rolling rails of the two boats. In return, the captain of the fishing boat hurled a much larger package onto the deck of the *Billy Budd*.

From a third craft, unmarked and as invisible as Block Island's shoreline, two men watched as much of the exchange through binoculars as the lights emanating from the rendezvousing boats allowed.

BILL RYAN

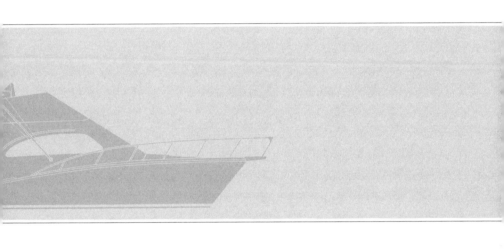

CHAPTER ONE

Job's Fishing Lodge consisted of ten shacks fronted by a two-story clapboard residence with the word ICE painted over the front door. Some years back the OFF had given way to erosion and no one had bothered to repair the damage. In fact, since the death of Job Ryan's wife, very little had been done in the way of upkeep either to the house or to the cottages. The misleading sign was of no consequence as there was not now, nor had there ever been, an office in Job's home. The business of renting cottages or the chartering of his boat, *Job's Patience*—both a rare occurrence of late—took place in the more homey atmosphere of the family kitchen.

Job liked to exaggerate to his fishermen cronies the number of summer people who had knocked on his front door in search of a bag of ice when riding along West Lake Drive.

Another mystifying sign was posted in the bathrooms of each of the ten cabins. This one cautioned guests not to clean fish in the bathtub. There was not now, nor had there ever been, a bathtub in any of Job's lodgings. Had the signs been posted in advance of future installations of bathtubs, one would be hard pressed to clean anything in them as they would have to be positioned vertically for the room to accommodate them.

Mrs. Ryan's fishnet curtains were also a casualty of her passing. These were not physically removed until they had been allowed to rot on their rods. Job Ryan lamented the fact that his daughter, Heather, was not the housekeeper her mother had been. "But the girl is the best mate in the whole damn fleet of commercial fishing boats working out of Montauk," Job Ryan often boasted.

Losing the restraining hand of her mother too early, Heather had grown as carefree and fetching as her namesake flower, which blankets Scotland's landscape with its delicate pink blossoms each spring. Her blond hair was bleached almost white in the summer months, adding a special luster to the dark eyes her mother claimed were part of their Indian heritage. Her nose was straight and small, her mouth a bit too wide, but one rarely dwelled on this minute flaw when assaying her slim waist, firm breasts and shapely legs.

One of the most popular girls at East Hampton High, Heather took none of her suitors seriously. She wasn't a tease, but rather a gregarious teenager who derived more pleasure from hauling in a ten-pound bass than being mauled at the East Hampton cinema on Saturday night. Heather was considered a perk by the fishermen who went out on *Job's Patience,* where her tomboy attire—jeans and rugby shirt—enhanced rather than hid her lithe figure, and her way with a rod and reel was the envy of the weekend anglers.

West Lake Drive is a few miles east of Old Montauk Highway as the crow flies and a few light-years away as real estate values fluctuate. The old highway that follows the coast with more ups and downs than an amusement park roller coaster is the address of the famous Gurney's Inn and Spa, several upscale motels and numerous homes of the rich and famous, all perched on a cliff towering over white, sandy beaches and the Atlantic Ocean.

The better motels on West Lake Drive are, of course, right on Lake Montauk, along with a number of marinas and commercial fishing docks. The lake's inlet at Gosman's Dock gives the fishing vessels a scenic waterway into Long Island Sound and the ocean.

Job's grandfather had built the lodge on the wrong side of the drive because the land there is more solid, and besides, "He never gave an inchworm's ass for waterfront property." To prove the wisdom of Granddaddy Ryan, Job boasted that the lodge had never been repaired or renovated "in all them years."

In his youth, Job Ryan had been the best catch in Montauk—the East Hampton village sometimes referred to as "America's last frontier." Besides being heir to the lodge, he was blonde, blue-eyed and gifted with a body he never tired of displaying on the dock, bare to the waist, as he scaled and cleaned his own day's catch for shoppers who met the returning boats in search of fresh blues, bass and flounder.

Many a vacationing housewife, left to her own devices from Monday to Friday, spent a few stolen hours with Job in cabin number ten, which he kept ready for these trysts. Such amenities as a choice of condoms—lubricated, ribbed, flavored, etc.—a Polaroid camera for those who would consent and surprising how many did, and a mini refrigerator to keep their recent ocean-fresh purchases fresh before transporting them back to home and hearth were the cabin's staples.

At near fifty, Job was still slim and muscular but the sun had darkened his fair skin, the elements had thickened it to the consistency of cowhide, his belly was beginning to expand to make room for the thirty or so cans of beer he poured into it every day and his golden hair, which he did not shampoo often enough, was streaked in unflattering shades of yellow and gray. The only part of Job Ryan that retained the vigor and appearance of a teenager was the lure of cabin number ten.

Like his appearance, the quality of Job's clientele had also deteriorated since his granddaddy's and father's days. In fact, the decline and fall of Job's Fishing Lodge could be viewed as a microcosm of America's social structure in a state of flux from the dwindling years of the twentieth century into the new millennium. In his lifetime Job saw his patrons segue from businessmen who read *Field & Stream* and came to the lodge for a week or weekend of serious fishing and relaxation among like-minded colleagues, to those looking to get away from wife and children, who went out on *Job's Patience* by day and frequented the rowdy Montauk bars by night for the sole purpose of finding female company not averse to accepting an invitation for a nightcap back at the lodge, to the new influx of Hispanic immigrants, mostly male and mostly illegal aliens, who slept in shifts, not unlike a Bowery flophouse of yore.

When Heather was twelve, Job and his wife, Carol, faced the fact that they would not produce another child. Although young Heather was already a competent hand on *Job's Patience,* her father thought a boy would be more acceptable to those all-male fishing parties who sometimes looked askance at Heather when they weren't openly ogling Job's fast-maturing mate.

It was Mrs. Ryan who suggested taking in a boy under the foster care program, proclaiming, "We get full-time help that pays his own keep and doesn't cost us a cent." Job could find nothing wrong with the idea and their application was looked upon favorably, thanks to Mrs. Ryan's housekeeping and Mr. Ryan's standing as a respected member of the Montauk commercial fishing community and the owner of a fishing lodge. The agency could not wish to send one of their charges into a more wholesome family setting.

The boy, Bill, had been left on the steps of the police station in Riverhead by a person or persons unknown. The examining physician placed his age at several weeks but his birthday was officially recorded as the date he had been found by an officer reporting for duty on the graveyard shift. Pinned to the blanket he came wrapped in was a note: *Please take care of Bill. I can't.*

By the time he was ten, Bill had lived with six sets of foster parents and had not been sorry to leave any of them. He arrived on West Lake Drive with a small cardboard suitcase that contained everything he owned. "You're big for ten," Job greeted him, seemingly pleased with this fact. Indeed, the boy was a good foot taller then Heather, who also seemed pleased with this fact.

"I'll fatten you up," Mrs. Ryan promised the scrawny boy, but in the few years she had left on this earth she saw Bill grow taller, but not one inch wider.

The house had three bedrooms on the second floor, the smallest of which was given to Bill. It contained a cot, a chest of drawers, a desk and a chair, all of which had seen service in one cabin or another over the years. A shower curtain had replaced the missing door of the room's one narrow closet. Bill liked it immediately, mostly because he didn't have to share it. In his last home he had slept in a room with three other foster children, in a bed with one who was a chronic bed wetter. His first night with the Ryans he bedded down with the window opened wide, breathing the invigorating aroma of salt air and waking to the wail of the Long Island Railroad's milk train as it left the Montauk terminal for New York. He prayed that these people would keep him a long, long time.

"The way the bastard takes to the sea, his father must have been a sailor or a bayman," Job told his wife a few weeks after Bill's arrival.

"There's no cause to call the boy that," she chided her husband. "He is what he is through no fault of his own."

Bill was Mrs. Ryan's pet and when she died of a heart condition that had troubled her most of her adult life, the boy lost the only real mother he had ever known. After the funeral, Job took Bill to a lawyer in East Hampton and began proceedings to legally change his name from Bill Doe to Bill Ryan. "This is what Carol wanted," he claimed before adding the caution, "Mind, I'm not adopting you. That would cost me your keep. But it's only right that you be given a proper name and mine is as good as any."

"Are we Irish?" Bill asked.

Job scratched his head in puzzlement. "Irish? We've been here so long we sort of lost track but Carol always bragged that she was part Indian." The boy liked the idea of being part Indian.

At twelve, Bill was as tall and muscular as most of the fifteen-year-olds in pursuit of Heather, and Job looked upon the boy more as a colleague than a foster son. When discussing life in general and the men who went out on *Job's Patience* in particular, Job would often remind his ward that "you can measure a man's courage by the length of his rod."

Thanks to that bit of homespun wisdom, Bill took notice of all the fishing rods owned and rented by the men aboard *Job's Patience*. When he reported to Job that they were all the same size, he was rewarded with a roaring guffaw, a slap on the back and an explanation. Job's rendering of the story at Bick's Clam Bar was the hit of the evening.

Bill and Heather were as close, perhaps closer, than natural siblings. They shared the loss of Heather's mother and Bill's champion as well as a love of the sea and the uncomplicated existence Job's Fishing Lodge offered the two robustly healthy teenagers. Job secretly harbored a wish that an attraction more physical than familial would one day develop between his daughter and foster son. A marriage between Bill and Heather would keep the business in the family and, "She wouldn't even have to change her name." But, perhaps wisely on the part of the youngsters, this was not to be the case. When Bill and Heather began to take a serious interest in the opposite sex, their looks went everywhere but at each other.

It could be said the Grim Reaper was almost solely responsible for the decline and fall of Job's Fishing Lodge. First the serious sportsmen of Job's father's day met their maker as inevitably we all must, and their sons' more affluent generation came to the Hamptons to fish for other things, all of them comfortably ensconced on dry, prime acreage. Then Mrs. Ryan's passing put an end to the care of not only her home but the cabins as well. The pride she took in their scrubbed bathrooms and clean sheets and towels had not carried over to her daughter, who could handle a fishing rod far better than the business end of a scrub brush.

Bill, with help from Heather and none from Job, did his best with the two commercial washers and dryers housed in a lean-to called the "utility room," but his best was not good enough to keep even the trade of the Saturday night revelers who had become the mainstay of Job's Fishing Lodge.

Job bragged that he never touched booze, but he more than made up for this abstention with his intake of beer. His daily ration went from a six-pack or two to a case since his wife's death. If you told Job he was a candidate for AA, he would reply none too politely, "That's for boozers and losers."

The cabins were now rented to Latinos who co-opted the space— and *Job's Patience* relied on what customers it could pick up at the dock in the summer where the competition for day-trippers was fierce, leaving Job short of ready cash during the long, cold winter months. Therefore, on a gray day in early March when a man knocked on Job's front door, not in search of ice, but to inquire about chartering *Job's Patience* for a party of businessmen from New York, Job Ryan couldn't have been more accommodating.

The group, about seven in all, were indistinguishable from hundreds of such fishing parties Job had welcomed aboard his boat in the last decade. Their attire was more Abercrombie & Fitch than seafaring, their picnic lunch was more liquid than solid and they appeared more interested in the traffic above the water than below it.

"Take us around Block Island," the man who was the spokesperson for the group ordered Job.

"This time of year we'd do better heading south of Block Island," Job advised.

"You know that, but maybe the fish don't," the man answered. "Let's head for Block Island."

Given the condition of Job's exchequer, he would have gone looking for fish *on* Block Island to please a paying customer. As the expedition moved away from the optimum fishing waters, one of the passengers took a very obvious interest in the boat's first mate. Bill Ryan was far from sophisticated but he had lived in the Hamptons long enough to know that the man was interested in things other than fishing instructions.

Now out of high school, Bill Ryan had grown into a tall, lanky young man with a head of dark curly hair and true brown eyes. His masculine appeal was more rugged than refined, a trait appealing to both women and men, not always for different reasons. When Bill's admirer pounced, he said, "I'm an agent."

"FBI!" Bill exclaimed in a grossly exaggerated expression of awe.

The man was not amused. "A theatrical agent."

"I'm not interested," Bill said, trying his best not to offend.

"But you haven't even heard—"

"I heard 'theatrical' and I'm not the theatrical kind."

Getting the message, the man said sharply, "I'm not interested in your butt, kid. I'm a legit theatrical agent. I develop talent."

"I don't think I have the kind of talent you're looking for. Do you want me to help you bait your line? That I can do."

The man shrugged. Taking out his wallet he said, "There are boys and girls in this town—hell, all over the world—who would fuck anything for the opportunity I'm handing you." He stuck his business card in the side pocket of Bill's jeans. "Take this. If you ever get some sense in that pretty head, call me."

That night Bill showed the card to Heather. "He wants to put me in the movies." Bill's boast was accompanied with an embarrassed grin.

"Strange," Heather answered, looking at the card, "the guys who hit on me come right to the point."

The Ryan family had learned, to their delight, that the boy they had taken in under the foster care system was a talented mimic, able to imitate both voice and nuance of television news anchormen as well as the characters on leading sitcoms. Shy, he had at first exhibited this skill only to Mrs. Ryan. Egged on by her, he finally got up the courage to treat Job and Heather to this remarkable gift, but never would he perform outside the confines of the family home.

Now, helping Heather set the table for dinner, Bill asked in a voice that was eerily indistinguishable from that of a teenage actor whose weekly television show enjoyed an audience of millions of teenage fans, "How do you think I'd make out in Hollywood?"

With a mischievous twinkle in her dark eyes she told him, "About like a minnow coming up against a barracuda."

CHAPTER TWO

Bill was in the utility room on a bright, windy day in March, when a black Mercedes came up the graveled drive and stopped at the front door. A tall, painfully thin man emerged from the car and entered the house. A half hour later, when the man departed, Bill entered the kitchen and asked Job, "Who's the scarecrow?"

Job took a can of beer from the refrigerator and pulled off the aluminum tab. "Don't speak ill of our salvation." Downing half the can in one swallow he continued, "He wants to charter the boat once a week for private runs."

"What's a private run?" Bill wanted to know.

"One that ain't open to the public, that's what."

Knowing from long experience that this was as much of an answer as he was going to get out of Job Ryan, the boy took a new approach and tried again. "How much?"

Job put the beer can to his lips once more and downed the second half. He shook the can to ensure that it was empty and, satisfied that it was, deposited it in a cylindrical container lined with a plastic garbage bag. This latest deposit was but one of many already in the container. When full, Job would haul the bag in the pickup truck to the IGA market and recycle the empties in return for the deposit due on each can.

"Like putting money in the bank," Job would often utter when feeding the kitty.

Job didn't seem to hear the question so Bill knew he would get no answer. That meant the rental fee was either astronomical or dirt cheap. But judging from the gleam in Job's eye and the way he had knocked back the Bud, Bill surmised the price was fan-fucking-tastic, as Job would have said if he didn't want to keep it a secret. The fact that he did want to keep the fee and the nature of the run a secret worried Bill.

Used to dealing with the taciturn Job, Bill tried again. "Who is he, Job?"

"Name's Avery. He's a big shot in New York. Keeps a place out here on the old highway."

"Avery what?"

"Just Avery." Job handed over Avery's business card.

Bill read aloud. "'Avery. One word says it all. Fashion Photography.' What does he want to do on the water, see what the fish are wearing?"

"He's not coming along for the ride."

The more Bill learned, or didn't learn, about this private run the less he liked it. "What's that supposed to mean?"

"Just what it sounds like."

"And what do we do out there? Play with ourselves?"

Job wiped his lips with a paper towel. His wife had broken him of the habit of using his sleeve for that purpose. "Don't talk dirty, kid, and don't tell me how to run my business."

Bill had no stomach for getting into an argument with Job late in the day, when the man was beginning to feel the cumulative effects of his imbibing. "Come on, Job, what's it all about?" Bill pleaded.

"We rendezvous with a trawler and exchange cargos. That's it." Job made it sound as mundane as if he had agreed to take on a gaggle of Boy Scouts for a half-day run and watch them heave off the deck.

"What's our cargo?"

"None of our business."

Paying the answer the respect it deserved, Bill went right on with, "And what do we take on, lobsters?" Job was eyeing the refrigerator, paying scant attention to his inquisitor. Not getting any answers, Bill figured he could ask anything he wanted to know. "Who put this Avery on to us?"

Job had no problem with this one. "Bick, over at the bar."

"And what was this big shot doing at Bick's place?"

"He's taking pictures of Montauk fishermen. Says he's gonna put them in a book. Says he's going to do for fishermen what Grant Wood did for farmers."

Losing patience, Bill shouted, "Who the hell is Grant Wood?"

"Beats me, kid."

"Did this Avery tell you Bick put him on to us?"

"That's what I said," Job answered.

"What did he do? Ask Bick for the name of a boat owner who was hard up for cash?"

"Maybe he asked for the name of the best damn fisherman in Montauk. Ever think of that?"

No, Bill hadn't thought of that because the guy seemed about as interested in fishing as the crew they had taken on last week. In Bill's mind a fashion photographer and a theatrical agent were cut from the same cloth. "Funny, he turns up a week after we take out those men who were as keen on fishing as I am on bird-watching. You think they sent him?"

"I think Bick sent him and what difference does it make?" Job gave up the struggle and opened the refrigerator, reaching for another beer. "Our first run is tomorrow. We sail out at sunset. I have to map out the coordinates for our rendezvous."

"You don't have to be a brain surgeon to know the whole thing stinks worse than yesterday's catch. I don't like it, Job, so count me out."

Job held fast to his unopened can of Bud. "Do like you want, but you'll be screwing yourself out of your ten percent."

Bill was aware that Job was baiting his hook but that didn't stop him from snapping at the line. "What does ten percent translate to?"

"Two hundred bucks."

"Jesus," Bill moaned.

There was never any doubt that Bill would accompany Job on the run and they both knew it. Job Ryan was crude, or crass, or maybe a good dollop of both, but he was a kind man who had given Bill a home and a name. Now, hard up for cash, Bill's foster father needed an ally he could trust and wisely opted not to go outside the family circle to find one.

Not wanting Heather actively involved in the intrigue, Job had placed his confidence in Bill. This bond between man and boy, all unspoken as was their way, was more binding than any legal adoption. The fact that Job was now leaning on Bill rendered the boy proud and grateful, far outweighing the distaste he had for the assignment. It wasn't a question of repayment but rather a show of sentiment both would have been loath to call love.

Job told his daughter as much as he had told Bill of their sudden change in fortune. She had as much taste for the mysterious private run as did Bill but being human, and young, asked at the supper table that night, "Are we going to be rich?"

"If we don't land in jail first," Bill quipped.

This got a narrow-eyed squint from Job, who laid down his fork and the law at the same time. In short, he told Heather and Bill that they were not to discuss the new assignment with anyone, including each other. It was his contention that the less said, even in the privacy of their own home, the less chance of a slip among strangers.

Job did not worry for a minute that his fellow fishermen might question him about a weekly run in the early evening hours with nary a passenger aboard. All East Enders of long standing, the men and their families kept their noses out of their neighbors' business. One's privacy was sacrosanct: a word they had probably never heard but whose meaning they adhered to vehemently.

There were still some who remembered the days when Montauk was the main port of entry for the illegal booze run in from Canada that supplied New York and most of the East Coast during Prohibition. Those fishermen looking to earn an extra buck were called rumrunners and stories are still told of the one who, being chased by the Coast Guard, abandoned ship, was picked up by a freighter and disembarked in Venezuela. And every Montauk resident knows where the popular Gin Beach got its name. Six decades later drugs replaced bootlegged gin but the beach remains Gin Beach and those who ply the drug trade are still referred to as rumrunners.

The man called Avery arrived at the house the next day carrying a locked suitcase, the size of which one might take for an overnight trip, and exchanged a few words with Job and the young people. The conversation consisted of little else but comments on the weather and the traffic on Montauk Highway now that the season was approaching. Heather and Bill treated the tall, frail man with his gray crew cut and skeletal appearance with a mixture of awe and fear.

The first encounter with the trawler *Billy Budd* went off without a hitch. A bag similar to the one Job tossed onto the deck of the trawler was tossed over to *Job's Patience*. For Bill, whose vicarious adventures had their roots in the exploits of James Bond and Jack Ryan, the moment was at once terrifying and exhilarating. Denying this would be unworthy of Bill's almost morose self-scrutinization. This penchant for introspection, however, was quick to point out that unlike his daydreams, he had been cast in the role of prey, not ally, of the avenging heroes. When the merchandise landed on the deck with a thud, Bill heard a door being shut and bolted, barring the way back to his carefree existence on West Lake Drive.

"You see how easy it is," Job uttered as he bent to retrieve the package.

Bill pretended not to hear the jubilant pronouncement as he watched the *Billy Budd* withdraw into the fog.

The following morning Avery showed up at the house, again carrying a locked grip, and exchanged it for the one Job had received from the *Billy Budd*. Avery told Job when the next meeting at sea would take place and with that established a pattern for the exchanges and meetings that was to go on, unaltered, well into the summer.

When alone, Bill and Heather speculated on the contents of both satchels.

"He brings money. What else?" Bill whispered. "In exchange for what we take on."

"You know damn well what you take on," Heather reminded him.

Had this conversation taken place within Job's hearing, the two would have been smartly chastised. Job had made it clear to both of them that they did not know, nor did they care to know, what was in the grip Avery brought or the one he took away. "We're employees, doing what we're told and getting paid for the job. Just honest people, making an honest living. What's in them packages is the responsibility of them who owns 'em. Like the Good Book says, you can't shoot the messenger for delivering bad news."

The analogy escaped Bill and he had no idea what "good book" Job had in mind. However, he did recall a teacher at East Hampton High telling the class that ignorance of the law is no excuse. He was sure that's what the judge would say to Job if they got caught trading packages on the Sound. Neither Job, his daughter nor Bill were ignorant of the drug scene in the Hamptons, so claiming ignorance would also be a bold-faced lie. But if the rationale soothed Job's conscience, Bill wouldn't press the issue.

In spite of Job's dictums, Heather and Bill continued to discuss the matter. "How much do you think is in that bag?" Heather asked, not for the first time.

"What difference does it make? It's not ours."

"But how much do you think is there? Enough to go around the world in style?"

Bill shrugged, uncaring. "Why do you want to go around the world? We have everything we want right here."

"Everything you want, maybe, but not me. You don't want to spend the rest of your life operating a fishing boat and renting rooms to illegal aliens, do you, Bill?"

Indeed he did. However, until that moment it had never occurred to Bill that he would ever do anything but work aboard *Job's Patience* and help run the fishing lodge. He assumed that Heather was Job's sole heir and right now it sounded as if she had no intention of keeping the operation going when Job passed on. He could never afford to buy out Heather, so the answer to her question was that he had no idea what the future held for him if Heather sold out.

Bill was saving as much as he could from his ten-percent share of their weekly take, and Job, he knew, was doing the same. They had discussed redoing the house and the cabins, turning the lodge into a first-class operation as soon as they had put away enough to sever their connection to Avery and the weekly private runs. It was the dream that sustained the Ryan men and enabled them to carry on an operation that was against both the law and their principles.

"I thought you loved this place," Bill countered.

"I do, Bill, but I'm not married to it—and neither are you."

Annoyed, Bill said, "Right now I'm just hoping to spend the rest of my life out of jail."

"Then stop the private run," Heather told him.

"I can't. Job needs the money and you know it."

"So we are a part of it whether we like it or not."

On that ominous note the conversation ended. Bill walked away thinking, *Damn Avery. Since he showed up here and we got some ready cash in our pockets everything has changed.* Like Job, Bill didn't give an inchworm's ass for change, and East Hampton was changing faster than he and any of the locals liked to think.

The way the villages were being invaded you'd think someone had struck gold in the potato fields. But the potato farmers had done just that, Bill reminded himself, with the price of their land, which had soared astronomically in recent years. Why plow the earth when you could sell it for millions? Everyone was getting rich and now Job Ryan and family had joined the caravan. No, Bill Ryan didn't give an inchworm's ass for change.

Either as an excuse for appearing at Job's Fishing Lodge every week or in actual pursuit of turning out an art book, the man called Avery, a camera dangling from his skinny neck by a leather strap, became a familiar figure around the marinas, docks and motels along West Lake Drive.

The East End fishing fraternity has long had a reputation for being good Samaritans on land as well as on sea. A story, one that many old-timers swear is true, has it that a German U-boat discharged two spies off the Amagansett coast during the Second World War. Thinking they were shipwrecked sailors, the fishermen who found them washed up on the beach took them in, fed them, gave them dry clothes and paid their fare for a one-way train ticket to New York. Note the words *one way* were always accompanied with a wink and a nod.

The old men liked to regale Avery with stories of hurricanes and sharks—mostly false—but their sons proved shy and usually grabbed a shirt to cover their bare chests as they hauled fish or swabbed decks with Avery's camera focused on them. It soon became apparent to the Ryans that Bill was Avery's favorite subject. The photographer never seemed to tire of pointing his camera at the boy and clicking away rapidly, running through a roll of film in record time.

Bill pretended not to like the attention but he couldn't deny the feeling of pride it evoked. He sometimes likened it to the way children with doting parents must feel when the important moments of their lives are being committed to film for the family album. It was a form of adulation Bill Ryan had grown up woefully lacking.

Now that Avery had made himself known to the fishing community, the curious and clever Heather thought she could make some inquiries about the man without drawing attention to the fact that she or the Ryans were connected with him in any other way but as fodder for his camera. From Bill she got the idea of a link between fashion photography and show business that led her to East Hampton's show business guru, Helen Weaver.

Helen worked in her father's video rental shop, once located on Main Street in East Hampton Village but due to a rent increase was forced to relocate to a mini shopping complex in the less prestigious region of the Springs in East Hampton Town. However, the sign over the shop's entrance still read MAIN STREET VIDEO. "The bandit can force me out but he can't make me change my name," Mr. Weaver declared of his former landlord.

Mr. Weaver's lament was fast becoming the war cry of other merchants forced out of their storefronts on Main Street for the same reason. Shops like Main Street Video and The Village Shoe Store were being replaced by such national logos as Polo, Banana Republic, London Jewelers and an enterprising retailer calling itself Cashmere Hampton.

What had also not changed at Main Street Video was its chief dispenser of videos, the pretty and pert Helen, the only child of Mr. and Mrs. Weaver. Helen was famous in East Hampton for her knowledge of films past, present and, one might imagine, future. Along with film reviews, Helen was also known to inject a bit of gossip regarding the celluloid stars, thanks to her religious reading of gossip columnists and entertainment magazines.

Helen was a few years older than Heather but they had managed to overlap in high school, giving them something more than just a nodding acquaintance with each other. Heather found Helen at her post and without preamble handed over Avery's business card.

"I heard he was out here, taking pictures in Montauk," Helen said, returning the card to Heather.

"Do you know him?"

Helen shook her head, putting in motion the ponytail she favored. "Not much to know. Fashion photography is stretching a point. He works for Freddy Parc."

Heather thought a moment and then exclaimed, "The underwear manufacturer?"

"One and the same. But I read the company is expanding, going into jeans and things like that. This Avery is what I think is called an in-house photographer for Freddy Parc Enterprises. Have you ever seen the underwear ads?"

"I'm not into men's underwear, Helen."

Helen laughed. "The ads have been pretty risqué. Some say even pornographic. But they made Freddy Parc a household word and no doubt a millionaire. This Avery is responsible for them."

"So what is he doing taking pictures of fishermen in Montauk?"

"Maybe he's expanding his horizons," Helen suggested. "Branching out and breaking away from commercial photography. It's been known to happen."

Heather wondered if Freddy Parc Enterprises knew just how far their in-house photographer had broken away.

Having reported what she had learned from Helen Weaver to Bill, he was not too astonished when one day Avery asked him if he wore Freddy Parc briefs.

"I can't afford them," Bill said, truthfully.

"If I give you a pair can I photograph you wearing them?"

"Fuck you, Avery," the usually placid Bill snapped back.

"Don't jump to conclusions," Avery said, "listen when you're being propositioned."

"One proposition from you is one too many," Bill answered.

Ignoring this, Avery went on, "Freddy Parc Enterprises is going to run a contest. A search for a male model to represent the line in a major ad blitz. I think you can be the lucky winner."

"I'm not interested, Avery, and I wish you'd stop pointing that camera at me."

Annoyed, Avery stated caustically, "There are a million guys just like you who would give their left nut for a chance at this."

Bill recalled hearing something very similar a while back, but whether he did or didn't, he still wasn't interested.

CHAPTER THREE

By midsummer the private runs and Avery's presence on the Montauk docks were both the norm rather than the exception. "Habit is second nature," Bill recited, "and nature is nothing more than habit."

"Where did you hear that?" Heather asked, obviously impressed with this bit of philosophizing.

"Read it someplace."

They were on the deck of the berthed *Job's Patience,* sitting in canvas chairs and passing a can of Coke back and forth. "Once, before you came, I was out with Job," Heather mused, "on a humid day just like this and everyone aboard was saying how the ocean was as calm as a lake. An hour later the sky went black as night and we were hit by a squall with waves washing over us that sent everything but the passengers into the drink." In spite of the hot sun, Heather shivered at the memory.

"You saying this is the calm before the storm?"

"I'm saying I'm scared, Bill, and I don't like lying to people," she complained.

"By 'people' you mean Ian Edwards," Bill said with a knowing smile.

Heather tried to negate the suggestion with a wave of her hand but the slight blush to her tanned cheeks defeated the gesture. Ian was a young man whose family had been engaged in commercial fishing in Montauk even longer than the Ryans. The Edwardses operated two boats that supplied seafood to fish markets and supermarkets from Montauk to as far west as the famous Fulton Fish Market in New York.

Ian, bright as he was personable, made it known that he intended to one day erect an establishment on the Edwardses' property to rival both Gosman's Dock and Disney World. First, he intended to marry Heather Ryan and to that end was seeing as much of her as she would allow.

"He asked me about the private runs," Heather confided to Bill.

"What did you say?"

"I told him we have a relative on Block Island and she wasn't doing well so Dad was keeping an eye on her. Only half a lie. My mother had a cousin who lived there but I think she's dead."

"Wasn't he curious to know why we went there at night?"

"I said we couldn't afford to lose a day's business in season," Heather explained.

This, Bill thought, would have been the case if Job did have to visit Block Island on a regular basis. "Did he believe you?"

"Ian believes everything I tell him," Heather bragged.

Looking at Heather reclining in a figure-hugging tankini, Bill conceded, "I can believe that."

"Can we tell Avery we want to stop making the runs?" Heather suddenly asked.

Bill watched a gull circle the dock and listened to the boat groan as the water's swell put its hull in contact with the wooden pillars that framed its berth. It was a sound as comforting to Bill Ryan as a mother's lullaby to her newborn.

"I've been thinking the same thing," Bill said. "Let's put it to Job."

"What about the money?" Heather reminded him. "The money to turn the lodge into a fancy motel."

"Hell," Bill said, "with that swimsuit of yours grabbing Ian by the short and curlies we can just add our oversized dory to his fleet and have us an operation like Mr. Onassis."

Heather flung the remaining contents of the Coke can into Bill's face before the two erupted into raucous laughter.

As it happened, Job had something to put to them. Or, more specifically, to Bill. Avery, it appeared, had once again made Job an offer he found difficult to refuse.

"All you have to do," Job informed Bill that night, "is carry the package from the *Billy Budd* one step further—to a house in Sag Harbor, every Sunday evening after dark. In fact, the later the better."

"No!" Heather shouted at her father.

"I'm talking to Bill, missy, so hold your comments till you're asked," Job scolded. It was clear that he had been drinking and the sheen of sweat on his forehead seemed to acknowledge that he was as nervous over this addition to the private run as was his daughter.

"Three hundred dollars," Job said, clutching the beer can that had become an almost integral part of his anatomy since prosperity had entered his home. "That's just for you, Bill. Yours to keep and do with whatever pleases you. Three hundred dollars for an hour's work, most of it driving from here to Sag Harbor and back home."

Bill shook his head as Job spoke. Did Job realize that the money Avery was waving under their noses was peanuts compared to what he must be taking in? And why was a fashion photographer, even one with only one client, involved in drug trafficking? And did Freddy Parc Enterprises condone their flack's moonlighting? So many questions and the only thing Bill knew for sure was that he and Job were as vulnerable and dispensable to the operation as fish in a barrel.

Bill, an avid reader, now shared what knowledge he had gleaned from his perusal of the subject. "Drug cartels are stacked like a pyramid with the suckers as cornerstones. That's us, Job."

Over the years, in all family matters, Bill had always deferred to Job, even when he knew the man was wrong, because he wasn't family and wisely refused to trespass on private property. Because of this, Bill's honest appraisal of their situation had Job looking perplexed and Heather smiling her encouragement at Bill.

"We never opened them packages, so we don't know what's in them." Job reiterated his old mantra.

"We all know what's in those packages," Bill countered. "It seems to me Avery wants to keep his hands clean while we dip ours in his crap."

"We never opened them packages," Job repeated, but even he was showing signs of having little faith in his own defense.

"That doesn't mean a thing, Job, and you know it. We get caught, we go to jail and Avery finds himself another patsy, which won't be hard with the way people around here are ready to sell their souls to keep up with the summer crowd."

"We've been making the run for weeks now and even the weather has been with us," Job insisted.

"So let's not press our luck," Bill advised.

It was the observant Heather, who knew her father even better than Bill, who asked, "When Avery made this offer, did he give you any choice?"

Job, his shoulders sagging, addressed the can he was now caressing with both hands like a penitent eager to confess his sins. He didn't hesitate a moment before announcing, "He told me the *Billy Budd* keeps a log of every meeting with *Job's Patience.* If the log was to fall into the wrong hands . . ." The disclosure seemed to remove an invisible weight from Job's hunched back as he straightened up in his chair, head high, looking to his children for either comfort or forgiveness.

"Jesus," Bill moaned.

Heather buried her face in her hands. Bill reached out and touched her arm. "We do what we have to do," Bill stated. "It's not your fault, Job. We both went into this with our eyes open."

"It ain't all bad," Job said. "There is a good side to it."

Heather looked at her father as if he had narrowed the gap between painfully distressed and certifiably mad.

"When the season ends, so do the runs. September the latest. We can start up again next year or not. It'll be up to us."

Bill and Heather exchanged a look that said it wasn't much but it was better than nothing.

"Like you said, Bill, we're in this together." Job seemed to rally now that he had set a deadline for ending their nightmare. This meeting was conducted, as were all family gatherings, around the kitchen table, and Job looked across its oval expanse directly at Bill, purposely excluding Heather, as he continued, "We make the Sag Harbor run together."

"Avery said only one of us, Job. For obvious reasons he doesn't want it to look like you and me and that damn package are joined at the hip."

"Then we'll take turns," Job quickly put in. "One Sunday you and the next Sunday me."

After this, all three were silent, perhaps trying to reconcile themselves to the ultimatum presented to them by the man Job had once called their salvation. A foghorn wailed in the distance, the sorrowful sound serving as a lament to Bill's and Heather's doomed hope of altering their course from *aweather* to *alee*.

Bill broke the hush when he said, "All we have to do is keep our fingers crossed from now until Labor Day."

Florence Walker looked more like the accommodating proprietress of a Sag Harbor B&B than a cog in the East End drug operation. Plump, with a flawless complexion and never without a cigarette in one hand and a glass of designer water in the other, she could claim to be on the good side of forty but was probably ten years older. Her house, each Sunday evening, was filled with people one might encounter at O'Mally's, an East Hampton pub and restaurant popular with the locals, ranging in age from late teens to candidates for Medicare. The only thing these people had in common was their ordinariness.

A caterer and a real estate agent had given their cards to Bill in the event he should ever be in need of their particular services. Business, and the name Avery, were never discussed at Flo's, so Bill had no idea of who did what, when or why in Flo's extended family. Baseball, summer traffic and the merits of Hollywood's latest blockbuster were the mainstays of conversation. It was so mundane, an intruder who had wandered in by mistake could believe that Bill had arrived with a couple of six-packs to join the party in progress.

Upon arriving Bill placed his package on the kitchen table, and with a curt nod to anyone in his path, he would attempt a hasty retreat from the house before Flo had time to greet him with a lecherous smile and a hand that encircled his waist as fingers slipped inside his jeans and tugged on the elastic band of his briefs. If caught he would wiggle, none too gently, out of her grip and tell her he was in a hurry to leave. On this particular evening nature forced him to make a stop in the bathroom, where he was relieving himself when he heard a woman scream. Seconds later he heard another scream—then a roar that for one crazy moment had him believing the television was tuned in to a baseball game and the home team had just scored a home run with the bases loaded in the bottom of the ninth. Shouts—cries— stampeding feet going in circles. Only one word, repeated again and again, made any sense. *"Police!"*

Still urinating, he pried open the small bathroom window and then wiggled through it, grateful for a body that had gotten him dubbed "the eel" in middle school. Landing on his face, he finished what he had come into the bathroom to do, wetting his jeans and the dirt he seemed to be kissing. When he rose he remembered to close the bathroom window before running, his penis still dangling from his fly, to the far end of the unkempt backyard. He crawled through a row of thick yews and came out in the rear yard of a house that fronted on the next street.

In the dark of an overcast midnight, he made it to the street without being seen, adjusted his fly, wiped his mouth and began walking slowly up the street. Lights were now going on all over the neighborhood and people were beginning to come out of their houses. Walking to the corner, then turning into the street he had just fled, he joined the crowd of spectators, some in pajamas and robes, watching a genuine police raid.

CHAPTER FOUR

FROM THE *EAST HAMPTON STAR*

DRUG RING SMASHED
IN MIDNIGHT RAID

A dozen South Fork residents, all charged with playing some role in a cocaine-trafficking ring here, were arrested on Sunday in a midnight raid by a platoon of town and county police officers.

Police said they had spent several months listening to conversations on the cellular telephone of the supposed ringleader and the telephone in her Sag Harbor house where her "employees" often congregated.

The alleged ringleader, Florence Walker, is a resident of Sag Harbor, where she has lived since leaving Queens, New York, five years ago. Ms. Walker and eleven other UpIsland residents were charged with felony conspiracy.

The police stated that the group was the county's main source of illegal drugs, dealing $5,000 to $10,000 a week in cocaine here. Ms. Walker is believed to have supplied the cocaine to the people who helped her distribute it.

Cross Section

The accused, allegedly working for Ms. Walker, are a cross section of the South Fork community: male, female, white, black, Hispanic, Asian—ranging in age from 17 to 60. Several were reported to be relatives of Ms. Walker.

They were arraigned en masse the following afternoon in a packed courtroom in East Hampton, giving their employment as waitress, construction worker, carpenter, lawn care specialist, real estate agent, etc.

Never Sold to Strangers

Lieutenant Christopher Oliveri, the East Hampton Town Police spokesman, stated that the cocaine distribution network operated on a strict policy of never selling to anyone they did not know. For that reason, undercover detectives could not purchase drugs from the alleged dealers and had to rely solely on wiretaps. Lieutenant Oliveri refused to comment on how Ms. Walker and the house in Sag Harbor came under suspicion but the *Star* learned that Ms. Walker had been arrested in New York City on drug-related charges ten years ago.

None Accused of Selling Drugs

Because undercover detectives were unable to purchase drugs from ring members, none of them could be charged with the sale of illegal drugs. A package in the Sag Harbor house containing 5 kilos of pure cocaine (approximately 10 lbs.) was confiscated by the police as evidence of possession with the intent to sell and prompted the felony conspiracy charge. As Lieutenant Oliveri described the operation, the cocaine was delivered to the Sag Harbor house where Ms. Walker would break it down into small packages for her couriers to distribute throughout Suffolk County. Lieutenant Oliveri stated that there was no doubt that the Sag Harbor operation was the chief supplier of illegal drugs to East Hampton.

The Lieutenant refused to comment, at this time, on where the cocaine found in Ms. Walker's home came from.

The Raid

The raid, several weeks in the planning, began at midnight, when officers armed with search warrants for Ms. Walker's house in Sag Harbor knocked at her door. An emergency services unit from the Nassau County Police Department entered first, followed by the Suffolk County narcotics unit.

"The accused did not try to resist nor did any try to escape," Lieutenant Oliveri told reporters. He also noted that many of the accused and their friends often spent the night and weekends at the Sag Harbor house. "We do not believe they were users," the lieutenant said in answer to a reporter's question. "This was a business operation, dealing in very small quantities."

CHAPTER FIVE

When he arrived back on West Lake Drive—filthy and scared—Bill gave Job a graphic description of everything that had happened and announced that he was through working for Avery. Job readily agreed, saying they had pushed their luck as far as it was likely to go. "If you didn't have to use the bathroom, you would have been out of there," Job concluded.

"No, Job. I would have met them coming in the door. That piss call was the luckiest thing that ever happened to me."

Job had waited up for Bill, as he did the few times Bill had made the Sunday night trip, but Heather had gone to bed. Hearing them in the kitchen, she came downstairs, wrapped in a terry robe. The moment she saw Bill she knew something had happened and he had to repeat the story, rapidly and with less detail, for her. Frightened, she sat close to her father and he put a comforting arm around her shoulders. "Are they going to arrest us?" she asked in a voice she did not recognize as her own.

"No one is going to arrest anyone," Job said. "Bill got away clean, and tonight we call it quits. Make us some coffee, honey."

It was one of the few things Heather could do in the kitchen with any competence and she obliged, even setting out the mugs, sugar and milk. They sat around the table looking as if they had all been charged with coming up with an answer to the riddle of life. None of them seemed to be having much luck. When they heard footsteps coming toward the house they jumped out of their chairs and crowded around the kitchen window. In the eerie predawn light they saw two of their tenants weaving toward the cabins.

"I've got to shower," Bill said. "I stink. Then I'm going to bed. We all need to sleep. Tomorrow we have to act like nothing's happened."

"Nothing has happened," Job protested.

"But it has," Heather insisted. "Suppose they come for Bill."

"Get ahold of yourself, missy," her father cautioned. "You act same as always or you stay in your room until you can. You hear me?"

"Keep away from the house and the boat," Bill added. "Hang out with the Edwardses. Ian likes having you there."

"I'm not leaving you and Dad," Heather countered.

"I'm not telling you to live there—"

"Stop bickering, you two," Job cut in. "We start pulling our oars in different directions, we go in circles." With this, Job reinstated his authority as captain of his ship and his house. "You wash, Bill, and you, young lady, go to bed. From here on we talk and act like this night never happened."

"I'm scared," Heather whispered, gripping Bill's arm.

"We all are, Heather," Bill responded.

Avery showed his face on West Lake Drive the Thursday following the Sag Harbor raid. The police action had been the talk of the town all week and that morning was featured prominently on the front page of the *East Hampton Star*. This made it unnecessary for Job to give Avery a reason why he wouldn't be making any more private runs.

Unperturbed, Avery told Job that some very important people would not look favorably upon this rash decision.

"Bill got out of that house a second before the shit hit the fan," Job said. If he was looking for sympathy from Avery, he wasn't getting any.

"So I thought when I didn't see his name in the newspaper." Job was shocked at Avery's comment, which came off more sardonic than caring.

Job Ryan—a big, crusty salt used to giving orders, not taking them—was beginning to feel uneasy under the gaze of this effeminate fop from the city. The mouse threatening the bull would have been amusing if the stakes were less intimidating. Job did not know who the important people were who would be unhappy to see him walk, but with those few words Avery had made it clear that Job would feel their wrath without ever seeing their faces.

"They've been good to you," Avery went on, "and there is no reason they won't continue to be. I'd have thought an old sea dog like you wouldn't head for port because of a cloudburst."

"Cloudburst! I hope you're joking, man. The people picked up in that house could be sent away for ten years, minimum. It was in the papers. Bill is scared, Avery, and so is Heather. What money we've put aside I'll give you back and repay the rest when I can. Just leave us be."

This meeting took place on the dock where *Job's Patience* was moored. Avery never discussed "business" in the confines of a room, or even on the deck of a ship. Job, to his chagrin, was both admirer and victim of this cunning. Anyone watching them would have thought the man with the camera hanging from his neck was a tourist seeking information regarding a half-day's fishing aboard *Job's Patience*.

The sky was a cloudless blue, the gulls were singing their particular paean to the sea's bounty and the locals were gearing up for the rush of visitors with cash to spare. One could not imagine a more unlikely ambiance for this malevolent exchange.

"The money is yours to keep, Job. We don't renege and we expect the people we do business with to do the same. You make the runs as usual."

The tone of Avery's words belied the bogus smile on his face. It was a side of the man Job had never seen before—cold, calculating, malicious. But then Job had never seen the man under duress. In the weeks he had been making the runs it had gone as smoothly as Avery had promised it would, and even if Avery had suspected Job and Bill were less than happy with the arrangement, he pretended not to notice.

Strange, but at that moment Job was thinking of the woman, Florence Walker. With Avery as an ally, she was lucky to be in the hands of the police with nothing more frightening to look forward to than ten years of free room and board. The fact that he was Florence Walker's supplier gnawed at Job like a stingray sitting on his chest.

"But the police are wise——"

"The police are wise to one weak link in a very long chain. The lady you read about made some very foolish choices in her hiring practices. Many of them family whom she thought she could trust but she didn't count on their big mouths. None of them know anything regarding the operation beyond the house in Sag Harbor. What little the lady knows she will keep to herself to protect that troublesome family."

The message was so clear, Job wanted to reach for Avery's throat. Instead he spit in the man's face but owing to his target's height the missile landed on Avery's shirtfront.

Avery glanced at the moist spot and boasted, "You see, Job, we're too big for you." Then he was gone—but not for long and certainly not for good.

Job answered the knock on his front door holding fast to a mug of coffee. "If you're looking for ice, we don't sell it."

"I'm looking for Bill Ryan," the young man answered.

"Who wants him?"

"Me. I'm Detective Evans from the East Hampton Town police. Is he here?"

Job started and a few drops of the hot coffee spilled over the rim of the mug and landed on one of his bare feet. Recovering, he said, "You gave me a turn."

The young man smiled kindly. "I'm used to it. It's the reaction I always get when I call on people who aren't expecting me."

"What do you want with Bill?" Job asked.

"No big deal," the detective assured Job. "Just want to ask him a few questions. Are you Mr. Ryan?"

At this point, Heather came out of the kitchen and into the front hall. She wore a T-shirt, jeans and sneakers. The detective tried to keep his eyes on Heather's face. "You're Eddy Evans," she stated.

"That's me," he answered. "Are you a friend of Helen's?" He spoke with the assurance of one used to being recognized as Helen Weaver's steady fellow.

"Yes. We were at school together and I see her at the store. I heard you two were engaged."

Eddy Evans didn't try to hide the pleasure he derived from being engaged to Helen Weaver. "Sorry I didn't recognize you . . ."

"Heather. I'm Heather Ryan."

"Helen has so many friends I'll need a scorecard to keep track."

"What are you doing in Montauk?" Heather asked, wondering if Eddy Evans was aware of the tremor in her voice.

"He's a policeman," Job answered, and before Heather could tell her father she knew this fact, Job ordered, "Go fetch Bill. He's checking the plumbing in one of the cabins. Then take my truck and pick up the supplies I asked you to get yesterday."

"What . . . ?"

"The list is on the kitchen table. Now go," Job ordered.

Glancing once at Eddy standing in the doorway, Heather retreated. Job didn't know if he should invite the cop in, or not. He decided against it, figuring that the man would go away sooner if they didn't treat him like an old friend.

He heard the kitchen door close with a bang. Heather had started on her fool's errand. There was no list on the kitchen table but he wanted her out of the house while the cop was there. Heather was never able to keep her face from telling people what was on her mind.

And from the look on the detective's face, he didn't believe there was a shopping list on the kitchen table, either.

"Are you Mr. Ryan?" Evans asked again.

"That's right. Job Ryan. Owner of *Job's Patience*. You went to the high school here?"

"No. I'm a Johnny-come-lately to East Hampton. But I went to Southampton College and liked it so much I stayed. My parents had a summer place here when I was growing up." Then Eddy addressed what he knew had prompted Job's question. "I'm a few years older than Helen and your daughter." Approaching thirty, Eddy was ten years older than his fiancée.

"You like to fish?"

"Not much. But I took a few courses in marine biology at the college."

Job drank from his mug, his hand considerably more steady now that the first shock of the police visit had worn off. "What's that got to do with fishing?"

"Not much," Evans told him.

Having reached an impasse they reverted to staring at each other for what seemed an eternity to Job and, no doubt, to Detective Evans, too. When the kitchen door once again made itself heard, Job muttered, "That'll be Bill."

Speaking as he approached the open door, Bill asked, "Why you standing out there?"

"Because no one invited me in," Evans answered.

The boy is too damn polite and has no sense, Job thought as he stood aside to allow the officer to enter. Both men followed Bill into the kitchen.

"Coffee?" Bill asked, pouring a mug for himself from a coffeepot any of the local antique shops would have loved to get their hands on.

"No thanks."

Bill added milk from the refrigerator but no sugar before taking his first swallow. He avoided looking at Job or the detective and appeared to address the dark liquid in his mug. "So, what can I do for you, Officer?"

"Detective Evans. Eddy Evans. You heard about the drug raid in Sag Harbor last week?"

"We don't know nothing about that," Job said.

"Sure. We read about it," Bill said. Turning, he spoke to Job. "I think he's here to see me."

"I am," Eddy Evans said quickly. "It's about your truck."

If Evans hadn't mentioned the drug raid, Bill would have been relieved but, as it were, the mention of his truck only made him more anxious. He drank quickly, which proved to be an error because the coffee seemed to go right through him. He felt his bowels loosen and became unsteady on his feet. "You want to sit?" he asked the officer.

"No, but you go right ahead. I seem to have come at a bad time."

Bill sat on a hard kitchen chair as Job went to the refrigerator. He prayed Job wouldn't open a beer at ten in the morning but when we pray the answer is often no. He was thankful that Job had the good sense not to offer one to the detective. "What about my truck?" Bill asked.

"The night of the raid we took down the plate numbers of all the vehicles parked on that street. Ten in all. Turns out most of them belong to people who live in the area or to people who had legitimate reasons for being there. A few, like yours, don't fall into either category. What were you doing in the neighborhood that night, Bill?"

"What night?" Bill asked.

Calmly, Evans repeated, "The night of the raid. Last Sunday, about midnight."

Bill knew he had to answer the detective but he had no idea what to tell him. He could say he was on his way to or from Southampton and driving via Sag Harbor. But what would he be doing in Southampton?

The detective withdrew a pen and notepad from his jacket pocket and stood, pen poised, looking down at Bill.

"I was on my way home, saw the commotion and parked to see what was happening." He hoped the explanation was more plausible than it sounded. Where might he be coming from? He could hear his heart beating when he suddenly thought of the Southampton movie house.

"That won't wash, kid, unless you own a working crystal ball. We took those plate numbers before the raid. Not after."

"Don't badger the boy." This was Job's second outburst since they had come into the kitchen.

"I'm not badgering anyone, sir."

"Quiet, Job." Bill looked up at the detective and wondered if the man could see the beads of perspiration that now covered his forehead. He was afraid that if he got up to get a paper towel he would soil himself.

Job put his beer can down on the table with a decided thud. "No—you keep quiet." Turning, he confronted the detective. "It was me using Bill's truck that night. Heather took mine to go visit a friend."

"Job . . ."

"The man knows we've got something to hide, so let me tell him what it is and maybe he'll leave us be."

"That's the most sensible thing I've heard since I knocked on your door, Mr. Ryan. What were you doing there on the night of—"

"I know what night it was," Job said, waving away the rest of the detective's statement. "I was visiting a lady."

"Fine. I'm not with the vice squad." His witticism went either unnoticed or unheeded. "Her name and address, sir, and I'll be on my way."

"None of your business," Job answered.

Evans lowered his pen. "Look, Mr. Ryan . . ."

"She's a married lady and that's all I'm saying."

Bill sat, staring at Job, not wanting to believe what he was hearing. "Job . . ."

"That's all I'm saying," Job shouted.

Seeing that the man meant it, Evans responded with a shrug that said he couldn't care less and pocketed his pen and pad. "I'm not part of the drug team, Mr. Ryan. Just giving them a hand at the height of the season. My job is to ask questions and report the answers back to my superiors—and that's just what I'll do. If they insist on verifying your story you'll hear from them, so maybe you should warn your lady friend."

"They can throw me in jail first." This declaration was remarkable in light of their position. Bill envied the older man as he recalled the analogy between rod and courage.

"As they say, Mr. Ryan, *bite your tongue,* because that's where you might end up if you don't cooperate. These guys play hardball." This obviously prompted Evans to say to Bill, "I used to watch you play basketball at the high school. You were good." With a nod to both men, Detective Evans took his departure.

Before the detective was out the front door, Heather came bounding in the back door. "I heard everything," she began, sounding as if she had just run a mile rather than standing inert with her ear cocked to the door. "You were great, Dad. Wasn't he?"

Bill collapsed over the table, his head falling onto his outstretched arms. Then he began to sob for the fools they all were.

CHAPTER SIX

Ignoring Bill's reaction to the detective's visit, Job griped, "The police play hardball. The crooks play hardball. And the slobs are the goddamn ball being tossed from side to side." He quenched his thirst with a long pull from the can he was holding and then put a hand on Bill's shoulder. "Get ahold of yourself, Bill. We got rid of him."

"Bill?" Heather was running her hand along Bill's spine as his torso lay across the tabletop. "Dad saved you. The cop believed him. Come on, we have to act like it never happened. Remember?"

Bill rose slowly, wiping his cheeks with the back of his hand. Looking at Job and Heather he began to giggle. Not recognizing hysteria when it stared him in the face, Job sighed, "See, it's gonna be okay."

When the giggles subsided, Bill looked at Job and said soberly, "It's over, Job. Don't you understand? It's over. They got me hooked and I can't break free."

"Come on, boy. There's no need for that kind of talk."

"Bill," Heather shouted. "What's wrong with you? Dad was helping you. Taking a risk for you. Now you—"

"No," Bill was moaning, "no. He told the police that he had my truck that night in Sag Harbor, visiting a lady he can't produce to back his story because she doesn't exist."

Job began pacing the room, kicking anything in his path. "Bull. They ain't ever gonna ask me to name that lady."

"Oh, but they are, Job. They damn well are. You can't produce the lady but the police can produce a dozen men to say you were sitting in Bick's Clam Bar that night. You were there, weren't you?"

"Bill, do you really think—" Heather cut in.

Paying her no mind, Bill went on. "You were there because you go there every night. I know that, Heather knows that and most of Montauk knows that. You were there and you stayed until midnight, at least, because you stay till near midnight every night. No way could you be in Sag Harbor that Sunday or any other Sunday.

"You tried, Job, and I know you did it for me but you can't come up with the lady to prove what you said and they can come up with a dozen men to say you're lying."

Still stroking Bill's back, Heather told him, "Maybe Dad is right. Maybe they won't ask him to name the lady. Pray that they don't, Bill. Pray."

"I'll think of something," Job was saying. "I'll talk to the boys over at Bick's and—"

"And tell them what we've been up to?" Bill cried. "Forget it. I have to get out of here. That's what I have to do."

"Out? Out where?"

Bill shook his head as if to clear it. Thinking aloud, he said calmly, "Tomorrow someone from the drug squad will come for that lady's name. When they don't get it, they'll pounce on the only other person who could have had the truck that night. Guess who? And no matter what I tell them, they'll want to know why I didn't tell it to the detective."

"I thought I was doing the right thing," Job pleaded.

"I know you did, Job. I'm not blaming you. I'm not blaming anyone. I'm the only one they can finger, so if I get away clean you and Heather will be in the clear. You've got to stop the private runs," Bill concluded.

"I can't," Job sobbed. "I can't."

Now Heather was crying. "Don't leave us, Bill. Please. And where can you go?"

"He ain't going no place," Job put in.

"I am, because if the police come after me I want to have a head start. I can move faster if I'm off this island."

Optimistic even through her tears, Heather cried, "Suppose the police don't come back?"

"That I doubt. But even if they don't, I'll still feel better someplace else. At least till this thing quiets down."

"Where will you go, boy, and what are we gonna tell people when they ask where you are? We have to tell them something."

Bill said nothing for a few minutes while Job and Heather held their ground, looking intently at him. Finally, a genuine smile appeared on Bill's face. "Tell them I got scouted by a theatrical producer and I took off to be a movie star."

"Damn," Job exclaimed. "That's worse than my story."

"I know, Job. But there is one important difference."

"What's that?"

"It's true."

MICHAEL ANTHONY REO

(ONE YEAR LATER)

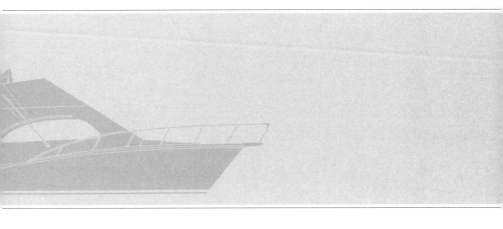

CHAPTER SEVEN

If one knew something about the theater—and Michael Anthony Reo did—he or she would notice scattered about Amanda Richards's home on Bluff Road in Amagansett many pieces of furniture and hangings that had appeared in a number of Amanda's plays and several she had neither starred in nor seen. Stage designers adored the actress and showered her with mementos as reminders of themselves and their work. When her New York town house began to take on the appearance of a prop storage facility, she wisely began to shift the overflow to her beach house.

Michael was the executive producer of Kirkpatrick Entertainment, a company his late father-in-law, Joseph Kirkpatrick, had spawned and nurtured from the early days of radio into the largest independent television network in America, WMET. When Kirkpatrick was alive and revered as an icon in the world of entertainment, his daughter and son-in-law claimed the title of "playcouple of the Western world."

Since Kirkpatrick's death, Michael and Vicky had abandoned drawing rooms in favor of boardrooms, with Vicky a major shareholder of WMET, a network now in the capable hands of Japanese and German interests, as well as the head of the prestigious Kirkpatrick Foundation. Michael, who had long harbored a desire to act, was following in his father-in-law's successful orbit as a producer. Armed with the savvy he had learned from his wife's father and in partnership with her, he was in the process of mounting his first film for Kirkpatrick Entertainment.

Michael sat in Amanda's great room, which offered a view straight across the dunes to the Atlantic Ocean. As he waited impatiently for Amanda to appear he tried to match various objects to their place of origin. The oil portrait of the actress, which hung over the fireplace mantel, he knew was from Amanda's latest hit, *Outrageous Fortune.* So, those rumors purporting that the portrait had gone from center stage to Amanda's attic where it would age grotesquely each time Amanda had a cosmetic nip 'n' tuck were untrue.

He rose when she came into the room, wearing a straight black ankle-length skirt and a white silk blouse that skimmed her slim hips. Her brown hair glowed as did her skin, which, as always, was covered with only a light dusting of powder and the slightest hint of color blended into her classically high cheekbones and perpetually pouting lips. A necklace of entwined gold threads and a pair of gold hoop ear-rings were her only accessories.

"Michael, how good to see you," she cooed, a moment before the lack of thunderous applause became apparent. She swept into Michael's open arms and returned his enthusiastic embrace.

"The tour went dark a month ago," he said. "Where have you been?"

"Repairing the damage. Even robots need maintenance, my dear. What are you drinking?" Michael made a move toward the bar. "No, let me," Amanda insisted. "Idle hands are an actress's nightmare. The perfect martini?"

"Bourbon, ice and a splash," he ordered.

"Why not? And I'll have the same." Playing bartender, Amanda complained, "The only social events in this town are fund-raisers for everything from preserving our farmlands to preventing the A&P from building a superstore on the main drag. I've been here a week and have been invited to no less than a dozen benefits."

"The hostesses, do-gooders and politicians have just twelve weeks to hostess, do good and secure votes," Michael answered, thinking that Amanda's lament was the cry of all the town's celebrated names, including his wife's.

"My neighbor up the street, the lovely Kathleen Turner, is associated with a shelter for battered women. Anyone with a recognizable name is asked to paint a scene—or whatever—on a ceramic plate which is then auctioned off at the benefit."

"Sounds like a worthy cause," Michael offered. "I take it you are hard at work with your brushes and easel."

"My dear Michael, I should be a client, not a patron, of the shelter."

Michael accepted his drink, as well as Amanda's comment, with a wry smile and, holding out a hand, requested, "Now, let me take a look at you." Amanda took the offered hand in hers, turning from left to right for his inspection.

"Sensational," came the verdict. "How do you do it?"

"That, sir, is my secret. What's yours?" Amanda referred to the seemingly eternal leading-man appearance of Michael Anthony Reo. He was in his early forties but, as they say in show business, he could play twenty-nine to thirty-five with very little help from makeup and lighting. His skin was still taut over a square jaw and his full head of straight, dark hair was as thick and vibrant as the day he graduated from New Jersey's Paramus High. Only his blue eyes—the gift of his Irish mother—which looked at the world with a dash of amusement and a large dose of cynicism, belied his youthful physique and boyish countenance.

Tonight, Michael wore a custom blue summer-weight suit and a tie that had never hung from a department store rack. "Genes," he assured her. "I don't do a damn thing that's good for me." To prove his point he accepted a cigarette from the box Amanda proffered, and picking up a lighter Amanda had used to ignite hundreds of cigarettes during the long run of *Outrageous Fortune,* he held the flame for her before lighting his own.

"Speaking of things beautiful, how is your lovely wife?" Amanda asked.

"Lovely, as a matter of fact. She'll be joining us at the theater. She said she would rather sneak in quietly than share me with the famous Amanda Richards."

"Share you?" Amanda cried. "I've been trying to seduce you for years and have been rewarded with a peck on the cheek for all my pains. If that's what Victoria calls sharing, I would hate to share a lifeboat with her."

Amanda Richards had made her availability known to Michael at their first meeting, some twenty years ago, when he was courting Victoria Kirkpatrick. He didn't take the bait not only because it would have been unfitting given the circumstances of his romance with Vicky, but also because he knew Amanda's reputation as a praying mantis— an insect species whose female cannibalizes her mate shortly after he has exhausted himself performing his marital duties. With Amanda Richards, it was an apt comparison.

"Married two decades," Amanda went on, "and still in love. Why, Michael, it's nauseating. Everyone we know has been married and divorced three times since you and Victoria said 'I do.'"

"Everyone except Amanda Richards," he reminded her. "You've never taken the plunge, Amanda, so you have no cause to comment on the joys and sorrows of conjugal bliss."

Amanda drained her glass and moved to the bar for a refill, snapping up Michael's still half-filled glass along the way. "My actor and socialite suitors have egos the size of an elephant's behind. Coupled with mine, there isn't a house in this world big enough to contain the two of us in conjugal bliss, as you would have it. I'm afraid the sorrows would woefully outweigh the joys."

"What happened to your Italian count?" Michael asked when Amanda had completed her task and handed him his bourbon.

"He went back to his Italian Contessa," she answered. "Sooner or later they all do, Michael. As dear Cole put it, '*a romp and a quickie is all little Dicky means, when he mentions romance.'* And he should know," she added with a toss of her head. The actress was famous for quoting popular Broadway lyricists, although she had never appeared in a musical.

Michael raised his glass. "Here's to Amanda Richards. Everyone's idol and no one's mate." With a gesture, Amanda returned the toast. "I take it you haven't succumbed to Joshua Aldridge's advances," Michael noted.

Amanda opened her brown eyes in mock surprise. "I didn't know he was making advances. Where did you hear that, pray tell?"

Michael shrugged. "Read it in one of the columns, perhaps. Or heard it at a party or at the club. This is East Hampton in season, Amanda, where a rumor a day keeps ennui away."

"My agent-turned-producer has too many irons in the fire to advance toward anything but an early grave—one hopes." Amanda's tone intimated that she would gladly clobber Joshua Aldridge with one of those irons to ensure her hopes were fulfilled. Not a good sign for the agent or, for that matter, Michael Reo.

Aldridge, an independent agent whose most prestigious client was Amanda Richards, had indeed turned producer. This evening, he was presenting his first effort, *Pale Sun, Bright Moon,* at the John Drew Theater in East Hampton. (Michael shuddered mentally each time the play's title popped into his head.) Michael had approached Aldridge about the possibility of Amanda playing a feature role in Michael's film and had ended up *volunteering* to escort Amanda to the theater this evening as Aldridge's producer duties would make it impossible for him to do so. But Amanda would be sitting with Aldridge, who had promised to assume the role of Amanda's date as soon as the curtain went up.

Michael had gotten the distinct impression that Aldridge and the actress were engaged in one of their famous battles. Amanda had just turned that assumption into fact. Michael had heard that Amanda had not been happy with her tour and had called Aldridge, many times, to come west and hold her hand. The agent, meanwhile, was operating a summer office out of his home in Wainscott, and the rumor of the day had it that Joshua Aldridge had discovered a bit of local talent in the form of a young man he was grooming for stardom, and an ingenue he hoped to turn into the next Amanda Richards. Hence, he had ignored Amanda's numerous cries for help and invested heavily in a play to showcase his discoveries. There were more reasons for Amanda's fury in this scenario than Michael cared to count.

When Michael had asked Aldridge if the agent thought Amanda could play a desperate fifty-year-old woman who seduces a young man, the agent had answered, "My dear Michael, Amanda Richards is a desperate fifty-year-old woman who seduces young men." He had also stated that if Michael needed a young man to portray the boy Amanda seduces, Michael might be interested in seeing Aldridge's new discovery, noting that Michael would have to be quick because, "Some very important West Coast people are already interested in him." Agents, Michael knew, talked this way and he discounted the comment.

In fact, Michael did need a young man for an important role in his film and Joshua Aldridge not only knew this, he also knew that Michael had found an actor for the part. Producer and agent had diplomatically skirted this issue for two reasons. The young man in question was not a client of the agent's but the godson of the producer. It had been the fear of being accused of nepotism that had prevented Joseph Kirkpatrick from indulging his son-in-law in an acting career and now Michael was resolved not to allow this to prevent him from furthering the career of his godson, Paul Monroe.

When Michael left Paramus, New Jersey, to seek a career as an actor in New York and landed the media mogul's daughter instead of a role in one of her father's television shows, more than the Hudson River divided him from his middle-class family who had joined the exodus from the Bronx to New Jersey in the forties. Michael's new life as an international bon vivant left little time for Sunday dinners in Paramus or excursions with his extended family to the New Jersey shore in July and August. But when his cousin asked him to stand as godfather for his son, Paul, Michael did so with pleasure and wrote out a check for the infant that was neither ostentatious nor chintzy. Thereafter, the name Paul Monrotti was placed in one of Joseph Kirkpatrick's secretary's suspense files where it popped out a week before Christmas and a week before the child's birthday as a reminder for a check, neither ostentatious nor chintzy, to be sent to Michael's godson.

When the boy's father called to tell Michael that Paul Monrotti was now Paul Monroe, the famous (some said infamous) model for Freddy Parc Enterprises, manufacturers of men's underwear, Michael met with Paul and was instantly taken with the boy's presence and determination to succeed in a field that had eluded Michael twenty years earlier. Paul reminded Michael so much of himself at nineteen that he had not hesitated a moment before offering to test Paul for a major role in the film he was producing for Kirkpatrick Entertainment. Charges of nepotism would not deter Michael's enthusiasm for his potential superstar.

The result of Michael's visit to the agent's Wainscott home was accepting two tickets to *Pale Sun, Bright Moon,* and getting cajoled into escorting Amanda to the opening.

Relieved that Amanda had given him a plausible reason to broach the subject of his script, Michael stated, "I trust one of those irons is the script I asked him to give you."

Amanda sipped her drink, obviously trying with some difficulty to refrain from draining her glass as quickly as she had her first. Amanda was a heavy drinker but one who held her liquor well, except when she was gearing up for a brawl. Then, all hell could break loose over the blandest of provocations. The next day Amanda would call those she had riled, blaming the booze for her behavior. Because she was a virtuoso of the performing arts, much was forgiven her.

Michael, who believed there was no excuse for common rudeness, did not agree with this maxim, yet here he was, courting the actress because he was in need of that special talent. The paradox of this didn't escape him. In fact, very little escaped Michael Reo's observations of the human condition—his own included.

"He sent it," Amanda stated. "By messenger."

Michael wanted to know where one got a messenger in East Hampton in July. Instead he asked, "And have you read it?"

Amanda moved about the room, tossing her cigarette into the fireplace's empty hearth, touching books, magazines and anything else that happened to be resting on a horizontal surface. Michael thought the only thing the scene lacked was a spotlight.

"I read it," Amanda finally answered, alighting on an ottoman that once held a theatrical King of Siam. "Couldn't resist. And . . ."

"And what?" Michael prompted.

"I loved it," Amanda announced, looking as if she were about to burst into tears.

"You could have fooled me," Michael answered, trying not to show his relief.

"I made two films." Amanda spoke as if confiding to a biographer. "One, a roaring success and an Academy Award. The second such a dismal failure it labeled me box office poison and unbankable, as they say out there."

"That was ten years ago, Amanda. People, and bankers, forget."

"Not this one they don't. It's become what is politely called a cult classic. Do you know what that means, Michael?" Not expecting an answer, she went on. "It means *'nice young men who sell antiques'* rent the videotape on the anniversary of my birth and laugh hysterically for two hours. *'First you're a vamp, then you're somebody's mother and then you're camp,'*" she concluded.

Michael silently named both lyricists Amanda had quoted without benefit of credit.

"In this case, Amanda, it's a stepmother. A very sexy stepmother."

"So sexy, she can't keep her hands off her stepson, who loves her to death—literally—because she was going to con him out of his father's farm, which the boy thought was worth a million but was off the mark by nine hundred and ninety-nine thousand."

"It's a true story," Michael said. "I dramatized the facts, of course, but the plot is based on a murder that took place right here in East Hampton last summer. I'm even using the detective who worked on the case as a technical advisor for the film."

"His time would be better spent looking for the boy who got away," Amanda answered.

"I was hoping the boy would turn up and audition for the role he created. He wanted to be an actor, I'm told."

"In lieu of that you've signed the underwear model who also happens to be your godson."

"I take it you got that bit of news from Aldridge," Michael responded.

"Really, Michael, it's common knowledge."

Michael fortified himself with a generous swallow of his drink before plunging in. "Paul Monroe, who was born Paul Monrotti, is my cousin's son. Vicky and I baptized him nineteen years ago and aside from sending the annual Christmas and birthday gifts, we've had no communication with him.

"As I'm sure you know, Freddy Parc ran a contest in search of a model to tout his underwear line. It was a public relations gimmick that seems to have paid off in spades. Paul, on his own, entered the contest and got the job. I didn't even know this supermodel was my godson until his father called me and told me so. I met with Paul and liked him immediately. He's got a bit of an ego, which is necessary in this business, and a lot of guts, which is even more of an asset, but he also happens to be a very sweet guy. He told me about his ambition to act and I set up a test. He's good, Amanda. Very, very good. He got the part because he's good, not because he's my godson."

Amanda laughed. "You sound like my favorite director, the late Josh Logan."

Michael thought for a moment and then said, "Of course. He gave Jane Fonda her first Broadway acting job and he was also her godfather. So what would have happened if Logan had not hired her because of who she was?"

"We would probably all be twenty pounds heavier," Amanda quipped.

It was Michael's turn to laugh. Show business gossip was so much fun because it was so innocuous. All the whispers and shouting and headlines didn't warrant a yawn twenty-four hours after the fact. Washington gossip, though just as droll, too often had dire consequences, tempering the fun with apprehension.

"I think, Michael," Amanda went on, "you want yourself, twenty years ago, for the role. The boy resembles you, in case you don't know."

Michael accepted the compliment with a shrug and a nod. "Vicky thinks so, too. I'm flattered. But he's not just a pretty face, Amanda; he's also talented."

"Today's audience will only see the pretty face, believe me. They'll also see me, old enough to be his mother, trying to separate him from his Freddy Parc briefs." Amanda shivered at the thought. "I don't like it, Michael."

"There's more to the story and the role than her relationship with her stepson," Michael protested. But this being neither the time nor the place to discuss the project, he suggested that they start for the theater if Amanda wanted to see and be seen before the curtain went up.

"You know the young man we're seeing tonight, Bill Ryan I believe he's called, also entered the Freddy Parc contest," Amanda said, reaching for another cigarette. Michael wondered what histrionic gestures actors would succumb to when cigarettes went out of fashion, as surely they must.

"I see you are up on all the latest scuttlebutt," Michael said, rising and preparing to leave.

"Thanks to Joshua's messenger," Amanda answered.

"I was wondering who delivered the script."

"Jan Solinsky," Amanda informed him. "All teeth and a Katie Hepburn accent. She aspires to the stage but right now she toils for Joshua in his summer digs."

"Where did he find her?" Michael asked.

"Would you believe she was ushering at the Bay Street Theatre in Sag Harbor. When she ushered Joshua to his seat, she charmed him with her teeth. My agent knows a patsy when he sees one and he's probably got her laboring for coolie wages. She arrived all gushing and breathless over meeting Amanda Richards. I poured her a drink and we sat down to some girl talk."

"Meaning you talked about men."

"Meaning we talked about one man. Joshua Aldridge. I learned what my agent has been up to while I was on tour, earning his bread and butter." Amanda paused for air. "First, he signed a boy he spotted out here—"

"Bill Ryan. I know. He's a friend of Paul's. In fact they met while vying for the Freddy Parc job. They were both finalists. If you can believe the hype, and Paul swears it's true, Aldridge found Bill Ryan on a fishing boat last summer."

"According to my friend Jan, it's true."

Michael shook his head. "What was Josh Aldridge doing on a fishing boat?"

Amanda killed another cigarette. This time in an ashtray. "Like you, Joshua has caught the producing bug, but unlike you he doesn't have a wife with unlimited funds and a great deal of leverage in the business. Joshua is courting angels and if they want to go fishing— well, as the money goes, so goes the producer."

Amanda Richards would not be the first, or the last, to allude to Vicky's fortune as the reason for Michael's ability to assume the title of executive producer for Kirkpatrick Entertainment with no previous experience except what he had learned at the knee of his famous father-in-law. The cries and whispers would only make him more resolute to succeed at the job and turn out a critical as well as a box office success that made it via an abundance of talent, not ready cash.

"Tonight's ingenue was in your show," Michael stated as if showing off his knowledge of the current scuttlebutt.

"Lisa Kennedy." Amanda named the girl with a noticeable edge to her voice. "She didn't come on tour with us. Schmoozing with my agent, no doubt. A pretty girl of limited talent," Amanda described Lisa Kennedy, "which is not an uncommon combination in my business."

"Paul tells me she's quite talented."

"So, he knows her, too."

"Didn't Aldridge's secretary tell you that Paul, Bill and Lisa are sharing a house just off Main Street in Amagansett? Practically around the corner from here."

Amanda sighed. "No, she spared me that. But she did tell me that your godson went to see Joshua regarding representation and Joshua turned him down. Joshua didn't like the idea of his boy coming in second in the Freddy Parc contest, I assume."

"I'm aware of that fact," Michael said, also aware of Amanda's pointed reference to his relationship to Paul Monroe. If the actress was intrigued with the haphazard interweaving of all these characters, perhaps it was because she saw the potential of a cataclysmic climax to the scenario. Maybe show business gossip wasn't as harmless as Michael believed it to be.

"Now I think we had better be on our way. There's a party following the show. Will I meet Paul Monroe there?"

"Sorry," Michael said. "Paul is at a command performance dinner at Freddy Parc's place."

"Freddy Parc? Does he have a house out here?"

"Everyone has a house in East Hampton, Amanda. Now we had better go."

Amanda left the room and when she returned she was wrapping what appeared to be a string of white feathers about her neck. "Summer furs," she announced.

Michael knew the line belonged to Blanche Dubois from *A Streetcar Named Desire*—and so did the boa.

CHAPTER EIGHT

The only difference between a Broadway opening and an opening at the John Drew Theater in East Hampton is that the latter is a dressier and more star-studded affair. In the lobby of the John Drew, Michael spotted a film director who had copped an Academy Award earlier in the year, a two-time Academy Award–winning actor, several actors of both sexes who were yesteryear's superstars and several who held that title today. It was indeed a tribute to Amanda Richards that her arrival precipitated a ripple of excitement among the show business elite and East Hampton society, causing many a sophisticated head to turn.

The "locals," who usually shunned such events at the John Drew, had turned out in force to see one of their own make the startling leap from fisherman to star attraction at the local theater house. The group, who congregated in a tight, exclusive clique, was well dressed, well behaved and noticeably unimpressed with the famous and infamous, including the lady with the white feathers draped around her neck. Michael wondered if Bill Ryan's family was among them.

While Amanda worked the lobby—waving, pecking cheeks and basking in the adulation of her peers—Victoria Reo greeted her husband with a whispered, "Where did she get the boa?"

"Do you remember her revival of *Streetcar* a few years back?" Michael whispered in return.

Vicky giggled. "Blanche's summer furs."

"In person."

Vicky wore a pink dress with a hemline just below the knee. The color and the length complimented both her blond hair and her shapely legs. She was a head shorter than Michael's six-foot frame, with a figure that was envied by women half her age. The Reos were among the handsomest couples in the crowd, a fact they exhibited with grace and a great deal of style.

"A lot of big names here tonight," Vicky noted, surveying the room. "Josh Aldridge must have called in all his marks."

"Not really," Michael answered. "This crowd would go to the opening of a door if they thought it would get them a mention in the press, even a local gazette like the *East Hampton Star*."

"With the direction this town is heading, Michael, a mention in the *Star* is on par with the *Los Angeles* and *New York Times*."

Without pointing, Vicky indicated a thin, pale face that towered above the crowd. "The giraffe with the gray crew cut. Isn't he Freddy Parc's photographer and gofer?"

"I believe he goes by the name of Avery," Michael acknowledged. "I also believe he's Freddy's former photographer and gofer."

"What happened?"

"I don't know. Paul told me he was on the scene when Freddy ran the contest but Avery didn't do the photography for the ad campaign. I assume Avery and Freddy came to a parting of the ways. I always thought his talent was a bit too esoteric for the general public, yours truly included."

"I remember meeting him mostly because I thought he was a bit fay," Vicky admitted.

"That puts you at the end of a long line."

"What did Freddy Parc ever see in him?" Vicky mused aloud.

They were interrupted by the CEO of a popular cable network

who said a few kind words to Vicky about Joseph Kirkpatrick but whose real intent was to try to feel out Michael and Vicky regarding the possibility of premiering their upcoming film on his network.

As the CEO recalled Joseph Kirpatrick's salad days—some stories true, some fabricated by the press and others fabricated by Kirkpatrick himself—the lobby's lights flickered to announce the start of Act One. Michael saw Josh Aldridge take Amanda's arm and lead her into the theater. He made polite sounds to the CEO, took Vicky's hand, and together they joined the first-nighters queuing up to enter the theater.

"Bill Ryan's performance was more than adequate," was how Michael summed up what the critics' reaction would be to Ryan's debut. Tall, almost painfully thin, dark hair and a shyness that bespoke the young man's sensitivity and vulnerability. These were probably the qualities Joshua Aldridge had spotted on that fishing boat, but Michael wasn't sure if these attributes could make Bill Ryan a competent actor, let alone a star. Time would tell.

Even if Michael had not already selected Paul Monroe for the role of the young man in his film, titled *The Hampton Affair,* he would not have considered Bill Ryan for the part. The young man in Michael's script hid his vulnerability behind a brash facade and was endowed with more grit than common sense—this was Paul Monroe's persona, not Bill Ryan's.

Amanda had not exaggerated Lisa Kennedy's beauty, but she had underestimated the young lady's talent. Kennedy wasn't simply more than adequate, she was very good, indeed. The actress had supported her leading man admirably while never upstaging him, a ploy Michael imagined she could execute with ease and charm.

"Well?" Michael said as he and Vicky patiently inched their way up the aisle along with a full house that had accorded the evening's effort three curtain calls.

"Ryan has possibilities if the right script and the right director come to his rescue—once again—his next time out. Kennedy is as beautiful as she is talented, and the director should have taken the curtain calls. He got Ryan to act up and Kennedy to play down, balancing a seesaw that looked a bit lopsided more often than not."

"Good girl. I'll make a critic of you yet."

"My dear husband, I cut my teeth on this business," she reminded him.

As if to prove her point, every celebrated name emerging from the theater who had not done so earlier now paid their respects to the daughter of the late Joseph Kirkpatrick and her husband. Many refused to express an opinion of the evening's entertainment until they heard Michael and Vicky give it their blessing. After that, it was generally declared a hit and an exuberant and rather loud crowd poured out of the John Drew to continue their chatter outside the theater.

It was a perfect summer evening with a sky full of stars and an ocean breeze that made the ladies' wraps and the men's jackets more serviceable than fashionable.

"Amanda said the party was at the James Lane Cafe," Michael said once he and Vicky were on the street and had broken free of the crowd.

"Must we?" Vicky questioned when they reached the intersection of Dunemere and James lanes. She was looking longingly toward their home at the south end of Dunemere Lane where Joseph Kirkpatrick had built a modest mansion separated from the Atlantic Ocean by the Maidstone Club and a good portion of its golf course.

"No, we don't have to, but I am courting Amanda and I need her agent's support, so I think we had better go and tell him how much we liked the show and Amanda how much we like her."

"Tell me what Amanda thought of the script," Vicky said, taking Michael's arm as they crossed Dunemere Lane and began walking down James Lane to the cafe.

As Michael spoke they meandered in a straggling procession along several blocks of East Hampton that artists and photographers have never tired of immortalizing in paint and film. The lane is flanked on the north by the old town cemetery, which gives way to the town pond—home to several families of ducks and two graceful white swans—and on the south, in order of appearance, the strollers passed an ancient windmill known as Hook Mill, the Mulford Farmstead, the Home Sweet Home cottage where it is said the poem of the same name was penned some three hundred years ago by its occupant, St. Luke's Episcopal Church and its faux Tudor manse and, finally, the James Lane Cafe, once known as The Hedges Inn when it was run by the grand master of restaurateurs, Henri Soulé.

Tonight the cafe had been taken over by Josh Aldridge, with chairs and tables gone and a buffet set up on one side of the room. The doors to the outdoor dining terrace stood invitingly open and both spaces were rapidly filling with a noisy, hyper crowd. Entering the cafe, Michael and Vicky were immediately in the bar area where Michael queued up for drinks as Vicky spoke to a friend.

While waiting, Michael noted that none of the locals he had seen at the theater made it to the festivities—had Aldridge snubbed them or vice versa? And he once more speculated as to the whereabouts of Bill Ryan's family. Michael couldn't imagine them missing the play or the party.

When, after an intolerable amount of time, Michael had not advanced one step closer to the bar and the drinks he had come for, he caught Vicky's eye and shrugged hopelessly. She nodded her under-standing and pointed toward the center of the main dining room where Joshua Aldridge now stood with his two young stars. They had not entered through the melee at the front door so must have arrived via a back door and through the restaurant's kitchen.

Michael was about to give up on the drinks and rejoin his wife when a voice behind him bellowed, "If Michael Reo is here, it must be where it's all happening."

Michael almost failed to recognize Tony Vasquez, mostly because the film director wasn't holding fast to a glass of vodka, or for that matter, any glass at all. Then Michael remembered hearing that Vasquez, who hadn't made a film in years due to his addiction to drugs, booze and women with similar preferences, had gone on the wagon. Thanks to his father-in-law, Michael was on a first-name basis with the box office elite on both coasts as well as across the Atlantic. "I came on two passes from the producer," Michael quipped.

"The author hasn't given us anything new," Vasquez said, "but Bill Ryan makes it all seem like something new and is the reason I'm here."

Michael was astonished. How had this has-been heard of Bill Ryan and known that he was being showcased in a summer theater three thousand miles from Vasquez's home turf? That a one-time respected Hollywood director would travel that distance to see a totally unknown performer open in an off-Broadway offering was too ludicrous for even a publicist's press release.

Vasquez seemed to be enjoying the puzzled look on Michael's face. "I've got something in the works, Michael, that's going to put me back on top and make Bill Ryan a household word." He stopped short, giving the impression that he had already said too much. "It isn't all gelled, so I can't say anything more but once we go into contract, remember that you heard it here first."

Michael scrutinized Tony Vasquez. Nice tan, but that went with his hometown. The suit must have set him back a couple of thousand but this didn't mean a thing. Show people often spent their last dime outfitting themselves to go begging for the money they were pretending they didn't need. But the man seemed to need Bill Ryan. Why? Even more curious, how did he know where to find Ryan and last but surely not least, Bill Ryan's talent, or lack thereof, did not warrent the attention of even a has-been like Tony Vasquez.

"Have I whetted your appetite?" Vasquez teased before moving on.

Michael wished he had something to wet his thirst. The bar was now more crowded than it had been earlier, so he gave up the quest and went to join Vicky. "It looks like a congratulatory line at a wedding reception," Vicky said as Michael approached.

Well-wishers were shaking hands with Aldridge and his protégés while lesser cast members hovered in the background. Michael thought Aldridge looked apprehensive, Lisa Kennedy nervous and Bill Ryan angry. In fact Aldridge and Lisa, on either side of Ryan, looked more like the actor's captors than his colleagues.

Amanda suddenly appeared before Michael and Vicky, holding two glasses filled with bourbon and crushed ice. "You both look like you need this," she offered along with the drinks.

"You have my undying gratitude, Amanda," Vicky said, giving Amanda Richards the obligatory peck on the cheek. "And how smart you look."

"Not as smart as you, Victoria. Pink is your color. Mine is black and white, like the handwriting on the wall. Speaking of which, what did you think of Joshua's sun and moon or whatever it's called?"

"Not bad, Amanda, you must admit," Michael said.

"I admit. How old do you think Lisa is?" Amanda asked, looking across the crowd at Lisa Kennedy.

"Nineteen," Vicky answered.

"Twenty, if she's a day," Amanda stated, "and I hate her for it." She turned to Michael and confided, "We came in through the kitchen. Trashy, but it has its advantages. Namely it leads directly behind the bar where I filled up and spotted you talking to Tony Vasquez. You know he directed my flop."

"I forgot that," Michael said.

"I wish the world would," Amanda lamented.

Vicky was about to speak when they heard Josh Aldridge shout, "Wait," while Lisa Kennedy reached out to grab Bill Ryan's arm and missed. Ryan pushed his way through the astonished crowd and fled into the kitchen and, presumably, out the back door.

Josh Aldridge's guests were treated to a second drama, one neither rehearsed nor anticipated, and like the good audience they were they fell silent, watched and listened, but had the good sense not to applaud.

Michael glanced at the majestic tall clock in the bar room. Midnight. "Maybe he doesn't want to keep his pumpkin waiting," he murmured into his wife's ear.

E D D Y   E V A N S

CHAPTER NINE

"Female. Caucasian. Five feet, four inches." Lieutenant Christopher Oliveri lowered the manual tape recorder and visually remeasured the corpse, head to foot. "Give or take an inch," he amended his first estimate. "No identification found on the body but she appears to be a local." Oliveri glanced at Detective Eddy Evans, who stood beside him in the small bedroom. Evans nodded in agreement with the last statement.

Oliveri knew the importance of first impressions at the scene of a crime before personalities, bureaucracy and politics began to compete with the facts. Hence the tape recorder. Christopher Oliveri, a ten-year veteran of the EHPD, trusted no one, including his own memory.

The girl reclining on the bed with a jockstrap tied tightly around her neck looked young enough to be Oliveri's daughter. The lieutenant, who was forty, did not record this assumption. In life she may have been a pretty young lady. Pretty, if one disregarded the unseemly red and purple blood vessels that now marred her tanned complexion, the result no doubt of the misplaced athletic supporter. Her sun-bleached hair and weathered skin attested to the fact that she had spent many hours outdoors—be it at work or play.

The eyes, in spite of their swollen condition, were closed. He didn't like touching the dead so could not record their color. "Hair straight, shoulder length, natural blond." Oliveri shrugged. The last assumption seemed gratuitous under the circumstances.

"Wearing jeans, a white blouse, no bra. Also no bag or backpack belonging to the victim in the immediate vicinity." He paused a moment and then added, "If she had either, it may have been removed by the perpetrator."

The lieutenant inspected the dead girl's feet. She wore sneakers without socks. The jeans were standard Levi's and the blouse of some synthetic fabric. Oliveri, whose gray suit was impeccably tailored, his shirt pima cotton and his striped tie silk, noticed such things.

A film director, without a moment's hesitation, would cast Christopher Oliveri in the role of a mafia prince. Brown eyes, olive skin, a beguiling smile that revealed a perfect set of teeth and a full head of dark hair, just beginning to gray at the temples, topped a five-foot eleven-inch body upon which not an ounce of excess fat appeared. Women found the lieutenant very attractive. When his wife teased him with this fact he protested that his good looks were more of an annoyance than a perk. She knew he was more pleased than vexed by his comeliness. So did he.

"Bedroom. Small." He continued to record, prompted by the activity that was now taking place in the room. A photographer, a print man and the medical examiner vied for space to perform their duties.

"Twin beds, the victim sprawled across the one on the right as you enter. The beds are separated by a chest of drawers. It's all the room can hold. One closet, contents indicate a male occupies the room." He knew that the male was now sitting in the front room of the two-bedroom Amagansett cottage, a few yards from the murdered woman.

The doctor was closing his black bag. "What can you tell me?" Oliveri asked.

"Dead. Strangled with a jockstrap," the doctor answered.

"For that you went to medical school?"

"For that question you went to detective school?"

"When?" Oliveri asked, ignoring the jibe.

"Hard to say," the doctor answered. "Isn't that what the doctor usually says in detective novels?"

The guy was a comedian. But this was East Hampton, in season, when everybody, including the ME, had an act. "Give me an estimate," Oliveri tried again.

"Rigor hasn't set in, so I would say the girl met her maker not more than three hours ago and not less than one."

Oliveri looked at his watch. It was midnight. The murder had taken place between nine and eleven.

"She looks like someone who has spent most of her life at sea," the doctor continued, "and judging from her appearance I would opt for a fishing boat, not a pleasure craft. The skin has been pummeled with an abrasive and I would say the abrasive material was salt air."

Oliveri once again looked to Eddy Evans for confirmation. The detective agreed with the doctor's assumption with an almost imperceptible nod.

"What the hell is she doing in an overpriced summer rental in Amagansett?" Oliveri exclaimed. "And dead."

"With a jockstrap tied around her neck," the doctor added. "In case you haven't noticed, Lieutenant, it's a Freddy Parc jockstrap. And if you think the kid sitting in the front room did it, think again. This is—or was—a healthy female, not unaccustomed to physical labor. The kid couldn't get a jockstrap, or anything else, around her neck without her permission."

"What makes you think she didn't give her permission?" Oliveri snapped back.

Ignoring this, the doctor ruminated, "The kid's very handsome. My daughters collect his pictures. It's embarrassing." With this the doctor gave the corpse a final glance, bowed his head as if offering a prayer for her untimely demise and walked out of the room. Oliveri waited for him to leave before addressing his subordinate. "You know her, Eddy?"

"I do. It's Heather Ryan. Her father runs a fishing boat out of Montauk." Evans, perhaps purposely, avoided looking at Heather's body as he made the identification.

"Is she a friend of Helen's?"

"Heather is—was—a year or two younger than Helen but they knew each other," Eddy answered.

Oliveri shook his head woefully. "What's happening to us, Eddy?" he sighed.

Eddy was silently grateful that only time precluded Oliveri from launching into a diatribe on *them*—the catchall term for all those who had discovered the Hamptons in the past decade, descending upon it like locusts, stripping it of all the charm they had come for in the first place and making housing and shopping unaffordable for all but themselves. This lyrical description of East Hampton's second home owners, summer renters, celebrities and the rich in general was compliments of Lieutenant Christopher Oliveri, verbatim. Eddy knew it by rote.

"Funny thing," Eddy said. "Her brother, Bill, is performing at the John Drew this evening. He went to New York a while back and made it as an actor. You must have heard about it, Chris."

"I think I did," Oliveri admitted reluctantly. He didn't like it known that he kept abreast of all the local gossip. He started out of the room and Eddy followed. They entered a narrow foyer that separated the doorways of the cottage's two bedrooms. Farther along, there was a bath to their left, and still farther, a kitchen on their right.

The foyer opened to the front room, which comprised half the square footage of the cottage and was divided into a living/dining area with sliding glass doors off the living area opening onto a small deck. The front door was directly in the center of the room, which boasted a cathedral ceiling, making it appear more spacious than in fact it was.

As the doctor opened the front door to leave, Oliveri caught a glimpse of the uniformed policeman stationed out front and he could hear, rather than see, the chatter of the crowd that was beginning to gather on the long driveway that led from Amagansett's main street up to the cottage. The late diners leaving fashionable Gordon's restaurant and Felice's pizza parlor, both directly across the street, had seen the police activity and couldn't resist following their meal with a floor show.

When the young crowd at Estia's restaurant and the Stephen Talkhouse cabaret at the far end of Main Street heard the news, Oliveri would need additional uniformed men just to clear the driveway. Amagansett, one of the five villages that comprise the town of East Hampton along with Sag Harbor, Montauk, Wainscott and East Hampton Village, did not as yet have a "celebrity tour" guide map as does Los Angeles, but word of mouth in the Hamptons seemed to work just as well, if not better. Therefore everyone crowding the driveway knew Freddy Parc's boy model occupied the cottage even if they did not know his name. It was only a matter of time before the local press picked up the scent. Oliveri wanted to get himself and the boy out before the media tried to force their way in.

The front room was furnished in motel modern, its hardwood oak flooring bare and polished to a high gloss. The area to the left of the front door as you entered held a table and six chairs. A sideboard stood beneath the dining area's two windows. It supported a huge teak fruit bowl, now empty, and a telephone.

The living area accommodated a couch, end tables holding lamps, and two club chairs, all surrounding a rectangular coffee table that looked suspiciously like a door propped up on four squat legs. A television set atop a tea trolley stood against the room's outside wall. Besides a police officer guarding the front door, the room also contained Paul Monroe.

Oliveri looked at the boy sitting on the couch and reluctantly agreed with the doctor's description of the popular male model. The kid was handsome. Like a Greek god, he thought, then shook his head woefully over this theatrical depiction of his chief suspect.

Paul Monroe was smaller than the officer had imagined him. Maybe five-seven or -eight, but perfectly proportioned as his nearly nude photographs confirmed. Well, nude except for the Freddy Parc briefs, currently positioned as the most popular brand of men's underwear in America. This marketing ploy was accomplished via a media blitz featuring Paul Monroe, sunning, running and sleeping in Freddy's underpants.

The campaign culminated with Paul's image, sixty feet high, hovering over Times Square, clad in nothing but Freddy's abbreviated shorts. Every weekend this season, East Hampton beachgoers were treated to a mini version of the Times Square billboard affixed to a banner and suspended from a monoplane that cruised the shoreline from Westhampton beach to Montauk. Many people, especially young girls and the regulars who frequented the gay beach at Two Mile Hollow in East Hampton, considered it an improvement over the planes toting adverts for suntan lotions, beer and hard rock radio stations.

Designer skivvies. Oliveri mentally dismissed the product and its designer. Rumor had it that Paul was ready to step out of Freddy Parc's briefs and onto the silver screen.

"Paul Monroe?" He opened with the obvious.

Paul's straight black hair was pasted to his damp forehead; his blue eyes were glossy with tears. When the police had arrived an hour earlier they had found him kneeling over the toilet bowl. He nodded in answer to Oliveri's question.

"That your real name?"

"Monrotti," Paul answered, standing so that he was now on eye level with his inquisitor.

Oliveri admired the gesture. Paul Monroe was frightened, but he wasn't about to cower. "Paul Monrotti?" Oliveri queried again.

"Yes."

"I'm Lieutenant Oliveri and this is Detective Eddy Evans. Now that we all know each other, introduce me to the dead girl."

Eddy was not surprised at the request. Detectives in general, and Oliveri in particular, did not give away information—they asked questions and imparted facts only when getting an answer that was contrary to those facts.

"I don't know who she is," Paul said.

"You live here, don't you?"

Paul nodded.

"Do you pick up girls on the beach or in bars and bring them here?"

"No."

"You called us at eleven. What time did you get home?"

"Maybe fifteen or twenty minutes before."

"What were you doing, looking at the body?"

"I got sick."

"So who's the dead girl?"

"I told you, I don't know."

"How did you get into the house?"

"With my key. And the door was locked."

Oliveri also knew that all the window screens were securely fixed to the sills and attached from the inside. The patio door was also bolted from within. The dead girl, and her murderer, had come in via the front door. "Notice anything strange when you came in?" Oliveri asked.

"Not until I went into the bedroom."

"Who else has a key to the cottage?"

"Bill Ryan and Lisa Kennedy. We share the place."

"And where are Mr. Ryan and Ms. Kennedy this evening?"

"At the theater. The John Drew in East Hampton. Bill and Lisa are appearing in the show that opened tonight."

"How come you're not over there applauding your roommates?"

"I had another engagement."

"So, how did the victim get in here? Do you figure someone blew her away outside the house and then slipped her under the door?"

"You tell me. You're the detective," Paul countered.

Oliveri tensed but kept his cool. "Do you own a Freddy Parc jock-strap?"

"No," Paul replied.

"Yeah, that's right." Oliveri nodded as if in deep thought. "You like to let it all hang out." Before Paul could reply Oliveri continued, "Who sleeps in the room currently serving as a morgue?"

Paul visibly shuddered. "It's my bedroom."

"Then Ryan and Kennedy occupy the other bedroom."

"That's right," Paul answered.

"Are they lovers?"

"Ask them, Lieutenant. I share the house, not their love life."

Oliveri waved a hand around the room. "Given the size of this place it would be difficult keeping out of each other's back pockets, let alone each other's love life."

"Are you getting off on this, Lieutenant?" Paul's wisecrack had Eddy Evans wincing.

Oliveri started and took a step toward Paul but stopped a moment before committing himself to a charge of police brutality. Then, to Eddy's amazement, the lieutenant began to smile. Paul's bravado and buckling knees were an infectious combination and if Christopher Oliveri had a son he would expect nothing less of him. "Just answer the questions, kid," Oliveri advised. "Now, who pays the rent on this cottage? Main Street, Amagansett, short walk to everything, including the ocean, two bedrooms, in season, ten thousand a month, minimum."

"I work for Freddy Parc Enterprises."

"What do you do for Freddy?"

"I'm a model. That's what I do."

"Tell me about it," Oliveri snapped.

"Please," Paul pleaded, his blue eyes glaring at Oliveri. "You know I'm the centerpiece of a multimillion-dollar ad campaign for Freddy Parc Enterprises."

Oliveri, of course, knew this, but he liked to push the envelope when questioning a suspect. It took the starch out of them. Eddy, who never intervened when his boss chose to control the interview, figured it would take a lot of pushing to intimidate Paul Monroe.

"Where were you tonight? Before eleven, that is?" Oliveri changed direction, another way to keep a suspect off his guard.

"At a dinner party."

"Where?"

"Freddy Parc's home, on Further Lane."

"I know where Freddy Parc lives." Oliveri looked purposely at the boy's attire. Jeans and dress shirt—sans tie—both of which would reveal Freddy Parc labels should Oliveri care to look. "Not a very formal dinner for fancy Further Lane. Martha would never approve," Oliveri scolded mockingly.

"Ms. Stewart was one of the guests."

Eddy suppressed a smile as Oliveri went in for the kill. "The dead girl is your roommate's sister. Does that jog your memory?"

"Lisa's sister?" Paul looked amazed.

"No. Bill Ryan's sister."

"That's not possible," Paul uttered, shaking his head as if to clear it.

"Not possible? Why?"

"Bill is an orphan. He has no family," Paul stated.

"He told you that?"

"Yes."

Oliveri turned to Eddy, and knowing better than to verbalize his ignorance in front of a suspect, the detective merely shrugged his shoulders.

"Do you know that Bill Ryan is from these parts?" Oliveri asked.

"Yes," Paul said. "He grew up in Montauk. He was a fisherman."

"Who raised him?"

"I think he was in foster care," Paul responded. "Look, Lieutenant, I haven't known Bill that long. Less than a year. I'm just telling you what he told me, and I never saw that poor girl before I saw her dead. I swear it."

"You haven't met the people who raised Bill Ryan since you've been here?"

"No. Never. He doesn't talk about them and I never asked any questions because it's none of my business." Paul sank back down on the couch. "This is a nightmare. There's a dead girl in my bedroom. I don't know who she is or how she got where she is. Would you please get her and yourself out of here and leave me alone?"

"I intend to do just that, Paul. Only you're coming with me."

"What? Where?"

"To the station house for questioning."

"I thought that's what you were doing here—now."

"Questioning you without reading you your rights. Why, Paul, how could I do such a thing? That's against the law."

Paul got to his feet. "I want to make a phone call," he demanded. "I'm allowed to do that. I know I am."

"You can make a call when we get to the station," Oliveri told him. "Do you know a lawyer in town?"

"No, I don't."

"So who are you going to call?"

"Michael Reo."

Oliveri rolled his eyes toward the ceiling before glaring at Eddy Evans. Eddy avoided the gaze as he politely guided Paul Monroe toward the front door.

Paul removed a handkerchief from his back pocket and pressed it against his face. "Are you going to be sick?" Oliveri cried.

"No," Paul shot back. "I don't want them to see my face."

"Why not?"

"Because I look like shit, that's why not."

CHAPTER TEN

Eddy brought a container of coffee to the lockup where Paul Monroe was being detained. "It's decaf," Eddy said, "so it won't keep you awake."

Paul, seated on the cell's cot, looked at the detective as if the man were crazy and then smiled a silent thank-you. After a star-studded dinner party where several guests, after several drinks, had told him they did not recognize him with his clothes on—an observation that was fast wearing thin—coming home and finding a corpse on his bed, being interrogated by Christopher Oliveri and now, at three o'clock in the morning, finding himself in jail and being offered decaf coffee for a nightcap by his captor had Paul Monroe feeling more like a candidate for a padded cell than Freddy Parc's supermodel.

But when being tendered a little cheer and solace by Eddy Evans, one could not help but smile in gratitude. Six feet high, one hundred and sixty pounds, crew cut atop, penny loafers below and a face that had God, mother and country written all over it, Eddy Evans was a man you could trust with your wife, daughter and wallet.

"I don't expect to get much rest tonight," Paul said, "but I appreciate the thought." Looking about he noted, "Quiet night. Am I your only customer or do you keep the serial killers in a dungeon below stairs?"

With a wave to the guard on duty Eddy entered the cell. Leaving the door open, he sat on the cot next to Paul. "You're all we've got to keep us company. It happens, but not too often in season. No luck with the phone call?"

"No," Paul answered. "They must have gone to the theater and then on to the reception after the curtain."

"You weren't invited to the reception? You could have gone after your dinner party."

"I wasn't invited," Paul admitted, and then shook his head in a manner that said he either didn't care or wouldn't have gone if he had been asked.

"How come?"

"Politics. It's a long story and it's as silly as it is meaningless to the reason I'm here." Paul sipped the coffee and took some comfort from the warm liquid and its familiar taste.

"You want to try again? I mean the phone call," Eddy suggested.

"Not at this hour," Paul declined. "No sense in waking up the house. Tomorrow morning is soon enough for them to get the news." Thinking this over, Paul asked, "Could Michael get me out of here if he came now? I told you he's my cousin."

Appearing reluctant to deliver the news, Eddy told him, "We can legally hold you for twenty-four hours without charging you."

"Charging me?" Paul exclaimed. "You mean for murder? For murdering a girl I don't even know?"

Eddy touched Paul's shoulder. "Don't get in an uproar. Unless something extraordinary comes up between now and tomorrow morning, which I doubt, you'll be out of here by high noon."

"So why did he bring me here in the first place?" Paul moaned.

"To make sure you don't disappear on us," Eddy said.

Paul again looked askance at the detective. "Mr. Evans, not many people know my name but my face and the rest of me is on display all over the country. Including a rendition sixty feet high in Times Square. Where could I hide and why would I want to?"

Eddy nodded in agreement. "It's true, but just suppose you did panic and run. We would have you back in no time, but Oliveri would look like a fool, an image that would not make him happy, believe me. He did what any cop would do. It's insurance."

"Does he think I killed her?"

"Put it this way," Eddy explained, "you reported the crime and you live in the house where the murder took place. Right now you're all he has and he's not about to let you go until he absolutely has to."

Paul put the container of coffee, unfinished, on the concrete floor and, still not convinced of Heather's identity, asked, "Is she really Bill's sister?"

"Her name is Ryan. Heather Ryan. As far as I know she's Bill Ryan's sister. Maybe the Ryans took Bill in as a foster child, as he told you, but he's been with them so long most people think he's Job's son. Job Ryan is Heather's father. I know this for a fact."

Paul, who was having a hard time keeping his eyes open, said, "I guess it's true, but Bill never mentioned them to me and I swear I never saw that girl until I saw her dead."

"Why do you think Bill lied to you?"

"He didn't lie, Mr. Evans. He told me, and Lisa, that he was an orphan, raised by foster parents. The end. He didn't give us any more information than that, and we never asked for more. At least I didn't. You hear stories about kids being abused in foster care and I figured maybe Bill wanted to forget the experience. Bill's a nice guy. A hick, but a nice guy."

Rethinking the latter description of his friend, Paul looked at Eddy apologetically when he asked, "Are you from out here?"

"Queens, New York," Eddy answered. "I've been here about a dozen years, which makes me an alien. Chris Oliveri is fourth generation, which makes him a newcomer. The Ryans are considered local, including your friend Bill."

"He's local, all right," Paul said with affection rather than sarcasm. "And if the girl is his sister, why wasn't she at the theater to see him perform?"

"That's just one of the many things we have to find out. The lieutenant was hoping you could tell us that."

"The lieutenant thinks I have the answers to all the questions," Paul said with scorn. After leaving the cottage, Oliveri had taken Paul to the station house on Pantigo Road and formally booked him. He then read Paul his rights and allowed him to make a phone call to the Reo house, which proved fruitless. Then Oliveri had continued to question Paul for almost an hour in the presence of Eddy Evans and a tape recorder before sending him off to bed down in the lockup. "The guy has a chip on his shoulder," Paul added.

Eddy sighed without making a sound. Paul Monroe was not the first visitor to East Hampton to make such a pronouncement after tangling with Lieutenant Oliveri for any reason from a chance meeting at a social function to being hauled into the station for a misdemeanor. The assertion was, in fact, true. Oliveri did have a chip on his well-tailored shoulder, which he balanced precariously in the faces of the summer hordes including, or especially, the rich and famous ones. However, this Eddy expressed aloud, "He's a good cop and an honest one. He would never try to railroad anyone, Paul, believe me. All he wants is to see justice done, and he doesn't give up until he's convinced the right person is paying for the crime. Corny, I know, but it's the truth."

"He thinks I did it," Paul stated as if to disprove Eddy's faith in Christopher Oliveri's crusade for justice.

Eddy was quick to answer. "We have some problems with this case, Paul."

"You have problems?" Paul shot back. "I have the problem, in case you've forgotten."

"What I mean, Paul, is you said the cottage door was locked when you arrived and you opened it with your key."

"Well, I did," Paul all but shouted. "That's the truth. I know everyone around here says they don't have to lock their doors but Lisa and I are city folk, Mr. Evans, so we lock. Would you rather I lied?"

Eddy was thinking that if Paul had lied and said he found the door open he might not be spending the night as a guest of the East Hampton taxpayers. "The front door was locked as was the patio door. The windows were open but the screens were all in place and secured from the inside. You told us there are three keys to the cottage. Yours, Bill Ryan's and the girl's, Lisa Kennedy."

"As far as I know, that's it," Paul told him. "You see, Joshua Aldridge, the man who's producing the play, rented the cottage for Bill and Lisa. I have something in the works with my cousin Michael Reo, and when he asked me to come to East Hampton Bill suggested I share the cottage with him and Lisa. That's when the rental agent had a key made for me. I told all of this to Oliveri a dozen times."

Eddy wanted to remind Paul that Heather Ryan had either walked or been carried into the cottage via the front door, but Oliveri had stressed that point repeatedly when questioning Paul. Eddy had come to the cell to soothe Paul's ruffled feathers, not to harass him further. "And the other two keys were at the John Drew Theater all last night," Eddy said.

"By now Bill and Lisa must be back at the house," Paul thought aloud, looking as if he were trying to envision their reaction to finding a policeman waiting to greet them. "Do you know what's going on there?"

"Sorry, Paul, I don't. We have an officer stationed there but we haven't been in contact with him. He would have told Bill and Lisa what happened when they got back home. We'll just have to wait till morning to know how they took the news, and we'll want statements from them, too."

Paul positioned himself on the cot so that he was able to lean his back against the wall. If he wasn't at ease, Paul was noticeably more relaxed since talking to Eddy Evans. This relative calm being the result of an old and reliable police procedure. One officer ruthlessly grilling a suspect and, later, another offering the prisoner a little TLC in the guise of father confessor. Oliveri and Evans were perfectly suited for the roles of the tough and tender inquisitors.

"I think I should tell you, Paul, that I know Mr. Reo," Eddy suddenly divulged.

Paul rubbed his eyes with the back of his hand and then tried to focus them on Eddy Evans. "Are you the cop that's helping him with the script?"

"Technical advisor," Eddy corrected. "I was involved with the case he's going to film."

"So you must have known my connection to Michael as soon as you learned who was living in the cottage."

"I did," Eddy admitted.

"Why didn't you say so?" Paul asked him.

Looking embarrassed, Eddy answered, "Because it has nothing to do with police business."

"You mean you're moonlighting with Michael and your boss doesn't like it so why remind him of the fact." The way he had literally stood up to Oliveri, Paul now made it clear to Eddy that he could give as well as take. And, like Oliveri, Eddy admired Paul's moxie.

"I mean, what I do on my own time is my own business as long as it doesn't interfere with my work." Eddy rose to leave. "Now why don't you try to get some rest. It'll be light in a few hours."

With some effort Paul raised his back from the wall and turned so that he was able to stretch out on the cot. He had removed his shoes but kept his jeans and shirt on. "I'll try, but don't count on it."

"If you have to use the bathroom, call the guard. He'll take you there."

"And back, I'm sure," Paul called as Eddy left the lockup and closed the door behind him.

As he passed the desk sergeant, the man said to Eddy, "The word is out and I've had a dozen calls since midnight, mostly from New York.

The press is going to pounce on us before dawn and it looks to be bigger news than when the rap star was giving his weekly parties with a cast of thousands."

"You know what rhymes with rap," Eddy tossed back.

"That's politically incorrect, Evans, but I'll pretend I didn't hear it. And get this, some joker has already dubbed the case 'The Jockstrap Murder.'"

"Where did you hear that?"

"From the reporters who called, where else?"

"And how did they know the modus operandi?" Eddy asked accusingly.

"Who leaked the *Pentagon Papers* to the *New York Times*?" was the answer he got. "They also say the kid is a relative of Mrs. Reo. Is it true?"

"He's Mr. Reo's cousin," Eddy said.

"He'll be out of here in the morning," the sergeant predicted with confidence.

"He'd be out of here even if he wasn't Reo's cousin."

"Ho, ho, no," the sergeant exploded. "Is he wearing Freddy Parc briefs?"

"Enough, Sergeant."

"Lighten up, Evans."

Eddy found Christopher Oliveri still sitting in the interview room looking as meticulously groomed as he had before they received the call from Paul Monroe that dispatched them to the Amagansett cottage.

His tie was perfectly knotted whereas Eddy seldom wore a tie; his suit jacket was not only on, but buttoned, and Eddy had discarded his jacket the moment they arrived back at the station house and right now he was not quite sure where he had left it. Oliveri's hair was neatly parted on the left and combed back with not a hair out of place; thanks solely to his crew cut, Eddy's hair was equally unruffled; and while a bit of five o'clock shadow was beginning to emerge on

Oliveri's face it only added a masculine charm to his healthy complexion; for his part, Eddy felt an overwhelming desire to step under a shower and subject his face to its hot needle spray.

Eddy envied his superior's unfailing ability to look like the guy in a police department recruiting poster, but there were times, like now, when he found the distinction as annoying as the antics of a precious child.

Oliveri admired Eddy's wholesome good looks and disarming charm. ("I bet you even wear a forty *regular* suit," Oliveri often groused. Eddy did.) But at times, like now, Oliveri bemoaned his assistant's too human qualities, such as looking beat after putting in a long day and showing too much compassion for those who didn't deserve any.

Oliveri enjoyed teaching and Eddy was eager to learn from his mentor. More important, they liked and respected each other, making their working relationship a winning combination for the EHPD.

"Anything?" Oliveri questioned as Eddy took a seat at the room's rectangular table.

"Nothing, Chris. He hasn't changed his story in any way and I believe him. He knows as much about this murder as we do."

Oliveri mulled this over before saying, "Not true. He knows one person who's close to the victim, therefore he knows more than we do, but he doesn't know what he knows. Understand?"

Eddy nodded. It was true. Witnesses to a crime very often failed to realize that the most seemingly mundane facts could be the solution to the crime. It was the detectives' job to probe and judge what was and was not relevant. "He did say that there was to be a party after the show tonight—or last night—but he wasn't invited."

"Why?"

"'Politics' was the word he used," Eddy said.

"Interesting. More blood has been shed over politics than any national disaster. Let's find out why Paul Monroe wasn't invited to the party and how much he may have resented being passed over. Also, why wasn't Heather at the theater and where was her father—what did you say his name was?"

"Job. Job Ryan. He runs the boat *Job's Patience,* out of Montauk. And," Eddy continued, "because Bill never mentioned the family, or foster family, Paul thinks they may have given him a hard time so Bill wants to forget them. Maybe Bill left Montauk after a falling-out with Job and Heather. Job's wife passed away some time ago."

"They have a falling out and the girl turns up dead. There's a lead. You think Helen can fill us in on the domestic scene at the chez Ryan?"

"She'll tell me as much as she knows, but remember, Helen and Heather weren't close friends, just acquaintances. Helen is on a first-name basis with everyone who comes into the shop."

"See what you can find out, Eddy." Oliveri began to tick off points, verbally underlining them by jabbing a forefinger in the air. "Under what circumstances did Bill Ryan leave Montauk? Why weren't the Ryans at the theater, cheering their actor relation? Why wasn't Paul Monroe, a friend and roommate, invited to the post-theater festivities? What is the relationship between Bill Ryan and Lisa Kennedy? If they are tight, as my daughter would say, is Paul Monroe jealous, and if so, of who or whom, Bill or Lisa?" Oliveri paused for effect. "How did Heather Ryan get into the cottage, alive or dead, if Paul Monroe didn't let her in, vertically or horizontally?"

It seemed to Eddy the answer to Oliveri's final question would solve the crime and he doubted if the lieutenant's other points would lead to that resolution. But a sidekick must learn to live in the shadow of his better and Eddy would rather chill out in Oliveri's shade than swelter in his heat. "Is that all, Chris?" Eddy asked.

"No, that's not all," Oliveri barked. Eddy recognized the tone and guessed what was coming. "I knew that sooner or later your relationship with Michael Reo would get tangled up with your work. Why didn't you tell me the kid was Reo's cousin before I had to hear it from him?"

"Because I didn't think it was germane to our investigation at the moment—and I still don't think it is."

"Don't you? Reo is involved in producing films. Our chief suspect is Reo's cousin who, you were so kind to tell me, Reo is going to feature in his film. Nepotism of the first degree. Bill Ryan is an actor. His girl is an actress. His sister, or half-sister or foster sister, is dead. The joint is lousy with artistic types and one corpse and you don't see a connection?"

"No!" Eddy answered.

What else could Lieutenant Oliveri do but laugh? "Okay, you win for now, but nosy around the potentates and see if you can learn who's doing what to whom, and why. More blood has been shed over a part in a film than politics."

BILL RYAN

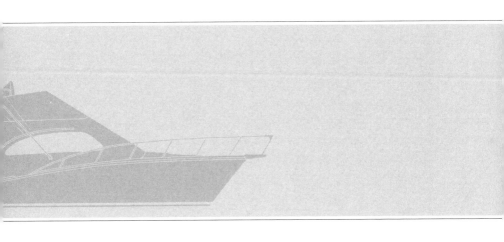

CHAPTER ELEVEN

Bill drove east in the rented Ford as if rushing to meet the dawn, which was just beginning to send streaks of purple light, like tendrils, across the dark summer sky. He sped past the intersection that linked the old Montauk Highway to the start of the new speedway, continuing on the ancient roller-coaster stretch of road that was now known as the scenic route between Amagansett and Montauk. He had either missed the turn or forgotten that it was the faster path to his destination. He knew only that, like a shark, he had to keep moving or he would die.

But he did want to die. He would have gladly turned into any of the driveways that led to the prestigious cliff dwellings on the old highway, crashing through the guardrail and cascading down to oblivion on the sandy beach below if, in exchange for his life, God would return Heather to the land of the living where she belonged. He couldn't imagine Heather dead. It just wasn't possible. But she was dead. The policeman had said she was. They had found her on Paul's bed. Her body had been taken away and the tiny bedroom sealed with a policeman guarding the door. And Paul was gone. The crazy bastards had arrested Paul.

Like everything Bill now possessed, the rental car was compliments of Joshua Aldridge, who had presented it to him and Lisa before they left the city for East Hampton. He was pushing it to its limits but had no idea what those limits were because he couldn't see the speedometer through the tears that kept spilling over his cheeks, coating his lips with their salty residue. He couldn't see much of the highway, either, but it made no difference. He knew the way, but even if he never got there, that would be okay, too.

About like a minnow coming up against a barracuda. Heather's teasing words played over and over in his head like some plaintive melody he was unable to shake off. *About like a minnow coming up against a barracuda.* And she had been right, as she had been right about so many things. So why was she dead and he still alive? Because no one goes after minnows, that's why. It's the barracudas that draw the sharks.

Like a minnow, Bill had moved with the current from the day he had fled Montauk and presented himself to Joshua Aldridge, theatrical agent, never dreaming that the flow would carry him back to his starting point. Once back he had to contend with the frustration of not being able to see the people he called his family, and the anxiety of having to appear on a stage, in front of an audience, for the first time in his young life. The anxiety had turned to terror when, the afternoon of the play's opening, Heather had called to say she had to see him—the sooner the better.

When he knew Bill was coming back to East Hampton, and there was no way of avoiding it, Job had decided that Bill should have no contact with the family. Job had let it out a year ago that Bill had left against Job's wishes. Like a child who covers his face to make himself invisible, Job believed the greater the distance, physically and emotionally, between Bill and himself, the safer they would both be from any connection between Bill's truck being spotted at the scene of the drug raid in Sag Harbor and Job's lame excuse for its presence there.

When the police never returned for the name and address of Job's alleged romantic interest in Sag Harbor, Job thought it best to count their blessings and maintain the status quo. The truth of the matter being that there is no rest for a guilty conscience, and the three, Job, Heather and Bill, lived in fear of a return visit from Eddy Evans or his superiors, whom Bill and Job believed to be the dreaded narcotics squad. Bill's last, brief contact with Job was to give Job the telephone number of the Amagansett cottage to be used for emergency purposes only.

If Heather had broken the rule and contacted Bill for a meeting it could only mean that the feared emergency had arrived. When the call came, Paul was out and Lisa was sunbathing on the deck. Telling Heather he could not see her that night because he was opening in a play was about as ludicrous as everything else that had happened to Bill Ryan since he left Montauk for New York. With Lisa in full view on the other side of the glass doors leading to the deck and a short distance from the telephone, he couldn't think beyond telling Heather he would call her back as soon as he could safely arrange a meeting.

Bill's first thought was to have Paul Monroe appear for him on the stage of the John Drew so that he could meet with Heather as early as possible. And why not? Paul, who had coached Bill since the day Joshua Aldridge had given Bill the script for *Pale Sun, Bright Moon,* knew all the lines and was an actor, not a mimic like Bill.

He dismissed the idea as impossible faster than he had conjured it up and did the next best thing. He had learned that, after acting, timing is the single most important element in the theater. The opening night curtain was to go up at seven and come down, after one intermission, at exactly nine. He had been told that Aldridge was giving a celebratory dinner party for him and Lisa after the show. Aldridge's date was to be the famous actress Amanda Richards. Bill had declined the invitation and both Lisa and Aldridge had thought it best not to force the issue. Their goal was to get Bill Ryan on the stage in front of an audience. Getting him to appear socially would have to wait its turn.

It was less than a ten-minute drive from the theater to the Amagansett cottage. He would take the Ford and Aldridge would drive Lisa home after their dinner party.

He called Heather, leaving a message on her answering machine telling her to be at the cottage at nine and wait for him there. "They lock the door," he told her, "but there's a deck. Wait for me there. I won't be more than ten minutes." Paul was going to Freddy Parc's and would not be at the opening. He doubted if Paul would be home as early as nine but to cover himself he told Paul that he was expecting an old girlfriend and not to be surprised if Paul found her waiting when he got home. Bill and Paul, as unlikely a pairing as Huck Finn and Little Lord Fauntleroy, had become confidants in the short time they had known each other.

But, as is the way with currents, the one carrying the minnow in its wake had unexpectedly changed course, upsetting Bill's plans and, he now believed, was responsible for the death of his beloved Heather. Between a technical problem with the lights and an audience who enjoyed chatting outside the theater on a lovely summer evening, the curtain went up a half hour late. Because of first night jitters the play had run over its allotted time and, due to its late start, ended at ten instead of nine.

After stage fright proved more harrowing then piloting *Job's Patience* through a hurricane, he had been forced to greet well-wishers who invaded the wings and dressing rooms after the curtain, preventing him from leaving the theater the instant he had taken his final bow. Then he had been told there was to be an opening-night party that he was obligated to attend.

Without even listening to his protests, he was practically dragged to the James Lane Cafe and wedged between Lisa and Aldridge, where he had to shake hands with people he didn't know and didn't care to know. But even in his fury he had not failed to notice that none of his people from Montauk, those who had attended the play, had been invited to the party. It was at this point that the minnow decided to buck the tide and go his own way.

He was still at the cottage, sitting on the couch in a state of shock, when Lisa came in a few hours later. When she saw Bill she thought he was having a nervous breakdown. When she saw the policeman and he told her what had happened, it was Lisa who looked on the verge of collapse. The scene that followed was surreal.

Lisa demanded to know who the girl was and Bill did his best to explain, telling her as little as possible and therefore not making much sense. "Sister? Sister?" Lisa kept exclaiming in bewilderment. "You never said you had a sister."

"She's not really my sister."

"Then what is she?"

It went on like this—Lisa posing questions and Bill evading any direct response—for what seemed like an eternity.

"Please, Lisa," Bill finally begged. "Not now. I'll explain later."

"Explain now or I'll go out of my mind. A murder? Here? And Paul arrested?"

"It's a mistake. They arrested Paul by mistake. I'll explain everything tomorrow. Now I have to go."

"Go," she screamed, hysterically. "Go where? First you run out on me at the cafe—and just how did you expect me to get home? Now you want to leave me alone in a house where a murder was committed a few hours ago. If you go, I'm going with you."

"I have to go to her father," Bill explained.

"Her father? The dead girl's father?" Lisa was in tears. "Bill, what is going on? What was the girl doing here, in our house?"

Even under duress Bill remembered not to say Heather had come to meet him with the policeman listening to their every word. "I don't know, Lisa. I don't know. Call Mr. Aldridge. Tell him what happened. Tell him to come here and get you. I'm taking the car."

"It's three o'clock in the morning," Lisa sobbed. "Please don't leave me here."

"I have to go, Lisa. I have to go." He repeated the words by rote, like the lines he had been forced to learn for the play, and for the second time that night, the minnow swam upstream.

He didn't want to think about Lisa now, or if Heather had been raped while he was shaking hands at a fancy East Hampton restaurant. Nor did he try to ponder why the bastard had carried her into the house or how he got into the house without a key. Least of all did he want to think about Paul. Why had they arrested him and what had he told the police? Paul had promised to keep Bill's date with a former girlfriend a secret, but the bargain, he was sure, did not include murder.

Regardless of how Paul identified Heather, the police would know who she was. If Paul talked, what reason could Bill give the police for his late-night meeting with Heather, and why he had lied to Paul about his relationship to her? If Paul didn't talk he would not have to say anything. But how could he know what Paul had said or not said? He had to meet with Paul before he was forced to give a statement to the police. But when, where and how?

To keep from screaming he kept repeating to himself that Heather was dead and he had to see Job. For the moment, that was all that mattered.

Bill pulled into the gravel driveway and stopped abruptly near the front door. Just as the car's engine died the wail of the Long Island Railroad shattered the silence. Bill Ryan rested his weary head on the Ford's steering wheel and sobbed—and sobbed—and sobbed . . .

"I killed her," Job said, "just as if I had tied that filthy thing around her neck."

They sat at the kitchen table, the empty third chair a glaring reminder of Heather's absence from the family gathering. When Bill arrived he found Job barefoot, in jeans and sweatshirt, moving aimlessly around the familiar room. "The police have been and gone," he told Bill, and then the two did something they had never done before. They embraced and shamelessly cried on each other's shoulders. When there were no more tears left to shed, they sat in silence, comforting each other with only their presence, as was their way.

Bill brewed a pot of strong coffee as the sky grew light. Pouring out two cups, he recalled the dawn following the raid in Sag Harbor when the three of them had sat in the kitchen drinking coffee and setting into motion the plan that, like a boomerang, had come back to haunt them.

"Don't say that," Bill answered Job's lament. "Looking to place the blame won't bring her back. What we have to do now is decide where we go from here. That's what Heather would say."

"We don't go no place," Job answered. "It's Avery who's going to his grave before the sun sets on Heather's."

"He didn't do it, Job. He was at the theater, watching me. He's got a couple of hundred people who can swear to that."

"Then it was one of his people who done it."

"And who are they, Job?"

"The devil, that's who."

Bill drank his coffee and tried to formulate a plan of action but his tired mind kept coming back to Paul and what Paul may or may not have told the police. He couldn't plan a move without a map indicating the location of the booby traps, which were too numerous to count.

"Why did Heather want to see me?" he thought aloud.

"To let you know she had decided to tell Avery I was finished playing his errand boy. She wanted to make a clean break even if it meant we would go to jail."

"What?" Bill cried.

"Now don't get antsy. Heather was no fool. She read up on things. She said if we went to the police and made a clean breast of things, they would go easy on us in return for our cooperation. That's what she said. Maybe we wouldn't have to do any time at all. In fact, she was sure we wouldn't." Here, Job got up but, to Bill's relief, he did so to refill his coffee cup, not to get a can of Bud.

"She was in the clear, Bill. You know that. After you went, I did it all alone. She wanted to help but I wouldn't let her. That's the truth."

Bill knew it was the truth. Since leaving for New York, Bill had talked to Heather at least once a week and she had kept him posted of the fact that Job, by himself, was still doing the private runs in fear of

Avery's retribution should he refuse to carry on. Did Avery know what Heather was planning, and if so, could he have ordered her death? Bill shivered as the brisk morning air invaded the kitchen through the screen door that was kept open all summer.

Or was Heather's death a result of the rush of people that now came to East Hampton to see for themselves why it had become a haven for movie stars and Wall Street moguls? DFDs, they were called by the locals: Down For The Days. It was their presence that made it necessary for the local shops to employ security guards to discourage shoplifters and other undesirables. Did those other undesirables include rapists and murderers, as well as college kids on a spree? Heather, alone on that deck some five hundred feet from tiny Amagansett's main drag, but as isolated as an atoll in the vast Pacific Ocean.

And did knowing who was responsible make any difference?

"It would be you and me taking the fall," Job was saying. "She wanted your permission to go to the police."

But the police had come to her, Bill thought, sadly.

"You see, Bill . . ."

"She wanted to marry Ian Edwards," Bill finished Job's explanation. "She told me she and Ian had an understanding."

"But she wouldn't marry him with this thing hanging over us," Job went on as if Bill had not broken his train of thought. "People are talking about my solitary evening runs. I know that and so does Ian. Heather wanted to go to him with a clear conscience and for that she had to stop the runs the only way she knew how."

"Did Avery know what Heather was planning to do?"

"I don't think she was that foolish," Job said, "but you know how Heather was. She never had a kind word for Avery and she couldn't keep her face from telling people what was on her mind."

"Then we can't be sure it was Avery who . . ." Bill broke off abruptly, allowing the unspoken words to hover between them as clearly as if he had shouted them aloud.

"We can't be sure of anything, kid," Job said. "Now you better get back to your house and that girl I hear you're smitten with. An actress, no less." Job wanted to add that he had had his share of visiting actresses but didn't think it was the time or place to do so.

"I'm never going back there," Bill protested. "I'm staying here where I belong, with you."

"Are you daft, kid? We dealt ourselves a hand and now we got to play it out. You got a new life going and I gotta square off with Avery. And you keep out of my face or I'll punch yours out."

The fury was directed not at Bill but at those who had caused Heather's death. Job had something planned and Bill suspected the worst. "Please don't do anything you'll regret," Bill advised. "We don't even know if Avery is responsible."

"Like I just said, we don't know anything, and until we do we stick to our original plan and keep our distance. Less said, soonest mended, Carol used to say, and that's how we'll play it. We keep our mouths shut and our eyes and ears open."

Bill doubted if even Job had a homily to salvage the fact that, thanks to Bill, Paul Monroe was now a loose cannon in their dangerous game. How soon could Paul's statement to the police be mended? "What about the funeral?" he asked Job.

"That's my job."

"You can't cut me out, Job. She was like my sister. More even. I want to be with you when we put Heather to rest."

Job Ryan knew when to raise the ante and when to fold his hand. "And you will be, kid. I promise."

They started when they heard the front door open followed by the heavy tread of booted feet on the bare floor. A moment later Ian Edwards marched into the kitchen wearing waders over his jeans, his blond hair uncombed and his blue eyes blazing with fury. Spotting Bill, the ire found a target. "What the fuck are you doing here?"

"Easy, Ian," Job began, standing. "You're in my house and Bill is here to pay his respects. You heard what happened?"

"It's all over town," Ian cried, choking back tears. A good two inches over six feet, Ian Edwards looked like the god Thor about to vanquish the unfaithful. "She was killed in the house he's sharing with the actress and the pervert who runs around half-naked. The place has one bedroom is what I heard."

Bill winced. He had grown up in a town where gossip and innuendo were as commonplace as the local weather report, but he had never been the subject of the hearsay. "That's not true," he said to Ian. "The house has two bedrooms, Paul is as straight as you, and you never heard anything like that from Heather."

"Who cares?" Ian shouted. "What was Heather doing there last night? She never told me she was going there."

"She came to meet me," Bill admitted.

"You? I heard you were on the stage with your lady friend."

When Bill looked as if he were about to get up and confront Ian physically, Job intervened. "Quiet, both of you. We'll have plenty of time to talk about the whys and the hows when we learn what the police have to say. Until then we act like family, not enemies."

"Has this got anything to do with your secret night runs?" Ian said, turning to Job.

To Bill's relief, Job didn't so much as flinch when he said, "It has to do with mourning my daughter."

"I loved your daughter," Ian reminded Job.

"We all loved her," Bill said.

"But she was carrying my baby, not yours," Ian sobbed.

Job stared at Ian, his eyes and mouth wide open. Bill, in spite of himself, felt an invisible hand lift a weight from his shoulders, sending it through the kitchen ceiling without making a sound. The plan he had been searching for replaced the burden. He could tell the police, in all honesty, why Heather wanted to see him so urgently and why he had kept the rendezvous a secret.

He thanked God—and Heather—and Ian Edwards.

CHAPTER TWELVE

Ian's announcement was met with awed silence but not paralysis, either physical or mental. After absorbing the news that made Heather's death even more poignant, Job went for a can of beer and Bill, busy formulating the plot that would save him and Job without throwing themselves at the mercy of the law, hardly noticed the man's surrender to temptation. This did not mean that the two were insensitive to Ian's grief or the double loss Heather's death now represented, but rather demonstrated that the need to survive, like old habits, dies hard.

After the dramatic disclosure, calmer heads prevailed and their shared grief had Ian apologizing to Bill for his harsh words. Bill accepted the apology with grace, happy to know that Heather's choice for a mate was both intelligent and considerate, and not the boor he appeared to be when he had arrived, still in a daze over the news of his loss.

Job sent Ian home to wash and shave, telling him that as soon as he heard from the police and had made the necessary arrangements for Heather's funeral, he would meet with Ian and the Edwards family. Before Ian was out the front door, Bill expounded to Job, "If Avery is behind all this, he's dug his own grave."

"That he did," Job answered, "and when he's done digging, I'll make sure he settles right in."

Bill shook his head in despair. "Promise me you won't do anything foolish, Job."

Job drank his beer and shrugged. "Depends on what you mean by foolish."

"I mean we're in enough trouble without adding murder to the list. It won't bring her back."

"I promise you this, kid. I won't lift a finger until we do the right thing by Heather and put her beside her mother in peace and with dignity."

It didn't give Bill much time, but maybe a few days would be long enough to talk some sense into Job and do what Heather had wanted most—stop the private runs and get Avery and his pals off Job's back. "Listen, Job. From today, and until this thing is forgotten, every eye in town, including those of the police, will be on you. You heard Ian. Your night trips are already being talked about. Try one now and you might have your neighbors, as well as the law, on your tail. Avery is no fool. He knows this, so for now you're out of his net.

"I also think that as long as the police are involved in Heather's death, Avery will keep his distance from you. Let enough time pass and he may forget to come back."

"But I'll not forget," Job cut in.

"Remember what you promised," Bill chided.

"I know what I promised."

"And here's what I'm going to tell the police," Bill said, conspiratorially. "Listen carefully . . ."

Bill found Lisa and Josh Aldridge waiting for him when he got back to the cottage. Lisa ran to meet him, welcoming him with an embrace and a kiss that not only assured him he was forgiven for abandoning her at the scene of a crime, but also suggested that she was sorry for her hysterical behavior. Bill was amazed by the fact that after going almost twenty-four hours without food or sleep he could still be embarrassingly aroused by the feel and scent of this beautiful woman and bewildered that she would think him worthy of her affection.

Lisa Kennedy was even more striking close-up than when seen from behind the footlights of a stage. A dark-eyed blonde with a tall, willowy figure, Lisa had made a respectable living gracing the covers of fashion magazines since the age of six.

"The only reason I didn't start sooner," she once told Bill, "was because my father insisted I graduate from kindergarten before I entered the world of tits and ass to bring home the bacon. Mother made up for it by enrolling me in a professional school where I spent more time with Mama, making the rounds, than in a classroom. I'm still amazed by the fact that I can read and write." What Bill did not suspect was that in the world of tits and ass, Lisa worked with wholesome, all-American young men who, in turn, liked to play with wholesome, all-American young men. When Josh Aldridge introduced Lisa Kennedy to Bill Ryan, she was as thrilled by Bill's reaction to her as he was by her obvious play for him.

Lisa's attire—shorts and a T-shirt bearing the logo EAST HAMPTON TOWN DUMP—made the statement that even casually dressed she could impress her paramour, or anyone else for that matter.

"Is Paul still in jail?" Bill asked when he had freed himself, however unwillingly, from Lisa's comforting arms.

"I called Paul's cousin Michael Reo this morning," Josh Aldridge answered Bill. "He's getting a lawyer and they're on their way to the police station. Michael has a lot of influence in this town."

"Why did they arrest him?" Bill went on.

"Let's all sit down," Lisa said. "I'll make you a sandwich, Bill. You must be famished."

"I don't want anything, Lisa. I'm more tired than hungry." Bill sank into one of the club chairs as Lisa and Aldridge took their places on the couch.

"They didn't arrest him," Aldridge told Bill. "They took him in for questioning. It'll all get sorted out."

"Have you talked to the police?" The question prompted Bill to pivot his neck awkwardly in an effort to peer up the hall that led to the bedrooms.

"The policeman is gone," Lisa told him. "I called Mr. Aldridge after you left and he came for me. I spent the night at his house." Bill looked at her apologetically but her understanding smile said there was no need for remorse. "When we got back here this morning a team of men were in Paul's bedroom and when they left, the guard went with them. The press was here, too, taking pictures of the house, but the police got rid of them."

"It's private property," Aldridge explained, "including the drive-way, so they can't come any closer than the street at the end of the drive. When I told them Paul wasn't here and wasn't expected they lost interest. By now they must know he's related to the Reos so they'll converge there and forget this place for now."

"Did you talk to the police?" Bill asked again.

"No," Aldridge said. "And I doubt if they would have told us anything if we did. But they wanted to know where you were. You'll have to contact them, Bill, as soon as you feel up to it."

"Did they say how she got into the house?" Bill questioned.

This got a puzzled gaze from Lisa and Josh Aldridge. "What do you mean?" Aldridge asked.

"They found Heather on Paul's bed. When Lisa and I left for the theater Paul was still here and he always locks the place like a tomb when he leaves. So how did she get in the house?"

"Well, Paul has a . . ." Aldridge began but stopped in midsentence.

In the silence, Aldridge and Lisa stared at Bill, who finally blurted, "Of course Paul has a key and he found her on his bed. The policeman guarding the bedroom told me that. But Paul didn't put her there. That's crazy."

"Take it easy, Bill. Let's wait and see what the police, and Paul, have to say before we start speculating on what happened," Aldridge advised.

Joshua Aldridge was at the half-century mark, give or take a year. His tan attested to the fact that he did a lot of work on his cell phone, either at the beach or on his patio in Wainscott. The tan contrasted sharply, and handsomely, with his gray hair, combed straight back and always so carefully groomed as to encourage the rumor that it did not grow out of his scalp. The rumor was abetted by the fact that many on Broadway considered the agent a phony, but in his business the label was more help than hindrance.

Phony or not, there was no question that Josh Aldridge had been very kind and generous to Bill Ryan. Believing he had a diamond in the rough, Aldridge had fed, clothed and even, for a time, housed Bill Ryan, while grooming him for a career on stage and screen. Bill's first test had come when Aldridge entered him in the Freddy Parc quest for the perfect underwear model. Bill, who met Paul Monroe at a gathering of the contest finalists, was relieved and happy when Paul had claimed the prize. Bill hid his feelings from Aldridge but now, as Aldridge reached out to place a reassuring hand on Bill's arm, Bill wished he had done more to repay Aldridge for his kindness, generosity and blind faith in Bill's talent.

"Why didn't you tell us about the family?" Aldridge now asked Bill. "I would have arranged for tickets to the theater and invited them to the party."

Remembering that the party was the reason he had failed to keep his date with Heather, Bill said with unconcealed disgust, "You should have told me about the party."

"Later," Lisa insisted. "We can talk about this later. You can hardly keep your eyes open. Get some rest, then we'll go out for a good meal and after that we can talk."

"She's right," Aldridge agreed.

"No," Bill cried. "I want to tell you about the family now." Before they could stop him, he took a deep breath and plunged right in. "I was taken in foster care by the Ryans in Montauk when I was about ten. Job and his wife had one child, Heather. After school and summers I worked with Job on his fishing boat, *Job's Patience,* and when I finished high school I was Job's first mate on the boat and caretaker of the cabins Job rented out. I was one of the family, or I thought I was.

"Last summer, Heather started going with Ian Edwards. His family owns a couple of fishing boats and as soon as Heather and Ian got serious Job started talking about joining forces with the Edwards clan. As a wedding present he would give Heather and Ian the boat, the house and the cabins, and retire. Where that would leave me, I didn't know, but I was stupid enough to think I would take over the business when Job retired or at least be given a half-interest in the boat and the property."

"You weren't stupid," Lisa exclaimed. "After all those years you had every right to a share in the business."

"My God," Aldridge joined in, "do you realize they were being paid by the state while you were working for them for nothing?"

They were falling for it hook, line and sinker, as Job would have said, and Bill knew what they were thinking: *Poor waif, orphaned twice in his short lifetime.* And the more he lied, the more convincing was his story. But even as he spun his tale of woe, Bill was resolved to tell them the truth as soon as this nightmare was over. They had been good to him, Lisa and Mr. Aldridge, and he loved Lisa, but Job was family and no one came before family.

"So I left," Bill told them. "They weren't too happy to see me go but there was nothing Job could do about it. I kept the card Mr. Aldridge had given me and when I got to New York I looked him up. The rest you know up to yesterday.

"Heather called me in the afternoon and told me she had to see me. You see, she was pregnant with Ian's baby and she didn't know what she should do."

"I don't understand," Lisa said. "If she was going to marry Ian, what was the problem?"

Bill had not anticipated this glaring flaw in his story. Burying his face in his hands he played for time. When he looked up, he fixed his bloodshot eyes on Lisa and answered, "You see, she didn't know if she wanted to marry Ian. Maybe there was someone else. I don't know. But she was desperate and I couldn't refuse her. Whatever had happened, we were still like brother and sister. I told her I would meet her after the show. I told her to be here at nine and wait for me on the deck but, as you know, we ran almost an hour over." He stopped short of telling them that he had told Paul he was expecting a late-night visitor.

Josh Aldridge leaned forward and said thoughtfully, "If Heather was going to leave this boy Ian, and if there was another boy in the picture, both of them might have a reason for doing her harm. You have to tell this to the police."

Bill almost shouted in protest. Thanks to his ineptness, his listeners were rewriting his plot and giving it enough twists to blow the cover off both himself and Job. What next?

It came when Lisa asked something that had obviously been on her mind since meeting Bill Ryan. "But why did you come to Mr. Aldridge? You are the most reluctant actor I've ever seen."

"Where else could I go?" Bill responded. "I didn't have much money and the only person I knew in New York was the man whose name was on the card I took with me." Regaining his confidence, Bill also confided, "But I had been thinking about becoming an actor since Mr. Aldridge gave me his card. I mean, doesn't everyone dream of becoming rich and famous? Trouble was, when I came face-to-face with the possibility of actually going on the stage I was scared to death. I know deep down I don't have the talent, and after last night I don't have the desire. I'm sorry I let you down, Mr. Aldridge. When I can, I'll make good on all you spent on me. I'll even write you an IOU and sign it."

Lisa and Josh Aldridge exchanged looks before both exclaiming, "But you were good last night," Aldridge assured him.

"You were great," Lisa said at the same time. "The audience loved you."

When the time came to bare his soul he would tell them that what had happened on the stage of the John Drew last night was an illusion. An illusion created by Paul Monroe along with the help of a dozen videotapes. And how he wished Paul was with him now to pull another rabbit out of the hat, but seeing as he wasn't Bill could only insist, "I'm not going on with the show. Not now and not ever."

Sensing the hysteria in Bill's voice, Aldridge tried to calm him with, "Okay, Bill. No one is going to force you to do anything you don't want to do. Now get some rest. Everything will look different when you've had some sleep and a hot meal. Lisa and I will stay with you until then."

When Bill awoke the summer sun had just set, leaving the sky tinged with its afterglow and the bedroom in semidarkness. His first thought was of a tender, juicy steak and a pile of French-fried potatoes or *pommes frites,* as Paul insisted on calling them. The anticipation of food and the pleasant memory of Paul's often hilarious *hauteur* (another of Paul's words) approach to life were almost instantly negated when the events of the past twenty-four hours flooded his newly awakened mind.

Heather was dead, Paul had been arrested and the story he had concocted to justify his late-night meeting with Heather had taken him no place but up the garden path. His concern with what Paul might have said to the police had been replaced with what Ian would tell them when Bill repeated his story to the police as Mr. Aldridge had suggested he should. And could he keep Job away from Avery until Heather's murder was solved and the culprit, whoever it might be, was taken into custody?

He heard someone puttering around in the kitchen but harbored no hope that Lisa was fixing dinner. Lisa Kennedy was the answer to all of a virile man's longings except the one prompted by his stomach. Getting up and not bothering to put on pants, Bill emerged from the bedroom and, consciously avoiding looking at the closed door to Paul's bedroom, walked down the hall and peered into the kitchen.

Lisa, pouring herself a glass of white wine, paused to eye Bill in his Freddy Parc briefs and said jokingly, "I thought you were Paul."

"You wouldn't say that if you were looking a little lower down."

She closed the few feet that separated them and presented her cheek for a kiss. "That's naughty."

"But nice," he assured her, taking the wineglass from her hand as his lips grazed her cheek. White wine before dinner was yet another of Paul's dictates, although he conceded that Campari and soda with a twist of lemon was far more chic but also far more expensive.

"I'm going to shower outside," Bill announced. Taking the wine with him he headed for the patio door, losing his shorts before making it to the deck. He sometimes wondered what his friends in Montauk would say if they could see him like this, naked and uncaring, with a beautiful girl like Lisa for company.

"The soap and shampoo are out there," Lisa called after him.

He went down the steps leading from wood deck to grassy lawn and into the shower stall that abutted the house on the outside wall of the bath. He turned on the spray as hot as he could stand it for a good minute before reaching for the shampoo. Later, when he had lathered himself from neck to ankles, the door of the stall opened and Lisa, her hair in two hastily woven pigtails, joined him. Already anticipating her arrival, he took her into his soapy embrace, raised one of her legs to his waist and entered, exploding before he was fully entrenched, physically releasing all the pent-up emotion that had been smoldering within him since he learned of Heather's death.

His urgency and need were her satisfaction; the act more titillating and memorable for its briefness. They clung to each other for a long time, allowing the shower spray to cool their passion but not their ardor.

When they had met, Bill was the virgin and Lisa the tutor, albeit one with limited experience. In the weeks that followed, Bill proved a quick study and the teacher was more than happy to turn over the reigns to her promising student. Bill Ryan did not disappoint.

Their idyll was as brief as Bill's performance. When they returned to the house and were dressing, Bill received three phone calls in rapid succession, each a reminder of what had happened and what lay ahead.

First Aldridge called to say he had posted notices at the theater stating *Pale Sun, Bright Moon* had been canceled until further notice; ticket holders would receive a full refund at the box office. And finally, he would see Bill and Lisa in the morning to discuss the play's future. Aldridge had not seen Paul Monroe but assumed he was with Michael Reo. Bill got Reo's phone number from Aldridge, and he dialed when Aldridge rang off and was rewarded with a busy signal.

The next call was from the police. They requested Mr. Ryan's presence at the station house at ten the following morning.

The third call was from a reporter for a tabloid who wanted a statement from anyone in the house regarding The Jockstrap Murder.

"The what?" Bill cried.

"The Jockstrap Murder, that's what. Have I got the right number? Is this Paul Monroe or . . ."

Bill, in his jeans, barefoot and shirtless, almost broke the receiver when he slammed it into its cradle just as Lisa came into the front room wearing a simple sundress that accentuated her lissome body.

"Did you hear that?" he said to her. "Some nut wants a statement on The Jockstrap Murder. It's indecent."

"It was inevitable that someone would hang a label on it, and that one is guaranteed to draw readers like garbage attracts flies. Get used to it, Bill," Lisa said with authority. "Paul is what is called a national figure, although I doubt if many know his name, and you and I will be dubbed 'the actor' and 'the model' respectively. It has all the ingredients of a racy detective novel."

"It's still indecent," Bill repeated.

The phone rang again and this time Lisa picked it up. She listened a moment, said nothing and hung up. No sooner did it disconnect than it rang again. She stopped Bill from grabbing the receiver and picked up the connecting wire, followed it to its wall jack and unplugged it. "These are the also-rans," Lisa said, "whose expense account doesn't include travel outside the city and if one has our number, they all have it. I'm sure they're the reason you were getting a busy signal at Michael Reo's. Now get dressed so we can go to dinner. We have a lot to talk about."

It was dark when they walked, hand in hand, down the long driveway and joined the early evening strollers in the village of Amagansett. Aside from Amagansett Square—several acres of retail shops, most of them national chains more interested in having a presence in the Hamptons than in turning a profit—the few blocks of the main thoroughfare, unlike East Hampton Village, are not a shopper's paradise. Four restaurants, Gordon's being the most celebrated, Stephen Talkhouse cabaret, several antique shops, a liquor store, a hardware store, McKendry's Bar and Vinny's Barbershop are its mainstays.

The Amagansett Free Library, housed in an original, shingled East End dwelling replete with a Camperdown Elm on the front lawn, is a favorite site for photographers. A wooden bench had recently been constructed around the trunk of the ancient tree bearing a plaque inscribed with the words OH, FOR A BOOK AND A SHADY NOOK.

Bill and Lisa had no trouble getting a booth at Estia's at this early hour and when their wine came it was Lisa who raised her glass and toasted, "I won't say cheers."

MICHAEL ANTHONY REO

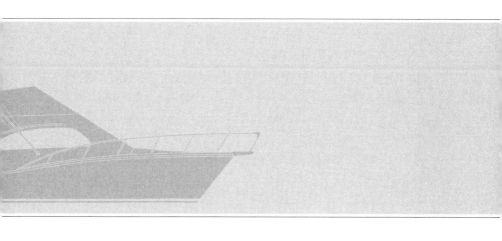

CHAPTER THIRTEEN

"Murder," Maddy broadcast, elbowing her way through the swinging door from the butler's pantry.

Michael lowered the Arts section of the *Times* and eyed his housekeeper suspiciously as she advanced toward the table toting a carafe of freshly brewed coffee. Vicky, he noticed, did not raise her eyes from that newspaper's Business section. *A true chip off the old block,* Michael thought approvingly of his wife. If their reading preferences were any indication of how they would conduct business at Kirkpatrick Entertainment, it bode well for the fledgling production company.

"Murder," Maddy repeated, placing the carafe on the table before she started clearing it of the breakfast dishes.

"Anyone we know?" Michael asked.

Maddy, a dish in each hand, rose to her full height of five feet two inches, squared her shoulders and responded, "Not unless we're socializing with groupies in an Amagansett rental." Her tone left no doubt that if the Reos were socializing with group renters anyplace in the Hamptons, she and her husband, John, would immediately give notice and retire. Having cared for Vicky's father for some forty years, the couple could very easily do this on the income Joseph Kirkpatrick had left them in his will.

However, such a move would cost them the two-bedroom, two-bath apartment over the garage of the Dunemere Lane house, and the prestige of being the couple who "did for" one of the richest women in America and her handsome husband. With Michael determined to return Kirkpatrick Entertainment to its glory days when the housekeeper and her majordomo husband had served caviar and champagne to celebrated names, John and Maddy were ready to dig in for another forty years.

"A young girl, just out of her teens, they say, strangled with something unmentionable," Maddy prattled as she gathered the dishes.

This remarkable statement caused Vicky to abandon the *Times* in favor of her housekeeper. "With what?" Vicky questioned.

"A gentleman's garment, Miss Vicky."

Fascinated by the conversation and repressing a grin, Michael prodded the housekeeper. "Give us a hint, Maddy."

"An athletic support, Mr. Michael." In her fluster she appeared to be putting the breakfast dishes back on the table as quickly as she was removing them. "It's the result of them group rentals, it is. Too many bodies of the opposite sex in too close quarters, if you ask me."

"A jockstrap!" Michael intoned without thought to propriety.

"Is it possible?" Vicky injected.

"I imagine it is," Michael said, "but it's got to be an all-time first even for East Hampton."

"They say it was the gentleman's garment what done it, Miss Vicky."

"Who are *they*?" Michael asked, as if he didn't know.

"Beg pardon, Mr. Michael."

"*They,* Maddy. *They* say, unquote."

"Why, Annie over at Barrett House told me. She called as soon as she heard about the murder."

"And how did Annie hear about the murder or is Barrett House now on the group-rental circuit?"

"Michael," Vicky interrupted, "it's none of our business."

"I'm just curious," he assured his wife.

Maddy followed these verbal lobs like a spectator at a tennis match, her position being in a direct line with the invisible net.

"Just be sure your curiosity doesn't get you involved in another murder. One per lifetime is sufficient, thank you."

"That was last year, Vicky. This is a new season," he joked.

Here Maddy, unable to refrain, offered the opinion, "It seems to me one murder should do for two seasons."

"And one lifetime," Vicky repeated, helping herself to a fresh cup of coffee. "Thank you, Maddy, that will be all."

"Yes, Miss Vicky." Maddy once again picked up the breakfast dishes and headed for the swinging door.

"But," Michael called after her, "first tell me how Annie got the news."

Maddy turned and eyed Michael with a look of gratitude, and for a moment Michael feared she would carry the dirty dishes back to the table. Instead she stood her ground, both hands full, and gushed, "Al Holiday, the man who oversees the Barrett property. He stopped at the firehouse before reporting to work and it was all the talk over there. The firehouse is next door to the village police, you know, and they got it straight from the town police."

"Are you sure Annie got the story straight?" Vicky questioned Maddy.

"I've never known Annie to be wrong," Maddy stated with pride. While Maddy was housekeeper to the CEO of the Kirkpatrick Foundation, Annie performed the same chore for the Barretts, a family that had been given a large slice of Long Island by King George III. In the hierarchy of housekeepers, Annie came out on top of the heap.

"When did this happen?" Michael wanted to know.

"Last night," Maddy told him, then elaborated for dramatic effect, "Midnight. Maybe it's a cult thing."

Vicky cautioned her housekeeper, "I wouldn't be spreading any rumors like that around town, Maddy, until the facts are known."

"Me, Miss Vicky? I never gossip." With that she once again elbowed her way through the swinging door and into her sanctuary where John was waiting to hear the Reos' reaction to the news. So as not to disappoint her husband, Maddy would embellish what little reaction the news had elicited.

The moment Maddy stated the time of the murder, Michael recalled the tall clock at the James Lane Cafe striking midnight as the lanky figure of Bill Ryan loped past it, on his way out the restaurant's kitchen door. Coincidence? Michael began to feel a bit uneasy and when the phone on the sideboard rang the sound jarred him vehemently. It stopped after the second ring when John took the call in the kitchen.

"Now who could be calling before nine in the morning?" Vicky wondered.

"It's got to be bad news," Michael said prophetically. "No one calls with good news before noon. It's an East Hampton rule."

It was John who stuck his face through the swinging door and announced, "For you, Mr. Reo. It's Mr. Aldridge."

"Amanda probably has the vapors after last night's debacle," Vicky said. "And I can't wait to hear what Paul has to say about his roommate's behavior last night."

"It will be acerbic but kind," Michael predicted. "I wish we had had a chance to meet Bill Ryan and the lovely Lisa. The Ryan boy reminds me of someone but I can't remember who."

After Bill Ryan fled, the greeting line had withdrawn in embarrassment and Amanda rushed to Josh Aldridge's side where she joined him and Lisa in circulating among the guests, making excuses for the actor's dramatic exit. Opening-night nerves, was the official excuse. The guests, noticeably more subdued, lingered for another hour or so, not wanting to break it up too quickly, lest giving the impression that Ryan's abrupt departure had put a damper on the party, which, in fact, it had.

"It's Mr. Aldridge on the line," John reminded them.

"Tell him Mr. Michael is not yet up and about."

"Oh, yes he is," Michael stated, both up and about to prove his point. He went for the telephone, which had been installed in the dining room by order of the late Joseph Kirkpatrick, who never liked to be more than an arm's length of the instrument, even when enjoying one of Maddy's sumptuous repasts. There was a telephone in every room of the Dunemere Lane mansion, including the master bathroom.

Michael greeted his caller, "Good morning, Josh." After this he was silent, listening to Aldridge speak for so long Vicky's coffee grew cold as she waited for her husband to say something that would give her a clue to the reason for the morning call.

When Michael did respond it was to say, "I'm stunned," which turned Vicky's apprehension to dread. This was followed by sound bites such as, "Yes . . . I see . . . I will, immediately . . . Thanks, Josh . . . Keep me posted and I'll do the same."

Michael replaced the instrument in its cradle and turned to Vicky, his face ashen. "My God, Michael, what is it?" she cried.

"That murder you didn't want me to get involved in has just landed on our welcome mat."

"The . . ." In her confusion Vicky struggled for the right word.

"Athletic support," Michael assisted.

"You're kidding," Vicky said hopefully.

Michael returned to the table where his coffee had grown cold while the plot of the film reviewed in his morning newspaper appeared insipid in light of what he had just learned. He poured hot coffee from the carafe into his cup and wished he could light a cigarette. He was one of those fortunate people who could enjoy a cigarette when the need or desire arose and not have another for a week, a month or a year. His wife, unfortunately, was addicted to the weed and had only just celebrated her sixth smoke-free month. For this reason, Michael never lit a cigarette when in the house with Vicky.

"Michael, if you don't say something, I'll go mad," Vicky urged.

He added a drop of milk to the coffee, stirred the brew indifferently and responded, "The dead girl is the sister of the young man who ran out of his own party last night—and Paul has been arrested in connection with her murder."

"Oh, Michael, no!" Vicky groaned.

"Oh, Vicky, yes!" he answered. "I'll tell you as much as I know if you'll stop staring at me with your mouth hanging open. It's most unbecoming." Michael continued to stir his coffee but made no attempt to raise the cup to his lips. "Apropos of nothing, it was a Freddy Parc jockstrap . . ."

When Michael finished relating what little he had gotten from Josh Aldridge, Vicky lamented, "Poor Paul. Imagine finding a body on your bed and then being accused of putting it there. Michael, you had better call his parents before they read about it in the newspaper or, worse, hear it on the television."

"I was thinking the same thing but first I'd like to see Paul and learn all the facts so I'll have something more than speculation to report to his father."

"You said the dead girl is Bill Ryan's sister?"

"That's what Josh thinks."

"Is there some doubt?"

"Josh knew Bill Ryan was an orphan but now Josh has learned the boy was raised by a foster family out here. That's what Lisa told Josh and she got it from Bill last night. It's all very murky, if you ask me."

"What are you going to do, Michael?"

"Call MJ and then go to the police station to see Paul, if they let me."

Mark Barrett, Jr., or MJ as he was called from childhood, was the young scion of the Barrett family and the latest Barrett to join the family law firm of Barrett & Barrett, with offices in the converted carriage house of the family mansion located on East Hampton's main thoroughfare. Actually, MJ was the only Barrett currently practicing law in

East Hampton and the sole occupant of Barrett House. His parents were separated, with his mother on an extended holiday in Italy and his father residing in the Barretts' New York pied-à-terre.

Michael and Vicky had been good friends of the Barretts and had watched MJ progress from prep school through Harvard Law.

"The ink is hardly dry on MJ's diploma," Vicky said regretfully.

"I have no choice," Michael answered her. "We can't get a New York lawyer out here on a moment's notice and I want to bail out Paul as quickly as I can."

"I doubt if MJ knows anything about criminal law," Vicky went on.

"MJ is East Hampton royalty and the police will respect that more than his knowledge or lack thereof of criminal law."

"Don't let Eddy hear you say that." This rejoinder had Vicky suggesting, "Why don't you call Eddy and see what he knows?"

"I intend to do just that," Michael said.

"And," Vicky added, "did it occur to you that Bill Ryan broke rank and fled just about midnight last night?"

"It occurred," Michael assured her. "I would like to know why and so will the police, I'm sure."

"Let the police figure it out, Michael. It's their job. We'll just make sure Paul is out of harm's way and then see if we can get him to move in with us as he should have done when he arrived here."

"Vicky," Michael sighed, "Paul is on his own for the first time and the last thing he wanted to do was move in with a couple old enough to be his parents."

"And look where it got him. In jail, that's where. And involved with all those murky people as you so aptly put it."

Michael was spared a response when the swinging door again opened wide enough to allow a chubby face with a ruddy complexion and crowned with silver hair, cut as short as a man's, to peek into the Reos' dining room. "Good morning, Mrs. Reo. Mr. Reo. I'm here."

And another county is heard from, Michael thought as Ms. Johnson announced her presence in the Dunemere Lane house. Ms. Johnson was, by profession, a registered nurse originally employed to care for Joseph Kirkpatrick when he had suffered a heart attack. She stayed on after his death to help Vicky with the letters, cards and flowers that had overwhelmed the household following the media mogul's demise.

At first hesitant with her midlife career change, Ms. Johnson was now a whiz at the computer, the fax machine and electronic mail, making her indispensable to Vicky in her role as president and chief mover and shaker of the Kirkpatrick Foundation. Ms. Johnson's timidity had fast given way to a zest for life in the fast lane. Bedpans and cranking hospital beds were as foreign to her now as starchy white dresses and shoes to match. When the Reos were in residence at the Dunemere Lane house, Ms. Johnson arrived three mornings a week at ten and left at four, always announcing her arrival by—well— announcing her arrival.

Vicky and Michael had no idea what Ms. Johnson did when she was not in their charge and somehow had never got around to asking.

"I'll be with you in a few minutes," Vicky addressed the face that looked amazingly like a smiling apple. "Maddy just brewed a fresh pot of coffee. Help yourself to a cup."

"Thank you, I will, Mrs. Reo."

"Maddy will frighten the bejesus out of Ms. Johnson with talk of our cult murder," Michael warned when the door closed on Ms. Johnson's smiling face.

"Don't worry about Ms. Johnson. She can hold her own. You should hear her fend off the crank calls we sometimes get." Vicky folded her napkin and prepared to rise from the table. She picked up a zippered leather case she had carried to the breakfast table that morning but had neglected to open. "No sense in me coming to the police station with you, and rather than pacing around here and jumping out of my skin every time the phone rings, I'd best be off to the salt mines and at least try to do some work."

"You sound just like your father."

"Is that so bad?"

"No, as long as you don't start looking like him."

Vicky shook her head, causing her blond hair, perfectly cut to follow the line of her jaw, to sway in a shimmering gold cascade. "That's more likely to be your fate than mine," she informed him.

The salt mines was the den turned into the summer offices of the Kirkpatrick Foundation and Kirkpatrick Entertainment. The founding father was gone but not forgotten.

The Dunemere Lane house contained two master bedroom suites, four guest bedrooms, breakfast room—now used exclusively by Maddy, John and Ms. Johnson, who brown-bagged it to the office—dining room, sunroom, drawing room, den and eight servants' warrens, long unoccupied, on the third floor.

Michael and Vicky had always made the south master suite their room, leaving the north suite empty since the old man's death. Although their bedroom was slightly smaller than the other, its southern exposure afforded a view of the Maidstone Club's golf course, the clubhouse perched on a dune and looking, especially when a thick fog rolled in off the Atlantic, like a Hollywood mockup of Wuthering Heights, and a sliver of the ocean itself on the horizon.

The phone rang as Michael entered the bedroom, and without a thought as to who it might be, he picked it up on the first ring. "Michael Reo here."

"Mr. Reo. It's Eddy Evans."

"Eddy! I was just going to try to track you down."

"You've heard about it, Mr. Reo?"

"I've heard. What can you tell me?"

"Officially, nothing, Mr. Reo. I hope you understand."

"I do, Eddy. No problem. But can I see Paul?"

"I'll see what I can do."

"Thanks, Eddy, and keep in touch—unofficially."

CHAPTER FOURTEEN

The town police are located on Pantigo Road, which is yet another name for Route 27—the others being Montauk Highway and Main Street, when it passes through downtown East Hampton. Michael drove the Land Rover, thinking the Rolls would appear conspicuous in the station house parking lot, causing the local guardians of the peace to look upon him with either awe or disdain.

In East Hampton, one is known by the car one drives and treated accordingly. There are those who rent, for the weekend, a Rolls or a Bentley or a Porsche to garner respect from those who rent, for a weekend, a Rolls, a Bentley or a Porsche. Passing each other on their way to and from Main Beach, these weekend millionaires wave and grin at each other, satisfying some primitive urge to see and be seen at their rented best.

At mid-season the uniformed police's tolerance level was probably at neap tide, making disdain the more likely reaction to Michael's visit, be it in a Rolls, a Land Rover or a ten-year-old Chevrolet.

The desk sergeant consulted a handwritten sheet of lined notepaper when Michael presented himself. Obviously satisfied, the officer nodded and pointed. "The interview room. We'll bring in your client."

Client? How had Eddy arranged this visit? Michael was overcome with a sense of guilt, which his surroundings did little to assuage. Avoiding eye contact with the men and women in blue he hurried to the interview room, relieved to find it empty except for two sets of folding chairs facing each other across a rectangular table. The small room contained one window, not barred but closed and probably locked. In films, the accused always sat with his back to the door so Michael took a chair facing the door. Should they learn the true reason for his visit he might have to change positions.

In a matter of minutes the door was opened by an officer who stood back to allow the prisoner to enter the room. Paul Monroe's blue eyes were swollen from lack of sleep, crying or both; his dark hair was uncombed and hung limply about his forehead and ears; his flawless complexion was pallid and in need of a shave.

"I'll be right outside," the policeman said, leaving Paul and Michael—one standing, the other seated—staring at each other.

"You look like hell." Michael finally broke the silence.

Paul slid into the chair he had occupied when being questioned by Lieutenant Oliveri. "Thanks. You really know how to make a guy feel good."

Michael reached across the table and took Paul's hand. "I'm all heart, but go ahead and cry if it'll make you feel better."

"Real men don't cry—but they do eat quiche. Can you get me out of here?"

"I called a lawyer. He was with a client but he promised to be here as soon as he's free."

"They told me my lawyer was here, meaning you," Paul said.

"Are you disappointed?"

"Not as disappointed as you must be with me," Paul answered. "This is going to be in all the newspapers and on TV. Freddy is going to love it."

"Freddy Parc thrives on publicity—good and bad—so forget him. It's you we have to take care of and I'm not disappointed in you, Paul;

in fact I think you're very brave. The fact that you're not comatose after last night is remarkable. I know I would be."

"I tried to call you last night," Paul explained, "but you were still at the party. I was going to call again this morning but then they told me my lawyer was coming so I thought I'd wait for him, whoever he might be. I'm so confused . . ." Exhausted, Paul's valiant and cocky facade was beginning to slip.

"You poor kid," Michael sympathized, thinking that Paul had probably not heard one kind word spoken to him since the police took him into custody. "Have they been harassing you?"

Embarrassed, Paul took a tissue from a box conveniently displayed on the table and wiped his eyes. Shaking his head, he assured Michael, "Not too much. The one you know, Eddy Evans, is pretty decent. Did he tell you what happened?"

"No. Actually Josh Aldridge called me this morning."

"Aldridge!" Paul sat up, suddenly alert. "What about Bill? Where is he?"

"I don't know," Michael said. "Aldridge told me the girl is, or was, Bill's foster sister, if that's the right description. What he knows he got from Lisa Kennedy, who, I believe, spent the night with Aldridge in Wainscott. According to her Bill went directly to see the dead girl's father and hasn't been seen since. Do you want to tell me what happened?"

Michael took the chair next to Paul but continued to support him by keeping a firm grip on the young man's hand. Paul dabbed at his eyes with the tissue and, more composed, told Michael everything that had happened from the time he left Freddy Parc's dinner party. Michael listened attentively and, when Paul finished, his first question was, "Why didn't you come to the party after leaving Freddy's place?"

"Because I wasn't invited." Paul smiled for the first time that morning. "You know Aldridge is pissed off at me because I beat out his boy for the Freddy Parc job."

"And Bill wasn't sore?"

"Bill? He was relieved. The thought of posing in his underwear riled him."

"He sounds more like an introvert than an actor," Michael noted.

"He doesn't want to be an actor," Paul told Michael. "Getting him on the stage was like trying to get a kid to eat his spinach."

"None of this makes any sense, Paul," Michael said in exasperation. "How did he get involved with Aldridge?"

"I told you, Bill was working on a fishing boat out of Montauk where Aldridge spotted him and gave him his card. Bill swears it's true and I believe him. Why would he lie?"

"Why, indeed. It sounds like something a press agent would concoct after too many martinis but I don't think your friend is the press agent type, so I'll buy it for now. But what Josh Aldridge was doing on a fishing boat is as big a mystery as to why Bill, who doesn't want to be an actor, left the fishing boat and went chasing after Aldridge. Do you know?"

Paul gave this some thought and Michael suspected the distraught youth was trying to decide how to answer. The young share secrets they are often unwilling to impart to anyone ten years older than themselves, considering their elders to be contemporaries of the guys who built the pyramids. In light of what had happened last night, Michael hoped Paul was telling him all he knew. He took heart when Paul answered, "I always thought Bill was running away from something."

"Why, Paul?"

"Mostly because he was so reluctant to come back here. He said it was because he didn't want to open in a show in the Hamptons and make a fool of himself in front of people he knew. I got the impression there was more to it than that."

"That's interesting," Michael said, "and you should tell the police. He's on the run and his sister is murdered. There's got to be a connection."

"I didn't say he was on the run, like he was being chased," Paul quickly objected. "And I'm just guessing. He's a nice guy and I don't want to say anything to the police before I speak to him."

With that, Michael was almost certain Paul was holding something back but given the boy's condition and their surroundings he wisely chose not to press the point. He would wait until he got Paul home, rested and fed before he attempted to gain his complete confidence. He had no doubt that Paul and Bill Ryan were confidants and hoped it didn't bode as injurious to Paul's case as it sounded.

"You didn't know anything about Bill's foster family before now?"

"I swear I didn't," Paul said.

"You don't have to swear, Paul. I'm not the police and I'll believe whatever you tell me."

"Thank you," Paul answered with a nod.

"Did you happen to meet any of Bill's old friends from out here? I mean the ones he was embarrassed to perform before."

Reluctantly, Paul shook his head. "No, I didn't."

"Strange, isn't it?"

Paul once again went to bat for Bill. "He's really a very good person, Michael. Way out of his element in New York and in show business, but he's ballsy, I'll say that for him. Freddy Parc had a luncheon at Tavern on the Green for the finalists and the press, where the judges picked the winner. Bill latched on to me in the green room where they kept us waiting for hours. In fact the first thing he said to me was that he hoped I would win. I thought he was being a bitch, but he wasn't. He really meant it.

"Aside from Lisa, who he met through Aldridge, he didn't know a person in New York his own age, so I became buddy numero uno by default. He looked up to me and trusted me, which made Aldridge unhappy because I had more influence with Bill than his agent."

"What about the girl, Lisa?" Michael asked.

Paul smiled and shrugged when he answered, "She's okay. And she's crazy about Bill. There's nothing introverted about him in the sack, let me tell you."

"Did he tell you that, or did Lisa?"

"No one had to tell me. I have two eyes and they work. Bill and Lisa are in love and good for them."

"What does Aldridge think about that?"

"Oh, he made the match," Paul said. "Lisa is so grateful for what Aldridge has done for her, she takes his advice as if it were written in stone. I think Aldridge uses Lisa to control Bill, which leaves me the thorn in Aldridge's side. You know he refused to handle me after I won the contest."

"You're better off with a big agency like ICM or William Morris. I'll see what I can do in that department. But tell me this," Michael said, getting back to the reason he was sitting with Paul Monroe in the interview room of the local police station, "if Bill is so ballsy, as you say, why is he allowing Aldridge and Lisa to manipulate him?" He waited for a reply and when none was forthcoming he said, "Maybe because Bill needed a safe harbor and Josh Aldridge was the closest port in a storm."

"Could be," Paul was forced to agree.

"What does Lisa Kennedy think of you?"

"We get along fine," Paul said, and as if explaining why, he added, "As soon as she was certain I wasn't after Bill, we became kissin' cousins."

And just who are you after? Michael pondered, scrutinizing his handsome and talented cousin. That, too, would have to wait for another time and place, neither of which might ever materialize.

"Your friend might be the world's most reluctant actor but he isn't the worst. He wasn't half-bad last night."

Paul couldn't suppress a grin. "Did he remind you of anyone you know?"

Amazed, Michael responded, "In fact he did, but I couldn't put a name to it."

"Bill's a natural mimic," Paul said with undisguised glee. "And as good as any professional I've ever heard. I'm sure the only reason he showed off for Lisa and me was to let us know he wasn't totally with-out talent. When he got the script for the show he was terrified. The few lines I heard him say were wooden to the point of death. Then I got an idea. Can you guess?"

Michael thought he knew the answer but didn't deprive Paul of elaborating on his own cleverness.

"He's built like a swizzle stick, right? So, I rented every Tony Perkins film I could get my hands on and had Bill watch them till he could do Perkins better than Perkins—and that's what you saw last night, Bill Ryan playing Tony Perkins."

"And it worked," Michael said.

"I know it. I sat through a few rehearsals, including the dress rehearsal the night before they opened."

"Does Aldridge know this?" Michael probed.

"He's never mentioned the fact, but he's no fool and he's savvy enough to know Perkins when he hears him. Aldridge wanted Bill to turn in a performance and I don't think he gave a damn how it was done. Lisa was in on it and never objected."

Michael imagined that these three young people had a hell of a lot of fun putting on their version of *Pale Sun, Bright Moon* under the noses of both the legitimate producer and director. But Michael wrestled with the bothersome fact that Josh Aldridge was desperate for Bill Ryan to succeed as an actor. Why, when there were hundreds of young men more talented and more eager the agent could be grooming for the big break? Did Aldridge want to prove that he knew a winner when he saw one? Perhaps, but Michael was not convinced.

"Look here," Michael pointed out, "Bill and Lisa are your friends and you happen to be sharing a house with them. You had to be at Freddy's for dinner, but what did they say about your not being invited to the party after the show, which you could have made?"

"Easy. Bill didn't know about the party. If he did, he would have made sure I was there or he wouldn't have gone. And before you ask, they didn't tell him about the party because they were afraid he would balk. He's not social, Michael, and after performing for an audience all he would want to do was go to bed and pull the covers over his head. Lisa told me what Aldridge was up to and asked me not to say anything to Bill. For the good of the show, as they say, I kept my mouth shut.

"I also figured it was Aldridge's way of trying to wean Bill away from me and have him socialize on his own. My guess was that Bill would refuse to go to the party. Did you notice any shackles when he arrived?"

"Two, in the form of his girlfriend and his agent," Michael told him. "They got him there, but he didn't stay long."

"What do you mean?"

"He broke free of his human chains and bolted just about midnight." Michael looked for any reaction to the news on Paul's pale face. If the time meant anything to Paul he was the consummate actor of all time.

"My guess is that he panicked," Paul said. "Bill Ryan is a rube, a hick, a clam digger from Montauk. Those first-nighters must have scared the tar out of him."

"There was a group of locals among those first-nighters," Michael informed Paul.

This, too, caused Paul to start. "Really? Was his family there? His sister?"

"I have no idea," Michael said. "But how could she be there? The curtain was late, a few minutes after ten, I think. If she was . . ." Michael left the thought hanging.

"I got home about eleven and she was there," Paul said.

"It's possible," Michael was thinking. "She could have left the theater and gone to the cottage—"

"Michael," Paul interrupted, "there's something you and the lawyer should know. I left the house after Bill and Lisa went to the theater. I locked up and when I got back, the door was still locked. I opened it with my key."

"How did she get into the house?"

"That's what Lieutenant Oliveri wants to know. The guy is a bastard, Michael, and he thinks I let her in—and did her in."

"With a Freddy Parc jockstrap, to boot."

"You heard about that?"

"I heard," Michael said, "and before the day is out the world will have heard. Freddy will run ads for the item in every men's magazine in the country."

"That's macabre," Paul said, wincing.

"No, Paul, that's retailing. And if you think Freddy will withdraw your ads, think again. He'll run them with a vengeance after today."

Paul looked as if he didn't know if he should be pleased or appalled at the suggestion but had little time to reflect on it when Michael stated, "I take it the only other keys to the house belong to Bill and Lisa." Paul nodded. "The lawyer I got is Mark Barrett, Junior. He's not much older than you and I've known him most of his life. We call him MJ. He said they can't hold you for more than twenty-four hours without charging you, and I doubt if they will do that. You just happened to be in the wrong place at the wrong time."

"That place is where I live at the moment."

"You're staying with us until further notice." Michael stood up. "I want to get back and call your folks before they hear it on the news. Now I can tell them I saw you and you're fine and not to believe everything they read or hear."

"Tell them not to come racing out here," Paul pleaded.

"I can't stop them but I can discourage them. You can talk to them when you get to the house. I've already told MJ to drive you to Dunemere Lane." Looking perplexed, Michael asked, "How did you get home last night?"

"Freddy's driver picked me up and took me home. I told that to the lieutenant."

"Did he drive up to the house?"

"No. I told him to let me off on the street, at the foot of the drive, and walked up."

"Too bad, he could have been a witness to the fact that she wasn't waiting outside the house," Michael said.

"She was already inside the house. But how did she get there?"

"We'll find out, Paul. I promise you that. Now cheer up. You'll be out of here in a few hours."

"Give me one reason to be cheerful," Paul said, also standing.

"Okay. Amanda Richards is this close to accepting the role in *The Hampton Affair*."

Paul greeted the news by throwing his arms around Michael and kissing him.

Trying to keep a low profile, Michael gave the officer outside the interview room a brisk nod before moving off. He could feel the policeman's eyes boring into the back of his head as he made for the exit. Before reaching it, he felt another pair of eyes focused on him, following his every step. Its source, he noted, was a well-dressed man, about his own age, in civilian dress—a perfectly cut gray summer-weight suit—who could have been a plainclothesman, a politician or an FBI agent on a snooping mission. Michael got the distinct impression that the man's gaze was less than friendly.

MJ Barrett was at the reception desk and just as Michael thought he could make it out of the station house without MJ seeing him the desk sergeant pointed and called out, "That's him, the kid's lawyer."

"That is Michael Reo," MJ said. "He called me and he is not a lawyer." Turning to Michael he asked, "What are you doing here?"

MJ was a pleasant-looking young man, with his mother's fair complexion and the Barretts' straight, ink-black hair, which always made Michael think the early Barrett settlers exchanged more than just trinkets and firewater with the Shinnecock Indians whose land they had usurped.

"Would you gentlemen please decide who's who elsewhere," the desk sergeant ordered. "People are trying to work around here."

Glancing about, Michael saw that they were indeed attracting attention, especially from the man in the gray suit.

"I'm here to see my client," MJ answered him.

The sergeant took a deep breath but before he exhaled Michael declared, "I'm the reason for the misunderstanding, Sergeant. Detective Evans—"

"Evans told me you were coming to see the prisoner, Paul Monroe."

"Did Detective Evans say I was Paul Monroe's lawyer, Sergeant?"

"I assumed—"

"And I confess I took advantage of that assumption, Sergeant. I don't think Detective Evans knew Mr. Monroe was restricted to one visit by his lawyer."

"I'll take care of this, Sergeant—and Detective Evans." The quietly modulated voice left no doubt that the speaker would do both— quickly and efficiently. Before he turned to confront the speaker, Michael knew, instinctively, that it was the man in the gray suit. And it was.

"Sure, Lieutenant." The sergeant appeared content to shift the responsibility to his superior.

Lieutenant? The infamous Lieutenant Oliveri?

"You may go, Mr. Reo," the lieutenant said. "We won't arrest you for taking advantage of our foolish assumption but don't try our patience."

Michael wanted to give the guy a good, swift kick in the arse but—when in doubt, keep your mouth shut, and your feet planted firmly on the ground.

"I'll take you to see Paul Monroe." The lieutenant addressed MJ in the same tone he had used to dismiss Michael.

"If you're not going to charge him, Lieutenant, I'm going to insist you release him."

"I'm not going to charge him, Mr. Barrett." Then he practically shouted, "Not now, that is."

EDDY EVANS

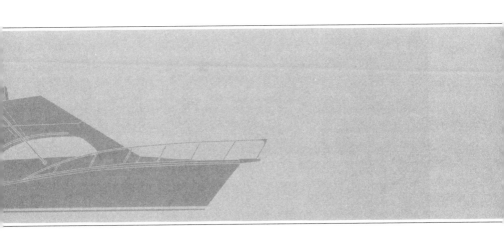

CHAPTER FIFTEEN

The moment Bill Ryan walked into the room, and not one moment sooner, Eddy recalled when he had last seen the boy and the reason for his visit to the Ryan home in Montauk. In the best of circumstances, the oversight would have disturbed him, but with Chris Oliveri next to him and Ryan being questioned in connection with the murder of the girl Eddy had also seen briefly on that occasion, the detective felt like handing in his badge and leaving the station house in shame.

The only comforting thought was that nothing had come from his encounter with Bill Ryan. It was related to the drug raid in Sag Harbor last year, he was sure of that, and Bill's pickup truck had been spotted in the vicinity of the house the narc people had broken into. Eddy remembered that Job Ryan, the man he thought was Bill's natural father, had the truck that night, visiting someone in Sag Harbor. Eddy reported what he had learned to the county narcotics unit, which was in charge of the case, and as far as he knew the older Ryan's story must have checked out because he never heard back from the narc squad.

Eddy remembered Oliveri giving information about the raid to the local newspapers, telling them as much as the county narc squad and the county police had told the East Hampton police, which was not much, and right after that Oliveri and his wife took off for Boston, where they had gone to bring their daughter home from her first year at college. Tying it in with his vacation time, the Oliveris had been away almost two weeks. Had they not, Chris Oliveri would have known about Eddy's visit to Montauk, its purpose, and remembered it the minute Eddy identified the body. Eddy had instantly recognized Heather because he had seen her in Main Street Video a few weeks ago, after which Helen had told him about Bill Ryan's success in New York and his forthcoming appearance at the John Drew.

Why he had not recalled his visit to the Ryans that day, Eddy could only attribute to the fact that when he was in Helen's company very little else penetrated his skull. This rationale did not distress the detective.

Eddy would have to tell Oliveri what he should have told him the night they went to the Amagansett cottage and brought Paul Monroe back to the station house. After being royally chewed out yesterday for clearing Michael Reo to see Paul, Eddy didn't relish the thought. He was aware of the fact that Paul Monroe was entitled to see only his lawyer, but Eddy couldn't see any harm in allowing the kid a visit from his cousin after being locked up all night and not knowing the reason why. Naturally, Oliveri jumped on Eddy's relationship with Michael Reo but Eddy boldly told the lieutenant he would have done it for anyone.

They didn't have one scrap of evidence with which to charge Paul Monroe and he was released a few minutes after Barrett came to get him. In the old days, whose demise Oliveri was quick to mourn, a more relaxed attitude existed between the police and the local population, especially those as well known as Michael Reo. The mourner, however, was quick to take up the new ways. To be sure, Eddy had not said that to Christopher Oliveri.

After working till sunrise the night of the murder and sleeping half the next day before reporting back to work, Eddy had not had a chance to speak to Helen about the Ryan family, as he promised Oliveri he would. Perhaps Helen could tell him something about Heather Ryan that would placate his boss, but he wasn't counting on it. In fact, he would rather Helen tell him that she had set a date for their wedding, an event Eddy was looking forward to with all the joy expected of a blushing bridegroom.

The stunning girl who followed Bill Ryan into the interview room was probably the catalyst for Eddy's vision of Helen in white. She had to be the actress Lisa Kennedy. With them was a distinguished-looking gentleman with gray hair who appeared to be the spokesperson for the couple when he introduced himself to Oliveri and Eddy.

"I'm Joshua Aldridge. The producer of the play now at the John Drew Theater here. This is Bill Ryan and Lisa Kennedy. I believe you wanted to see them in connection with the tragic death of Heather Ryan."

"How do you do, Mr. Aldridge," Oliveri spoke, but didn't extend his hand. In fact, neither did Aldridge. "We do want to see them, however not in tandem. If you and Ms. Kennedy would wait outside, we'll begin with Mr. Ryan."

"Of course," Aldridge said, taking the girl's arm. Before leaving she touched Bill Ryan's cheek to register her support but Eddy found the gesture most sensuous. If she was the reason Bill had left Montauk for New York, Eddy concluded the young man had made the right choice.

"Have a seat, Bill," Oliveri invited the moment the others had gone.

A tall drink of water, Eddy thought, looking at Bill taking the chair most recently vacated by Paul Monroe, and as nervous as a virgin on her wedding night. (He had to stop dreaming up those similes.)

"I'm very sorry about Heather," Oliveri began to Eddy's relief.

"Thank you . . ." Bill hesitated.

"Oliveri. Lieutenant Oliveri. This is Detective Eddy Evans."

"I know Mr. Evans," Bill said, giving Eddy a cursory nod but not looking him in the face.

"You do?" Oliveri exclaimed, but caught himself before elaborating on the disclosure. Oliveri was caught off guard and the man did not like to be caught off guard, especially when conducting an interview involving a murder.

Eddy gave Bill an apathetic smile while hoping White's Pharmacy sold cyanide tablets over the counter.

"How is Job taking it?" Oliveri continued in a solicitous manner.

"Very hard," Bill answered.

"We saw him yesterday but we didn't bother him—"

"What did he say?" Bill cut in, then looked at Eddy and Oliveri as if he were sorry he had.

"You'll have to ask him that," Oliveri said, a slight edge to his tone. "Before we begin, Mr. Ryan, this interview is being taped." Oliveri indicated the recorder he had switched on when the door opened to admit Bill and his companion. "Is that clear?" Bill nodded, and Oliveri cautioned, "Please say yes, Mr. Ryan. We can't record a gesture." When Bill complied, Oliveri read Bill his rights and asked, "Do you want a lawyer present?"

Bill shook his head, then, remembering Oliveri's admonition, said, "No, sir."

"What did you and Job discuss yesterday morning when you went to the lodge?"

"Heather."

Oliveri waited, but it was all he was going to get from Bill on that score.

Seeing the puzzled look on Bill's face, Eddy said, "Job told us you were there yesterday morning."

"As I was saying," Oliveri quickly put in, "we went to the lodge mainly to go through Heather's things." Hearing this, Bill shuddered and Oliveri remonstrated him with. "She was the victim of a vicious crime and knowing as much as we can about her will help us find the person who murdered her. I'm sorry if our job offends your sense of decorum, Mr. Ryan."

"I understand," Bill said.

"Job will have to identify the body today and hopefully the shock will have worn off and he can answer a few questions for us, as we're hoping you can do now. And if it's any consolation, she wasn't molested in any way," Oliveri declared.

Bill nodded and mumbled, "Thank you."

For an actor, Eddy thought, he's about as verbose as a clam, unless he thinks the silents will make a comeback.

"What time did you leave the house in Amagansett to go to the theater the night of your opening?" Oliveri was now all business and Bill Ryan responded by sitting up in his seat, like a student being called upon by his teacher.

"About five," Bill answered.

"Did you go alone?"

"No. I went with Lisa. She's in the show with me."

"What's your relationship to Lisa Kennedy?"

"None of your business," Bill snapped, startling Oliveri. Eddy wanted to laugh but didn't dare.

Undaunted, Oliveri proceeded, "Did you leave anyone in the house when you left?"

"Yes. Paul. You must know that. How is Paul?"

"Fine, I imagine. At least he was when he left here yesterday. Haven't you talked to him?"

"No," Bill said. "I tried to get him last night but the line was tied up all evening. This morning I got the housekeeper and she told me Paul was still asleep. Then we had to come here."

Fool, Eddy reflected, he's elaborating instead of simply answering the question, which, of course, was Oliveri's goal.

"The press is staked out at the Reos' Dunemere Lane house hoping to get a snap of Paul Monroe in his jockeys. Do you know who the Reos are?"

"Paul told me her father owned WMET," Bill said.

"He was a mogul, Mr. Ryan. A media mogul. Between Paul's half-nude photos and the Reos' notoriety, the press is having a field day. I'm afraid they're not at all interested in you."

"That's fine with me, sir."

Funny, Eddy had no doubt but that the boy meant it. If Bill Ryan is an actor, he was unique to the profession.

"Paul is sharing the house with you and Lisa Kennedy, is that right?"

"Yes."

"How come Paul didn't attend your opening night?"

"He was invited to dinner at the home of Freddy Parc. He's the—"

"I knew who Mr. Parc is. In fact the world knows who Mr. Parc is. Paul would rather go there than see his roommates in a show?"

Bill shifted his long frame in the uncomfortable chair. "He had no choice. He works for Freddy Parc. Paul called it a command performance."

"I understand there was a party after the show." Without waiting for a reply Oliveri asked, "How come Paul didn't come to the party after his command performance?"

"I don't know," Bill answered.

"You don't know? Didn't you ask him if you would see him there? I mean, you must have discussed the party with him."

Bill looked embarrassed as he once more shifted his weight in search of a more comfortable position. "I didn't know about the party," he bluntly stated.

The phrase "that makes the cheese more binding" was the thought that came to Eddy's mind. Eddy Evans was at home with clichés. They said it all in as few words as possible and everyone understood their meaning.

"Was it a surprise party, Mr. Ryan?"

"You might call it that."

"What else might I call it, Mr. Ryan?"

Without hesitating, Bill responded, "If I had known about it I would have told Mr. Aldridge I wasn't going. That's why they didn't tell me. Did Paul know about the party?"

Oliveri gave this some thought and decided there would be no harm in answering truthfully. "He told us he wasn't invited, so I guess he knew about it."

"It could also mean he didn't know about it," Bill pointed out, and Eddy was again taken with Bill Ryan's spirit. Bill Ryan might be a rube, but he was nobody's fool.

"How come your family, or foster family, wasn't at the play or the party?" Oliveri, it seemed, was trying to get answers to as many of the questions he had laid out before Eddy the night of the murder.

"They didn't like the idea of my leaving Montauk for a try at acting."

"They were sore at you?"

"I guess," Bill said, treading carefully.

"So how come you ran out on the party to meet Heather?"

The question, Eddy knew, was intended to unnerve Bill, but it missed the mark. The boy obviously knew it was coming.

"Did Paul tell you that?" Bill asked.

"Paul?" Oliveri's torpedo boomeranged and landed square on his lap. "Paul told us he didn't know you had a sister," he shouted. "He said he never saw the dead girl before he discovered her body and he didn't know what she was doing in the house."

This had the effect Oliveri had hoped to garner when he said he knew Bill had run off to meet Heather. Flustered, Bill shouted, "It's true. Paul didn't know about Heather. I never told him about her and he didn't know I was meeting her."

"So why did you ask us if we got our information from him?"

Looking on the verge of tears, Bill did his best to explain and failed miserably. "I don't know why. I don't. I wasn't thinking. I'm upset about Heather and I don't like being here. It was a mistake. Paul doesn't know anything about this. I swear to that."

It was time for Eddy to move into the driver's seat. "Do you want some water, Bill?" Eddy commenced. When Bill shook his head, Eddy continued. "You and Paul are good friends?"

"We met in New York. Paul sort of showed me the ropes. Yeah, we're good friends."

"And you share the house in Amagansett?"

"Mr. Aldridge rented the house for Lisa and me. Then Paul came out because he has something in the works with his cousin Mr. Reo. He was going to stay with the Reos, but I asked him to share our place. There is another bedroom." He knew it was the wrong thing to say almost before the words were out of his mouth.

Oliveri grinned contentedly. Eddy did not pursue the obvious but rather took a detour leading to the same place. "And what did Ms. Kennedy think about Paul sharing?"

"She likes Paul," Bill told them. Then he admitted sheepishly, "And she likes Paul's relatives. Lisa is very ambitious."

"Did Lisa know about your foster family in Montauk?"

"No. Neither did Paul or Mr. Aldridge. All I told them was that I was an orphan and raised in foster care."

"And they didn't ask about your family when you arrived back here?" Eddy persisted.

"No. They did not."

"And Paul didn't know you had a date to meet Heather that night after your performance?"

Bill sighed audibly and once more changed positions, managing to look more uncomfortable than ever. "I swear that Paul did not know Heather existed and he didn't know I was going to meet her the other night. I would say that in court and I know that perjury is a crime."

After a long pause that seemed to give Bill's statement the solemnity of a prayer, Eddy said gravely, "I'll be honest with you, Bill. We know you broke away from the party because the Chief, the Chief of Police that is, was a guest and your exit wasn't exactly discreet. I mean it's no secret. And we know you were going to meet Heather at nine that night because we played the tape on her answering machine and listened to your message."

There was another pause before Bill spoke. "I thought I could get back to the house right after the curtain. We ran late and after that everything got screwed up."

"We figured as much," Eddy said. "What did Heather want to see you about that couldn't wait for a more convenient time?"

"She was pregnant," Bill answered.

Eddy looked pleased. "We learned that yesterday. Were you the father?"

"Fuck you," Bill shouted and jumped out of his chair. "She was my sister and I haven't seen her in a year."

"Easy, son, easy," Oliveri broke in, also standing. "This is our job. We ask questions to get at the truth, not to embarrass or insult you."

When Bill was back in his chair Oliveri nodded at Eddy to continue. After apologizing, Eddy asked, "Who is the father, Bill?"

"She was going to marry Ian Edwards."

"Did he want to marry her?"

"Yes. Of course. They were engaged."

"Then I don't understand her urgency to see you."

Watching him closely, Eddy again got the impression that Bill was prepared for the question. "I think she wanted me to break the news to Job. If they got married in the fall, the baby would be born five months after the wedding."

"Strange she should turn to you after your falling out," Eddy noted.

"We were close, Heather and me. Raised like brother and sister. Who else could she go to for something like this? I was glad to get her call and I didn't want to put her off and have her think I didn't care, so I made the date for that night. It would be a reconciliation for the three of us was what I thought. How was I to know—"

"Okay," Eddy said, "and it makes sense. You don't think Ian Edwards meant her any harm?"

"Never. He loved Heather. Everyone who knew her loved her," Bill sobbed, then he surprised both Oliveri and Eddy when he shouted, "How did she get into the house?"

"Funny, we were going to ask you that." Oliveri was back in the driver's seat. "You had your key with you at the theater?"

"I did. And Lisa had her key with her. I already asked her that," Bill told them.

"That leaves Paul Monroe."

"That's crazy," Bill exploded.

"Then how did she get into the house? Paul told us he locked up when he left and the place was still locked when he got back. Obviously someone is lying," Oliveri accused.

"Not Paul," Bill insisted.

"Do you own a jockstrap?"

"I used to. When I played basketball at the high school."

"Was it a Freddy Parc jockstrap?"

"No. Of course not."

"Why did you leave Montauk and go to New York?" Oliveri got in quickly, and Eddy could see the question, as before, made Bill falter. The boy was so transparent, it was pathetic.

"I told you, to try my hand at acting. Mr. Aldridge came out on the boat and told me he thought I could make it as an actor. He gave me his card. That's the truth. Ask him."

"Don't worry, we will. So just like that you decided to give up fishing for acting. Some career change."

"Look, Mr. Oliveri, Job was in financial trouble. I mean we were broke. The competition was stiff and business was way off. When Mr. Aldridge said he thought I could make it as an actor, I grabbed the chance. Actors make big money. Millions. I did it to help Job and repay him for what he did for me."

"But you said Job was sore at you for leaving?"

Bill shook his head and ran his hand through his curly hair. "Job didn't see it that way. He's old and didn't understand what I was trying to do. He thought I was running out on him."

"That's all," Oliveri suddenly announced. "You can go. Tell Ms. Kennedy we will be with her shortly."

Bewildered, Bill began to rise. "That's all?"

"Yes. Unless you have something more to tell us?"

"No—no. I don't," Bill muttered. He backed away from the chair as if it were an instrument of torture. "Will you want to see me again?"

"You're not planning on leaving town yet again, I hope," Oliveri said.

"No. I'll be right here."

"Then I'm sure we'll be seeing you again, Mr. Ryan. Now please tell Ms. Kennedy we won't be long."

When the door closed, Oliveri switched off the recorder and exclaimed, "He's lying through his teeth."

"Selective lying, if you know what I mean. And he's scared out of his wits."

"I know what you mean, Eddy, and I think 'petrified with fear' would be a more apt description of our fisherman-turned-actor. Perjury, my arse. Paul knew about that meeting. What do you think?"

"I have to agree but I don't see a conspiracy. I think one of them made up a story—I don't know why—and then both of them tripped all over it."

"Ever hear of Leopold and Loeb?"

"Come off it, Chris. This is East Hampton."

"That's right. I forgot. This is the place where even murder weapons have a designer label. Now will you tell me about your more than nodding acquaintance with Bill Ryan?"

"You won't like this, Chris."

"Try me, laddie, try me."

When Eddy told his story it left Oliveri more pensive than sore. Instead of chewing Eddy out he quietly intoned, "The kid said Job Ryan was in financial trouble last year. Let's see how his bank balance has fared since then. And have you had a chance to talk to Helen?"

"You're kidding? I haven't had time to look at myself in the mirror since this thing broke."

"You're not missing much," Oliveri told him.

"Thanks. I'm seeing her tonight unless we have another murder."

"Don't rattle the beads, Eddy," Oliveri cautioned, looking at his watch. "Now go tell the producer that we'll get to him later and bring in the Kennedy girl. And, Eddy, I think you should question Ms. Kennedy. That will keep your eyes on her face and your mind off the rest of her."

Eddy blushed.

CHAPTER SIXTEEN

"My, don't you look sexy," Jan Solinsky sighed as Eddy, just out of his shower, wrapped a towel around his middle. "I must say you look even better at thirty than twenty. A little more hair on the chest, perhaps, but great pecs—and what legs."

"I wish you would call before you come here or at least knock before you invade my home. Christ, Jan, this is my bedroom."

"Call? Knock? Why, Eddy, this used to be my home and my bedroom, too. Remember?"

The house in the Springs, a section of East Hampton on the bay side favored by the locals and artists of all stripes, had been Eddy's parents' summer home. Eddy's father, a dentist, had purchased it when Jackson Pollock was paying his grocery bills at the Springs General Store with his paintings rather than ready cash, and before Willem de Kooning's outhouse toilet seat was sold at auction for a king's ransom, and when the split-rail fence fronting the Fort Pond home of artist Silas Seandel had not yet been replaced with one sculpted by Seandel himself. In short, at a time when a neighborhood dentist could afford to buy a second home in East Hampton.

When his father retired and his parents moved to Arizona, Eddy inherited the house along with a mortgage incurred to transform the summer bungalow into a year-round dwelling. Now engaged to Helen Weaver, the extra income his moonlighting job with Kirkpatrick Entertainment offered would go a long way toward paying down that mortgage and refurbishing the house from bachelor quarters to a home more suitable for his young bride. Eddy was on a roll and the only cloud on his horizon was the return of his former lover to the East End.

"I just want to report that Amanda Richards has accepted the role in *The Hampton Affair*. My role, I may add."

"Your role? You know what you are, Jan? Nuts, that's what you are. You never had a role and Amanda Richards is the most famous actress in America—maybe the world."

"I might have had the role if you had put in a good word for me with Mr. Reo."

"I told Mr. Reo you were an actress and he said he would keep you in mind."

"They all say that!" Jan complained.

"And, if you're employed by Mr. Aldridge, I don't think you should go around broadcasting his business."

"I understand you met him today," Jan said.

"I'm not at liberty to discuss it. Now will you get out of here so I can dress."

Jan smiled, displaying a perfect set of teeth that were bestowed upon her by nature and not a cosmetic dentist. This week Jan's hair, which she wore short, was an attractive auburn shade. Next week, who knew? She kept her hair short because she favored wigs, all of them fashioned after trademark hairstyles of famous film stars. Sitting on Eddy's king-size bed she said, "You used to love for me to watch you dress."

"Well, I'm a big boy now, so get off my bed and out of my hair." This was said with very little conviction because Eddy Evans had neither the desire nor the gumption to be mean or petty. He was, as Amanda Richards might plagiarize, "just a lug you love to hug, and hold against your heart."

"Tell me, Eddy, do you still have those boxer shorts I gave you one

Valentine's Day? The ones festooned with little red hearts and little cupids with wings. I must remember to tell Helen that those shorts turned you into an animal that night. Oh, Eddy . . ."

He took two giant steps across the room, almost losing his towel. "Don't you tell Helen anything, Jan. What passed between us is past, get it?" The statement lost its sting as Eddy had to grip the towel to keep it from falling to the floor. "Helen is very young," he added.

"She's twenty-one going on forty, Eddy, and she did have an affair with that boy who killed his stepmother. A murderer on the most-wanted list."

"He's not on the most-wanted list, but we'll get him anyway. I know the guy, and he won't be able to resist coming back here when they start filming the story of his life. He has more ego than brains."

"And won't you be happy to see him in jail and out of reach of the loving arms of his old girlfriend."

With a groan of frustration, and almost forgetting to keep a firm hold on his towel, Eddy responded with, "You left me once, Jan. Why don't you do it again? For old times' sake."

She had left Eddy to pursue an acting career in New York, where the only thing she did that even vaguely resembled the life and times of an actress was marry and divorce an incipient actor. However, she did not return to East Hampton in defeat, but rather with a new master plan for achieving her goal. The *Bay Street Theatre* in Sag Harbor had proved a great success, drawing big names on both sides of the footlights, and even serving as a showcase for Broadway-bound vehicles. Jan hoped one of those "vehicles" would provide her return transportation to the Big Apple.

She began her association with the *Bay Street Theatre* as a volunteer usherette. From there she got on the payroll working in the box office. When the agent Joshua Aldridge told the company's manager that he was in need of a part-time secretary to get him through the rigors of presenting his showcase at the *John Drew,* Jan Solinsky got her first big break—or what she liked to think of as her big break. And when Eddy got the job as technical advisor with Kirkpatrick Entertainment for a film project to be shot in East Hampton, Jan knew that her decision to return was nothing less than divine intervention in her quest for stardom.

Ogling Eddy's naked torso she teased, "You're not bad, Eddy, but the murderer—what was his name? Gary . . ."

"Galen. Galen Miller."

"What a lovely name. Galen. He was a hot number. And you know Paul Monroe is going to play his character," Jan stated, rather than asked. "He's related to Mr. Reo."

"I don't discuss my employers' business, be it Mr. Reo or the police department, with strangers."

"Strangers?" Jan shrieked. "Eddy, I used to share this bed with you." She ran her hand lovingly over the blue quilted bedcover.

"Please get out of here, Jan, and leave me in peace."

"I will if you tell me what Paul Monroe said when you arrested him."

"Who wants to know?" Eddy countered.

"I do."

"Are you on a reconnaissance mission for Mr. Aldridge?"

"Why do you ask such a thing?" Jan fluttered her false eyelashes and pretended to be shocked by the question.

"Because Mr. Aldridge has a vested interest in the case, that's why. His stars and their roommate are under suspicion and his play is closed. I think he's anxious to keep his ears to the ground and he's found the perfect snoop in you, thanks to your police connection—me."

"I'm hurt, Eddy."

"Good. Now get out of here. I have a date."

"With Helen?"

"No, with Amanda Richards. She wants to marry me."

"I met Amanda, you know," Jan said with pride. "We had a long talk. I think we have a lot in common."

"Like your ages," Eddy suggested.

"Bitch," Jan snapped. Calling her a contemporary of Amanda Richards incensed Jan Solinsky far more than Eddy's entreaties to get out of his life and stay out. Jan claimed to be Eddy's age, however he had long suspected that she was his senior by at least two years. Brushing aside the slight, Jan advanced to the next pressing topic on her agenda. "Effervescent" was a word Eddy often used in describing Jan's chatter—bubbles rising to the surface, exploding and immediately replaced by more bubbles.

"The murder is the talk of the town," Jan gushed. "When the *Star* comes out on Thursday it will be the lead story. And you know it closed our show. The girl was Bill Ryan's foster sister. Do the police have any leads?"

"If we do it will be in the *Star* on Thursday."

"Meanie," Jan said, showing Eddy a ladylike tip of her tongue. "Have you heard about the other man?"

Eddy adjusted his protective towel. "What other man?"

"It's being said that the girl, Heather, was in the family way. She was engaged to one man, the father presumably, but may have been in love with another."

For the first time since she arrived, unannounced and without knocking, Eddy listened attentively to what Jan was saying. "Where did you hear that?"

With a dramatic toss of her head, Jan explained, "In this town, who knows? On the checkout line and the farmer's market, browsing in Bookhampton or across the bar at O'Mally's, where the locals dish the dirt after work."

"She was going to marry Ian Edwards," Eddy stated.

"Is that what Bill Ryan told you?"

"Stop pumping me, Jan."

"My, you do have a way with words, Eddy."

Jan's interest in Heather Ryan's murder was prompted by Heather's connection to Bill Ryan and, consequently, to Joshua Aldridge. If she could be of help to Mr. Aldridge during these trying times he would certainly be indebted to her, and that could only help her career. Jan had counted on Eddy's connection to Michael Reo for a possible film role, and now Mr. Reo was involved in Heather's murder via Paul Monroe and Paul's connection to Bill Ryan, which brought her back to Bill's link to Joshua Aldridge to complete the circle. Divine intervention? What else?

"I have a theory about the murder," Jan now babbled.

"And I have to get dressed," Eddy reminded her.

"Oh, go on and dress. I won't look. Why should I? I've seen it."

Tongue-tied with embarrassment, Eddy marched back into the bathroom.

"I think," Jan shouted to be heard, "that Galen is back in town wielding a jockstrap."

"That's crazy," Eddy shouted right back.

"Why? The fact that Michael Reo is going to film his story is no secret, and you said Galen couldn't resist coming back when they did."

"And why did he do in Heather Ryan?"

"He mistook her for his old flame Helen Weaver."

"That's ghoulish," Eddy barked. "Now get out of here. You are a box office attendant and a part-time secretary, so if Amanda Richards has accepted the role, you can concentrate on selling tickets and taking notes."

"There are other roles," Jan stated.

"If you mean the young girl, forget it. You're too old."

"I'm twenty-nine, Eddy."

"Thirty, Jan. Don't you remember how we used to celebrate our birthdays together? Born one week apart and in the same year—or so you claimed."

"Now you have an attitude," Jan called back.

"And I'm going to have a stroke if you don't get out of here. And mind your own business, Jan."

She let out a scream that had Eddy calling from behind the door, "Now what?"

"Freddy Parc briefs. They're adorable, Eddy."

"Keep out of my drawers, Jan!"

Eddy walked into Main Street Video and, as always, he was noticeably aware of his beating heart when he gazed upon his future wife. Helen Weaver had straight, dark hair that fell to her shoulders when she didn't have it tied back in a ponytail. Her eyes went from brown to gray as the day progressed from bright sun to twilight. Her figure— she favored shorts and T-shirts in the summer—kept the men and boys browsing titles in Main Street Video long after they had made their selections. A fair complexion and a sassy air completed the picture that had Eddy Evans counting his blessings. For their date tonight, Helen had chosen a summery cotton dress in pale blue and white sandals with a sensible heel.

Customers who depended on her reviews, recommendations and movie gossip followed Main Street Video all the way up Springs Fireplace Road, rendering the move from East Hampton's Main Street negligible to Mr. Weaver's gross receipts.

Helen was also known to comment, often negatively, on the films currently on view at the East Hampton Cinema. This did not sit well with the theater's owner, who once offered Helen passes for herself and her policeman beau if she would keep her opinions to herself. To her credit, Helen has never bartered her reputation as one who has her finger on the pulse of America's filmgoers for a few pieces of silver.

"You have scruples, Helen," her father griped, "I don't. Get a couple of passes for your mother and me or forget a big wedding. I'll give Eddy a ladder, but he probably won't know what to do with it." Mr. Weaver's bark, incidentally, was far worse than his bite.

Helen's love of films, her comeliness and her involvement in the story Michael Reo proposed to film had Eddy worried that Helen, like Jan, would be bitten by the acting bug. When he confronted her with his fear she assured him that she had no interest in making a fool of herself, as she put it.

"Actors are very special people," she told Eddy, "and film actors even more so. Whatever it is they have, I don't possess and I know it."

"Aren't you even curious as to who will portray you?" Eddy asked.

Michael Reo often said, most likely with a thought to libel suits, that *The Hampton Affair* was pure fiction based on fact and not a documentary. Yet those involved in the actual drama knew that they would have to be represented, however fictionally, on the screen.

"Aren't you curious as to who will portray you?" Helen countered.

Without a moment's hesitation, Eddy answered, "No. Because it's not me. The detective in the script is a creation of some writer's imagination. The only thing we have in common is a badge inscribed East Hampton Town Police."

With a knowing smile, Helen said, "And the girl is not me and the boy is not Galen. It was our drama, Eddy, and one I would rather forget than act out." She shuddered as if the very idea was repugnant. "It would be like some weird form of psychodrama. No thank you. Let the actors do it and any resemblance to persons living or dead is purely coincidental."

In spite of this conversation Eddy still secretly harbored a fear that if Mr. Reo saw Helen, he would offer her the role instantly. Eddy was so in love with Helen Weaver that he would think less of Mr. Reo if he didn't do just that. So it was not by chance alone that Helen had not as yet met Michael and Victoria Reo.

The store was devoid of customers when Eddy arrived and Helen was perched on a stool behind the counter. Eddy leaned across the expanse and kissed her cheek. "I can't wait much longer," he implored.

"Oh, Eddy," she sighed. "All I can think about is poor Heather Ryan. It's the talk of the town. I didn't call you because I didn't want to bother you. Do you know who did it?"

The warning bell over the door jangled as two customers entered the shop. Aware of the discretion a policeman's companion must exercise in public, Helen quickly changed the subject. "I'm thinking about a fall wedding."

"This year?" When Helen nodded, he begged, "Name the date."

"I will, Eddy. I promise. Before the summer is over, I'll set the date."

"Do you love me?"

"No. I'm marrying you for your money—and you're late. Dad is in the back brewing coffee, and the girl, for a change, didn't show up."

"The girl" was any one of a number of local girls Mr. Weaver hired in the summer to deal with the seasonal increase in business. Their working hours were spotty, to say the least, what with the lure of the beach, a new boyfriend or the latest and hottest pub in Montauk to entice them into playing truant morning, noon or evening. Mr. Weaver, and the other shops, might go through a dozen such workers in a summer, very often ending up in September with the one who had started in April.

"Jan barged in on me, as usual," Eddy explained his lateness, "She's upset because Amanda Richards has agreed to do the film for Mr. Reo."

"Poor Jan," Helen said, shaking her head. "Did she really think she was in competition with Amanda Richards?" Much to Eddy's chagrin and thanks to Jan's insistence, Jan had befriended Helen Weaver.

"Amanda Richards is a great choice," Helen said. "She hasn't made a film in years. Her last one was a bomb, directed by Tony Vasquez, who's in East Hampton as we speak."

"What's he doing here?"

"Don't know. Maybe Mr. Reo is after him to direct."

"If he is, he hasn't mentioned it to me."

"You're a technical advisor, Eddy, not an assistant producer."

"But do you think I could model underwear?" Eddy whispered, accompanied by what he hoped was a bawdy wink.

"Stick to detecting, Eddy, it pays better."

"But it doesn't answer my question."

"Ask me no questions, and I'll tell you no lies."

Mr. Weaver emerged from the back room that served as a storage area for the videocassettes and doubled as a functioning kitchen with a sink and a two-burner range mounted over a mini refrigerator. He carried a mug of coffee and the moment he saw Eddy he asked, "What's new with the murder?"

A nod from Helen clued Mr. Weaver to the fact that they were not alone in the shop. "You are officially relieved of duty," Mr. Weaver quickly told his daughter, "and enjoy the evening. You have my permission to elope tonight, Eddy, so gather ye rosebuds while ye may."

"Sorry, Mr. Weaver, but Helen wants a big, expensive wedding at *The Waterside* in Sag Harbor, but I'm trying to talk her into the *Waldorf Astoria* in New York."

"A pox on your house, my son," Mr. Weaver called after the departing couple.

Taking the back roads through Sag Harbor and Noyack—a course the summer crowds were fast learning, judging from the number of cars on the country roads bypassing East Hampton Village, Wainscott and Bridgehampton—Eddy didn't rejoin Route 27 until they arrived in Water Mill and parked in the village parking lot, which afforded direct access to the back door of their destination, Meghan's Restaurant.

Presided over by host Steve and bartender Jeff, Meghan's is one of the Hamptons' best kept secrets if one is interested in an unpretentious ambiance and the best burger and fries (potatoes or chicken) on the East End.

Having discussed nothing but the murder on the ride to Water Mill, and assuring Helen that Heather Ryan had not been raped, they had not exhausted the topic as they settled into a booth at Meghan's. After ordering wine for Helen and a gin and tonic for himself, Eddy asked Helen if she had heard any rumors about another man in Heather Ryan's life besides Ian Edwards.

"Never," Helen answered. "Where did you hear that?"

Not wanting to bring Jan Solinsky into the conversation, Eddy said it was something they had come across in their investigation.

"You know I only saw Heather when she came into the shop," Helen said. "But when she did, especially this past year, she always asked me about our wedding plans and told me she and Ian were close to setting a date. Now that she's been murdered with a jockstrap I guess all the

rumormongers can't wait to make the crime more sordid than it probably is. Is the jockstrap supposed to belong to the other guy?"

Eddy didn't answer until the waitress had placed their drinks
before them and left. "I never thought about that, actually. Cheers."

"Did it belong to Paul Monroe?" Helen asked.

"I shouldn't tell you, but Paul says he doesn't own one."

"What about Bill?"

"He was an athlete in high school and . . ." Eddy put down his
glass, "This is embarrassing, Helen."

"Oh, Eddy, don't be such a prude," she scolded. "Jan told me you
were quite a rake in the old days."

"Don't believe anything Jan tells you, and those days were not so
long ago." Making his point, Eddy went on, "One more question about
the Ryans and then we'll talk about nothing but us. Okay?"

"Shoot," Helen said.

"Do you know why Bill left Montauk?"

"To become an actor," Helen said. "Heather told everyone he was
discovered."

"How do you get discovered?"

Helen laughed and with great glee launched into one of her old-
time Hollywood stories. "Lana Turner was discovered sitting on a stool
at a soda fountain."

"But not on a fishing boat out of Montauk, eh?"

"No, Eddy, not on a fishing boat."

The waitress was back and, without having consulted the menu,
Eddy ordered medium-rare burgers with well-done fries for two, and
an order of fried onion rings to nibble while they waited for the main
event.

"I just thought of something," Helen said when the waitress
departed. "Remember that drug raid in Sag Harbor last year, when you
went to see Bill Ryan because his truck was parked in the vicinity of
the raid?"

"I remember," Eddy said somberly, but did not elaborate.

"Old man Ryan said he had used the truck to visit a girlfriend and we tried to figure out who she was." Helen laughed at the memory. "Well, just about that time, Heather came in the shop and asked me about Avery."

"What's Avery?" Eddy said.

"Avery is a who, not a what," Helen informed him. "He's a photographer and he used to work for Freddy Parc."

"Freddy Parc?" Eddy pricked up his ears, as they say.

"Avery photographed those early underwear ads for the Freddy Parc company that were considered in very bad taste."

"The current one is not exactly fit for a church calendar," Eddy got in.

Their onions came and, taking one, Helen said, "Is Paul Monroe as adorable in person as he is in his photographs?"

"Who wants to know?"

"Your future wife, that's who."

The retort obviously pleased Eddy, who conceded, "He's cute. Now tell me more about this Avery."

"Not much more to tell. Heather asked me about him because he was taking pictures of the fishing folk in Montauk. I think she said he was going to publish them in book form. That's all."

"Does he still work for Freddy Parc?" Eddy wanted to know.

"I don't think so. I know he didn't do the layout for Paul Monroe because I read who did but can't recall his name. I'm sure it wasn't Avery."

"But Heather was asking about him."

"She was, Eddy."

Interesting, is what Chris Oliveri would have said.

"Interesting," is what Eddy said, just as their dinners arrived.

CHAPTER SEVENTEEN

It was Eddy's day off and he had intended to work on cleaning out his basement in preparation for having it made over into a recreation room. It was to be a surprise for Helen and the fact that a television star had just purchased the Further Lane home of a singer/compser for a reputed forty million dollars did not discourage Eddy from creating a more modest castle for his bride.

However, Eddy's day off had been scheduled before Heather Ryan's murder and he had worked with Chris Oliveri long enough to know that at the start of a case, especially a murder case with a high profile like Heather Ryan's, thanks to the people involved, there was no such thing as a day off.

He had also promised Mr. Reo that he would pick up the necessary applications for permits to film in various locations in East Hampton and deliver them to the Dunemere Lane house this afternoon. That, too, was before the murder, but Eddy saw no reason why he couldn't get the applications, deliver them to Dunemere Lane and check in with Oliveri after that. Chris had told him to nosy around their cast of characters to see what he could learn, so he wasn't exactly doing Michael Reo's bidding on police department time.

Eddy brewed a pot of coffee before starting out and an hour later drove his unmarked police car around the circular drive of the Dunemere Lane mansion, parked at the front door and rang the bell, all in the easygoing manner he would have employed to call upon a split-level in Suburbia, USA.

Maddy opened the door to him with a warm smile. "They're out on the back patio, just finishing breakfast. I'll get you a plate, Mr. Eddy."

"No thanks, Maddy, I can't stay long."

Since meeting Eddy, Maddy doted on the young man, always ready with an offer of food and drink when he called at the house. Eddy would decline with his winning smile and a pat on his flat stomach, stating his goal was to keep it that way. John liked to corner the detective and pump him for additional information regarding the crimes and misdemeanors that appeared every Thursday in the *East Hampton Star*'s Police and Courts column. Eddy always responded by simply embellishing the printed word but making it sound as if he were giving John privileged information.

When Michael began working on the script for *The Hampton Affair*, he had interviewed Eddy Evans for details regarding the drowning of Betty Zabriski Miller by her stepson, Galen Miller. Eddy, who broke the case—inadvertently with Michael's help—was not only cooperative, but gave Michael a very sensitive and poignant account of the life and times of local boys like Galen Miller to whom the glitz and glitter of East Hampton is like a Fifth Avenue store window. They can look but they can't afford to go in and buy. In this case the dividing line is not made of glass but composed of solid asphalt and known as Route 27, the highway that separates the south or ocean side from the north or bay side, in the town of East Hampton.

Real estate agents often run ads for homes proudly proclaiming them as being "south of the highway and north of a million bucks."

Michael liked Eddy Evans and thought Eddy's tall, masculine physique and clean-shaven smile brought back fond memories of the

Cleaver and Nelson families, little Beaver and his brother and dozens of young Hollywood actors of the past who ogled, blushed and stammered when in the presence of the film's *femme fatale*. After Eddy's meeting with her husband, Vicky Reo had proclaimed, "He's the kind of guy people clung to like a garment gone out of fashion but far too comfortable a fit to abandon to the Goodwill pile."

All the foregoing made Eddy Evans a very integral, if sometimes reluctant, part of Michael's preproduction team. From the start of their working relationship, Eddy feared that Michael's offer to take him on as technical advisor, for a very tempting fee, conflicted with his position with the East Hampton Town Police. Michael had convinced the detective that this was not the case but his unauthorized visit to Paul Monroe at the police station—arranged by Eddy—had in fact validated Eddy's fears and derailed Michael's assurance to the contrary.

"Working on the case?" Maddy asked expectantly. With Paul Monroe in the house, there was no doubt as to what case Maddy had in mind.

Eddy answered with his polite brand of subterfuge. "As a matter of fact, it's supposed to be my day off."

"Then you should be on the beach, taking the sun," she scolded.

"The beach? I'm a local, Maddy, and, like the gulls, we leave the beach on the third of July and don't return until September."

"Get on with you," she laughed. Leading him through the house she stopped suddenly and asked in hushed tones, "Did you find any trapdoors in the cottage where that poor Ryan girl died?"

That gave Eddy pause. "Trapdoors? I don't believe so, Maddy. Why?"

"Just a notion of Ms. Johnson, the lady who helps Miss Vicky in the office. Ms. Johnson is a reader of mysteries by Miss Marple and Harriet Vane, if I got the names right," Maddy informed him. "We hear the cottage was bolted from within but it must have been built over a basement or crawl space with access to the outside. She thinks that's how the murderer escaped—through the trapdoor and out the basement."

Eddy guessed correctly that the staff had heard about the locked cottage from the Reos. Did the rich know that those who serve also listen?

"You should check under the rugs and the closet floors and every inch of the floorboards for a trapdoor," Maddy recommended.

"But how did the murderer and the poor girl get in the house before he made his escape?" Eddy asked. "The place was locked by the occupants before they left for the evening."

Maddy thought about this but had no answer other than, "I'll have to ask Ms. Johnson. I'm sure she'll know."

"And they don't have a butler, so he didn't do it."

"Butler," Maddy cried. "Wait till John hears that."

Crossing the den, Maddy opened the patio doors and called out, "Mr. Eddy is here."

Michael and Vicky were at the table where they had just finished eating and were now relaxing over their coffee. "Bring Eddy a cup," Vicky called after Maddy.

"No," Eddy protested. "I had my coffee and I can't stay. I only wanted to drop these off." He handed Michael the envelope he had carried in.

"It's his day off," Maddy announced from the doorway.

"I'm sorry," Michael said. "Why didn't you tell me?"

Embarrassed, Eddy waved away Maddy's disclosure. "No problem. I had to go to the clerk's office to apply for a permit of my own," he half-lied. He did need a permit for his basement job but he had not applied for it that day. "And I see the press isn't camping out on Dunemere Lane this morning."

"Too early for the working members of the fourth estate," Michael said. "But they'll be back."

"Sit with us for a few minutes," Vicky invited. She looked cool and very pretty in white shorts and a pale blue blouse on this warm July morning. Michael was also in shorts and a polo shirt. Both of them were barefoot.

Seeing Eddy's gaze, Michael explained, "You have to excuse our appearance, but we never dress for breakfast alfresco."

Taking the offered chair, Eddy answered, "I wouldn't either if I ever ate breakfast at home, which I don't."

"That will change when you're married," Vicky guaranteed. "Have you set the date?"

"Not exactly. But Helen is thinking about this fall."

"A lovely time for a wedding," Vicky told him.

Holding up the large envelope Eddy had given him, Michael said, "I'll give these to our man who's scouting locations."

The more Eddy learned about the preparation necessary to making a film before a camera turned, the more amazed he was with the number of people involved in the operation. "Don't forget, you have to be very specific about dates. The police will give you all the help they can, but they have to know where and when you'll be filming well in advance."

"That's what I thought," Michael told him, "which is why I wanted to have the applications when we start mapping out our schedule."

"I hear Amanda Richards is going to be in it," Eddy said.

Vicky looked surprised. "Where did you hear that? She only committed to us yesterday."

"Eddy has a spy in Aldridge's office," Michael joked. "Am I right, Eddy? Amanda told me the name of Josh Aldridge's secretary and the fact that she aspires to the stage. Later, when I recalled you saying you had a friend who wanted to act, I realized they were one and the same person. Jan? Am I right?"

"Yes, sir. Jan Solinsky. She told me about Amanda Richards." Eddy looked uncomfortable and Vicky thought he was at his most charming in that guise.

"Eddy, I'm sorry if I got you in a jam the other day," Michael said, finally broaching the subject foremost on all their minds but which both sides were loath to discuss given Eddy's precarious juggling act between the police department and Kirkpatrick Entertainment.

Anything that can go wrong, will, was Eddy's take on the effect Heather Ryan's murder had had on his ability to keep one ball in the air and the other two in each hand.

"It's not your fault, Mr. Reo. It's mine. I never should have told Ken, the desk sergeant, to put your name on the visitors' list."

"So I am to blame, Eddy, because I asked you to do it," Michael said.

Eddy shook his head. "No, sir. It's my fault for not telling you I couldn't do it."

Michael suppressed a smile. Eddy was playing the martyr while clearly labeling Michael the devil's advocate. Anyone who confused Eddy's boyish grin with complacency would be making a serious error.

"Did you know Paul was allowed only a visit by his lawyer?" Michael couldn't help asking.

"Let's put it this way, Mr. Reo. I didn't ask and Ken didn't tell me."

"'Don't ask, don't tell' doesn't seem to be working with any of our uniformed services," Michael acknowledged with a wink that eased the tension somewhat.

"How is Paul?" Eddy asked.

"He'll live," Vicky said. "He's gone to see Bill Ryan, who finally got in touch with Paul yesterday afternoon. I think you saw Bill and Lisa yesterday morning," Vicky added. "I imagine the two have a lot to talk about."

"Are they back in the cottage?" Eddy asked.

"Paul is staying with us," Vicky answered. "We promised his parents we would keep him until this thing is settled. I believe Bill Ryan is back in Montauk, with the girl's father, and Lisa is a guest of Amanda Richards, thanks to Josh Aldridge. They're using the cottage as a meeting place."

"And wouldn't Eddy like to be a fly on the wall," Michael said.

"Do you know something I don't, Mr. Reo?" Eddy questioned.

"If I did, I would tell you," Michael said. "But do you tell me everything you know?"

"Michael, really!" Vicky cried.

"It's okay," Eddy assured her. "We don't know very much, Mr. Reo, and I'd tell you anything that wasn't deemed confidential by the department. I can say Heather Ryan wasn't raped."

"So," Michael thought aloud, "someone only wanted to silence her." This had Eddy thinking when Michael told him, "I believe I ran into your Lieutanant Oliveri when I was at the station house."

"I know you did," Eddy said.

"He's leaning on Paul because of that damn key. Am I right?"

"We have no idea how the girl or her assailant got into the cottage. Paul had the only key that seems to have been in the right place at the right time," Eddy asserted.

"Paul didn't do it, Eddy," Michael stated emphatically.

"I don't think he did, either, Mr. Reo. And trust me, Chris Oliveri won't harass Paul unless he has the kind of solid proof you can take to the DA. Paul was in the wrong place at the wrong time with the only key out of three within the immediate vicinity. You can't blame Chris Oliveri for leaning, just a little."

"I don't think Eddy is supposed to be discussing the case, Michael," Vicky reminded her husband.

Eddy said with a shrug, "We're not discussing anything that hasn't been in the New York papers, and everyone is going to have a theory from trapdoors to a fourth key no one knows about—yet."

"Oh, dear," Vicky laughed, "Maddy told you about Ms. Johnson's solution."

Eddy rolled his eyes skyward to say that she had.

"If we pool our resources, Eddy, we might have a better chance at cracking the puzzle and catching the bastard," Michael suggested.

"I'm willing to listen to anything you have to say," Eddy assured Michael.

"It sounds like a one-way street," Michael teased.

"Michael?" Vicky again cautioned him.

So absorbed were the three with their give-and-take conversation, neither Vicky nor Michael had touched their coffee. Now, Michael sipped from his cup as he waited for Eddy to reply.

"I said I would tell you anything that wasn't of a confidential nature," Eddy repeated.

"Why did Bill Ryan leave Montauk for an acting career he couldn't care less about?" Michael asked, "or is that confidential?"

"Ask him," Eddy responded promptly, "I'm sure he'll tell you just what he told us."

"I haven't had the pleasure of meeting either Bill Ryan or the pretty Lisa Kennedy, but I suspect the young folk are holding out on us, Eddy, and I'm sure you do, too," Michael said.

Eddy had expressed a similar theory to Chris Oliveri and now he pounced on Michael Reo for confirmation. "What makes you think that?"

"Nothing sinister," Michael quickly injected. "Just the way Paul and Bill were so anxious to powwow. Not surprising, given what happened since last they met, but I just had a feeling Paul might be holding back until he'd talked to Bill. I'm sure I'll know more when Paul gets back, including what Bill told you yesterday."

If Michael thought he was going to get a preview of Bill's statement to the police, he was wrong. "If Paul is holding back," Eddy said, "I would tell him the best way he can help his friend and himself is to tell us everything he knows."

"I'll pass that on," Michael promised. "Are you going to interview Freddy Parc?"

"Why should we?"

"To make his PR people happy," Michael replied with a cynical air. "Freddy has been on the horn with Paul a dozen times to tell him that his corporate pundits believe a 'no comment' is the most blatant comment of all. Therefore 'no comment' is all that Freddy will comment as he takes ads in all the popular magazines for his briefs and his jockstraps. A retailer on a roll has no conscience."

Eddy tried for a laid-back approach when he asked, "Will Avery take the photos for the ads?"

This had Vicky and Michael exchanging glances. "How do you know Avery?" Michael answered with a question of his own.

"I don't know him, but he works for Freddy Parc, doesn't he?"

This time Vicky answered. "We don't know him, either, Eddy, except for a few chance meetings at social events. I believe he took the early photos for Freddy's underwear line. The ones that caused a lot of comment—"

"And got Freddy Parc Enterprises on the map," Michael cut in. "But he didn't take the photographs for Paul's ad campaign, which makes me think Avery is no longer on Freddy's payroll. I always thought Avery was a hanger-on with little talent except for trying to elbow his way into the trendy set and not very successful at that, either. What's your interest, Eddy?"

"Interest? None. He was taking photographs in Montauk last year of our fishing community. I think he was gathering material for an art book."

Wide-eyed, Vicky exclaimed, "An art book? Avery? That I have to see."

"Avery was at the theater the other night, watching Bill and Lisa do their turn, so he's in town, or was a few days ago. Did you know that, Eddy?"

"No, I didn't," Eddy said, getting out of his chair. "Now if you'll excuse me, I'll be on my way. Don't forget to tell the boys, and Lisa Kennedy, that if they know anything that might help us solve Heather's murder—better late than never."

Eddy took a detour on his way to the station house and stopped at Brent's, a glorified delicatessen on Route 27 in Amagansett. Mornings, Brent's is the favorite rest stop for the local laborers of all trades who help themselves at the self-service coffee bar and pick up a bagel or a sweet roll to go with their beverage. They return at lunchtime for heros, accounting for the pickup trucks constantly vying for space in Brent's inadequate parking facility.

Brent's is the working man's farmer's market, the upscale bazaar in Amagansett, where those who can afford it shop for vegetables picked that morning or indulge in power breakfasts in the flower garden, where they can see and be seen sipping caffe latte, iced cappuccino or herbal tea.

Eddy poured himself a coffee and selected a buttered roll while waiting on the checkout line. He avoided looking at the New York newspapers on display at the exit door that headlined THE HAMPTON'S JOCKSTRAP MURDER in four-inch black type.

Arriving at the station house on Pantigo Road, Eddy found a note waiting for him from Chris Oliveri.

I'm at a meeting in Riverhead and should be back around six this evening. Meet me at my place and I'll buy you a beer.

It was a typical Christopher Oliveri message. Short and to the point. It was also an order, not an invitation to have a drink with the lieutenant. Eddy prayed that Oliveri wouldn't call him on his wedding day with a similar message, giving rise to a conflict Eddy didn't even want to think about.

Riverhead is the county seat and the site of Suffolk's municipal complex, including the county jail and the courthouse. It wasn't unusual for an East Hampton officer to spend the day in Riverhead, usually appearing at a criminal trial on behalf of the prosecution, or attending meetings on subjects as diverse as traffic control and child abuse. For this reason Eddy did not suspect Oliveri's meeting in Riverhead had anything to do with their subsequent meeting. In the world according to Christopher Oliveri, the reason for the urgent meeting could be anything from a break in the Jockstrap Murder to a two-dollar item on Eddy's expense sheet.

Eddy could go home and start on the basement or stay in the office and face the paperwork that consumes more of a policeman's time and energy than any criminal act. Removing the lid from his container of coffee and taking off his jacket, he opted for the air-conditioned ambiance of the station house over sorting rubbish in a dank hole under his house.

Before he began shuffling the papers on his desk, Eddy savored the last few minutes of conversation he had shared with the Reos. When Mr. Reo began to nibble on the bait, Eddy did not reel in his line as is the wont of novice fishermen, but instead had calmly stood up and announced, "Now if you'll excuse me, I'll be on my way," leaving his catch frustrated and curious, a plight Michael Reo would not tolerate for very long. Mr. Reo would learn everything there was to know about the man called Avery, and who was in a better position to do that without making waves than the socially connected Michael Reo and his charming wife?

Mr. Reo, not being young and foolish, would pool his resources with Eddy, and the detective might just learn the reason for Heather Ryan's interest in Avery and pass it on to his boss if it was worth the telling. *The most seemingly mundane facts could be the solution to the crime,* Eddy remembered, unwrapping his buttered roll.

BILL RYAN

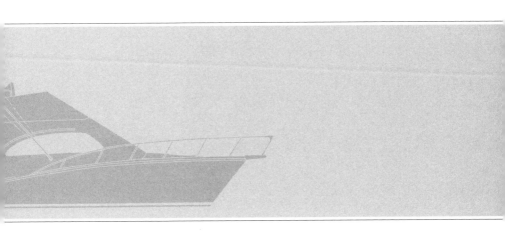

CHAPTER EIGHTEEN

Young, extremely attractive and talented, they came to the Amagansett cottage on the eve of success, but the dawn had brought murder, not stardom, to Bill Ryan, Lisa Kennedy and Paul Monroe.

They sat around the coffee table in the front room, the bright sun pouring in from the glass patio doors in sharp contrast to the dour expressions on their comely faces. Three cans of beer decorated the top of the table but the trio appeared more determined to find a solution to their plight by discussing it rather than drowning it.

"I screwed up," was Bill's take on the situation and had been since Paul had come to the cottage to meet with him and Lisa. "Now the police know you lied to them, Paul. I'm sorry."

"Who lied?" Paul said. "I told them I didn't know who Heather was and I didn't know what she was doing in our house. That was the truth."

"And I backed you up as far as that goes, but you didn't tell them you knew I was meeting a girl here after the show." Then Bill insisted, "You were smart enough to keep quiet about it and I was dumb enough to think you told them." Bill Ryan looked as miserable as he felt. He obviously had not slept properly these past two nights and since being questioned by the police his face appeared gaunt while his broad shoulders seemed to sag under some invisible burden.

"What I don't understand," Lisa addressed Bill, "is why you had to lie to anyone about anything."

"Because of that damn party," Bill responded. "If you had told me about the party, I would have told Mr. Aldridge I wasn't going because I had a date to meet Heather."

"That won't wash, Bill," Lisa told him. Like Paul Monroe, Lisa looked as fresh and pert as this breezy, sun-drenched July afternoon. "Regardless of the party, why didn't you tell me you were meeting with your sister after the show? In fact, why didn't you tell me, or anyone, that you had a family in Montauk?"

"He did tell me about his date but he said it was with an old girl-friend, and I figured that's why he didn't tell you," Paul got in. "I didn't tell him about the party because I was told not to. I know how to keep my mouth shut."

"How did you think he was going to keep his date with a girl if he had to go to the party?" Lisa asked.

"I wish you wouldn't talk about me as if I weren't here," Bill grumbled.

"Sorry," Lisa apologized, "but I'm just trying to make some sense out of this and so is Paul—and the police, I'm sure."

"I guessed Bill wouldn't stay five minutes at that party whether he had another date or not. And he didn't. He ran out of the joint." The thought of Bill running out on the first-nighters had Paul chuckling and, unable to help himself, Bill joined in.

"I don't see the joke," Lisa said, annoyed. "You left Mr. Aldridge and me with egg on our faces . . ."

"If I got here sooner, Heather would be alive," Bill all but shouted, precipitating a silence that had Paul reaching for his beer and Lisa looking tearful.

Bill took the moment to recapitulate his case, but if it was for the benefit of Paul and Lisa or himself, not even he was sure. "I didn't tell anyone about my foster family because they were sore about me leaving them when times were bad and I didn't think they wanted to see me. When Heather called and told me she was pregnant and asked if we could meet, I thought it would be a good time to patch things up. That's why I didn't want to put her off until the next day."

Turning to Lisa, Bill went on, "You were going out with Mr. Aldridge after the show, or so I thought, but I figured if Paul came home before I got here, I should tell him that he might find someone waiting for me. Rather than explain about the family, I told him I was meeting an old girlfriend. It's as simple as all that," Bill concluded.

"Nothing about this is simple," Lisa maintained. To Paul, she said, "Bill told Mr. Aldridge and me that he thought Heather was desperate to see him because she might not have wanted to marry the father of the child she was carrying. That there was another man in her life."

Bill looked more miserable than ever. "I wasn't thinking," he explained to Paul. "I don't know why I said it. Heather never told me that, I just suspected that might be the reason, but it wasn't. She wanted me to break the news to her father, Job. That's what it was all about."

Looking incredulous, Paul asked, "So what did you tell the police was the reason for Heather's call?"

"That she wanted me to break the news to Job," Bill stated.

To Lisa, Paul began, "And when the police asked you—"

"The question never arose." Lisa cut right to the point. "They just asked me, and Mr. Aldridge, about our movements the night of the murder and if we had ever met Heather or knew she existed. All we did was tell the truth—as we knew it."

"We're all telling the truth," Bill stated. "It's the questions that are unclear."

"Well, I like that," Lisa said with a smile.

"Bill, do you know anyone who would want to harm Heather?" Paul questioned.

"No. And she wasn't raped. The police told me that. It must have been some lunatic."

"Some lunatic who knew Heather would be waiting for you, alone, on the deck that night, and with a key to the house? How did she get in here?" Paul groaned. "You and Lisa and your keys were at the theater, leaving me with the only floating key, which makes me Lieutenant Oliveri's most promising suspect. I didn't let anyone in, so who did?"

"They can't prove a thing," Lisa said, "and you have no motive. Heather was a complete stranger to you."

"Tell that to Oliveri," Paul answered. "I think it was someone who knew she was going to be here. What about her boyfriend? Do you know him?"

"Ian," Bill said. "His name is Ian Edwards and he loved Heather. He didn't do it and he doesn't have a key to this house, but we'll find out who does, Paul, if we have to search all of East Hampton. And no matter what happens, you're safe. I can promise you that."

"I wish I had your confidence," Paul replied.

"My beer is warm," Lisa announced, getting up. "Who wants another?"

"I'll have one." Paul raised his hand. "Bill?"

"No. Not for me."

Lisa went into the kitchen as Paul told Bill, "Michael has a friend on the police force. Eddy Evans. He's a detective."

"I know him," Bill said.

"You do? How?"

"He questioned me, along with Oliveri," Bill said tersely.

Lisa returned with a can of beer for herself and Paul. Taking the beer from her Paul said, "I'm going to tell Michael everything we discussed here, if that's okay with you. I'll ask him to pass it on to the detective by way of explaining the little discrepancies in our stories. What do you think?"

Bill nodded his approval as Lisa said, "It can't hurt."

"It's better than doing nothing," Paul noted, hoisting his can of beer as if toasting the agreement. "How is Heather's father doing?" he asked Bill.

"Taking it hard. So is Ian."

"When is the funeral?"

"I'll call you tonight and let you know," Bill said. "Job and I are sitting down with Ian later today."

Addressing Lisa, Paul said, "And how are you getting on with Amanda Richards?"

"She tolerates me," Lisa said, "but beneath the armor is a heart of gold, or so she says. Have you met her yet?"

"No, but I can't wait. You know she's agreed to do the film for Michael."

"So she told me. And, Paul, Amanda said there's a smashing ingenue role in it. Put in a good word for me, love."

As usual, Bill felt like an eavesdropper when Paul and Lisa started discussing business. Suddenly they weren't the girl he loved and the boy he considered his best friend, but characters he vaguely recalled from a dozen forgettable films. Often, in his imagination, he had played at mimicking both of them.

"Didn't you tell me Aldridge has something hot going for you and Bill after the show closes?" Paul wondered aloud. Then, turning to Bill, he asked, "What about the show?"

"What about it?" Bill said.

"Paul wants to know when you'll be ready to go back into the show," Lisa said.

"Never," Bill replied.

Another silence followed. Paul sipped his beer and Lisa continued to stare at the can in front of her. It was Paul who screwed up the courage to counter Bill when he said, "If you were working at any other job, even on that fishing boat, you would take time off after what happened but then you would go back to work like everyone has to do. Think about it, Bill."

"You owe it to Mr. Aldridge," Lisa added. "His money as well as his reputation is riding on this showcase, which he did for you."

"I never asked him to," Bill protested.

"You came to him," Lisa answered, "and he didn't turn his back on you."

Visibly flustered, Bill got up and left the room. The next sound was the bathroom door closing and being bolted. Paul got up, too. "Maybe you should wait until after the funeral to discuss all this," he said to Lisa, "and with Josh Aldridge present. Now I have to get back to Dunemere Lane and play hide-and-seek with the paparazzi."

"And don't you love it," Lisa accused, getting to her feet. "How do you like living with your rich and famous cousins?"

"I consider it a rehearsal for the rest of my life," Paul said with a theatrical bow.

"I wish Bill had your ambition—and your balls."

"I'd say that between the two of you, you've got enough of both."

Putting her hands on Paul's shoulders she kissed the tip of his nose. "I'm so afraid, Monrotti."

"Of what?"

"Losing him."

"Then let go," Paul recommended, returning the kiss.

"Paul is gone?" Bill said when he came back into the room.

"Yes. He said not to forget to call him about the arrangements."

"Lisa, I'm sorry," Bill sighed. "I don't know what's going to happen or what I'm going to do or not do. I'm all torn up inside and I can't stop the hurting."

With a finger she touched the two tears that trickled from his sad, brown eyes. "Later, Bill. We'll talk about it later. I spoke too soon."

Sounding like he would explode if he didn't get the words out, Bill suddenly cried, "If something horrible happened to me, would you leave me and go back to New York?"

"Something horrible has already happened," Lisa told him, "and I'm still here."

"That's not what I mean," he pleaded.

She kissed his lips to silence him. "Nothing is going to happen to you. You're upset and talking nonsense."

Next he posed, "If I asked you to give up acting to become the wife of a fisherman in Montauk, what would you answer?"

"Later," she protested. "I said we would talk later, when all of this is behind us and we can think rationally about the future. Now we'll only say things we may both regret."

Then she was in his arms, being crushed by the force of his embrace and marveling at the fire that ignited deep within her as rapidly as his arousal reared between their tightly pressed bodies.

"Not here," he whispered. "Not in this place."

She took his hand and led him to the patio door and the lure of the outdoor shower stall.

Bill drove Lisa to Amanda Richards's house on Bluff Road before heading back to Montauk. He refused an invitation to go in and meet the famous actress. "I don't know what to say to famous people," was his excuse.

"One day you're going to be as famous as Amanda," Lisa foretold.

"Yeah, for hauling in a fifty-pound bass."

Without answering, she kissed him and got out of the car. He watched her trim figure in jeans and a T-shirt climb the steps that ran, ladderlike, along the middle of the hill that served as Amanda's front lawn. Covered with sea grass, cedars and arborvitae in no particular pattern or order, Amanda Richards declared it "going back to nature." Others declared it too cheap to employ a landscaper to design and a gardener to maintain a more formal front lawn.

Before driving off, Bill turned in the opposite direction to gaze across the dunes at the Atlantic, his view interrupted by bicyclists and Rollerbladers who reluctantly shared Bluff Road with automobiles in the summer months. He breathed in the salty air, grateful for the respite, however brief, from the events of the past few days.

Driving east to Montauk, Bill thought of all the mistakes he had made since leaving Job in that early dawn, and outlining his plan to keep Job and himself out of harm's way. First he had embellished his story to Mr. Aldridge and Lisa as to why Heather wanted to see him, all but implicating Ian in her death.

The next day, when he walked into the interview room at the police station and saw Eddy Evans, Bill had almost passed out with fear. Did Evans remember questioning Bill last year in connection with the drug raid in Sag Harbor? How could the detective forget? Would he realize that Bill had left Montauk right after that? Why shouldn't he? Then Bill had all but told Evans and the lieutenant that Paul knew he was meeting a girl that night when Paul hadn't disclosed the fact to them.

Bill remembered not to repeat the story of leaving Montauk because he was afraid Ian Edwards would inherit Job's property when he married Heather, and lucked out when Oliveri and Evans confined their questions to Mr. Aldridge and Lisa to their movements the night of the murder. Bill could only hope this took the heat off Ian and Ian's imaginary competitor for Heather's affections.

As promised, Bill would keep Paul safe even if he had to confess everything, as Heather had been ready to do, to clear his friend.

When he didn't find Job at the lodge, Bill instinctively drove up West Lake Drive toward Gosman's Dock and turned into Bick's Clam Bar, a one-story shingled building sandwiched between two marinas. Its weather-beaten facade, batten door and unadorned octagonal windows rendered it as classic a seascape outbuilding as any East End artist had ever portrayed on canvas.

The L-shaped structure contained a dirt-floor patio in the crook of its elbow that boasted a dozen tables and chairs, few of which matched, and an unobstructed view of the dock and the marine traffic on Lake Montauk. Besides clams on the half-shell, proprietor Bick served steamers, baked clams and a Bonacker classic known as Old Stone Highway Fish Stew that some claimed to be the best damn chowder in the world.

The catch of the day was also a staple and if you brought the kids, Bick could always produce grilled hot dogs and fries to keep them quiet. Bick's Clam Bar was strictly a local establishment and both Bick and his customers worked at keeping it that way.

Bick himself was behind the bar when Bill entered and he left his post to greet the boy he hadn't seen in a year with a hug and the words, "We're all sorry as hell about what happened, Bill, and anything we can do you just ask."

"Thanks, Bick."

"And we hear you're headed for Hollywood," Bick quickly lightened up.

"I'm headed for Job," Bill rebutted. "Is he here?"

Bick jerked a thumb toward the indoor array of mismatched tables and chairs. Seated at the only occupied table was Job Ryan. Bill's heart lurched perilously when he saw the scrawny neck and towering gray crew-cut head of the man sitting with Job.

CHAPTER NINETEEN

The short walk to the table left Bill breathless and he gasped when he spat at Avery, "You dirty bastard."

"Just sit," Avery said, "and pretend you're happy to see me."

Job took hold of Bill's hand and squeezed it painfully until Bill was seated. "Just do what he says," Job ordered. The glasses on the table revealed that Job was drinking shots with beer chasers. Avery had a cup of coffee in front of him, untouched, but he had removed the saucer and was using it as an ashtray. To tell him that smoking was prohibited in restaurants in the county would be ludicrous to say the least.

"I was out with my camera, saw Job and am paying my condolences," Avery said, fingering the camera dangling from his neck by its leather strap.

"He called me," Job countered, "and told me to meet him here."

"I didn't think it would be wise for any of us to be seen conferring at the lodge." Avery amended his first rendition of how his meeting with Job had come about.

Bill looked at Avery with an abhorrence that seemed to please rather than terrify the man, and only the restraining hand Job now kept firmly on the boy's knee prevented Bill from physically assaulting the photographer. "We're finished with you." Bill attacked verbally instead.

"So just get the fuck out of here and leave us be—you and the scum you front for."

"Just listen to him," Avery said in a foppish tone he knew annoyed both Ryans. "One short year in the big city and he's talking like a west-side toughie." Then, without a pause, he cut to a tone that had Bill Ryan cringing. "Well, you listen to me, my friend, and you listen good. The both of you were pleased enough to pocket the money the scum doled out every week and if you hadn't been scared into running the minute a cop knocked on your door, maybe you and Job would be enjoying the summer with money in your pockets and your sister still among us."

"What has my leaving got to do with what happened to Heather?" Bill hissed.

"Fool." Avery spoke with contempt. "Everything is connected but you don't know where the seams are joined, so stop treading on other people's nerves."

Job gave no indication that he was privy to this conversation, his face as rigid and noncommittal as a death mask. He wasn't drunk in spite of the whiskey and beer he had consumed, for not even that lethal combination could assuage his fury. Was he thinking of that day on the dock when he had confronted Avery and had been told not to make waves if he knew what was good for him and his family? He had heeded the warning but Heather was dead. Heather was dead. He clung to Bill's knee with a viselike grip.

"Do you think I didn't know what Heather was up to?" Avery was now telling them. "Her face was an open book and for the illiterate she mouthed the words. I watched in amusement as all of you played out your little charade of avoiding each other like the plague, but when I found out that Heather wanted to meet with you I knew she was about to make her foolish move."

"How did you know we were going to meet?" Bill exclaimed.

Avery took a cigarette from the pack on the table, inserted it into a holder and lit it. He did not exhale into Bill's face but rather directly over it—the gesture more horrific than the spoken word. They had bugged the phone at the lodge. Bill knew that as sure as he knew Heather was dead and he was a minnow gaping into the jaws of a barracuda—and he was scared. He had run before and now he wanted to run again. God forgive him, but he didn't want to die, too. He wanted to live. He wanted to return to his old life on West Lake Drive. He wanted to marry Lisa. He wanted a miracle he didn't deserve.

"I didn't kill her," Avery said, as if he were talking about an object and not a human being—not Heather. Job stared at the man and almost crushed Bill's knee in the process. "I was at the theater, watching you imitate some bygone movie star. How clever. Tell me, was that Paul's idea? Pretty Paul. Amazing how you two became such fast friends after he bested you for the Freddy Parc contract." Avery puffed on his cigarette, reverting to the role of effeminate popinjay, which no longer fooled Job and Bill Ryan.

"Do you know why you lost, Bill? I'll tell you why. Because the judges, the so-called fashion editors, insisted on interviewing all the contestants besides looking over their photos. Josh hired me to do your composite and it was every bit as good as Paul Monroe's. But in the flesh, Billy-boy, in the flesh you are as dull as a Buddhist monk in meditation and pretty Paul shines like the star he's going to be, thanks to Freddy and Paul's connection to the Reos. As I said, it's all connections, and if you were not destined to be connected to Freddy, I saw no reason to stay where I wasn't appreciated except for the goods I could deliver to jazz up Freddy's parties. So I left Freddy, and not a moment too soon.

"The contest was supposed to launch your career but you lost, so poor Josh had to come up with the showcase that closed after one night. But you did win the heart of Lisa Kennedy. Not bad for a fishmonger from the sticks."

Avery could have been talking a language Bill and Job had never heard, let alone mastered. They sat motionless, looking at the speaker with an odd mixture of hate and awe. "I don't understand," was all Bill could say.

"Of course you don't, and that's my point. You don't understand anything, therefore you should do what you're told if you know what's good for you. Before you arrived I was saying to Job that, for the moment, all sea voyages are suspended. You are both too close to the murder for comfort and the police will be watching you. I will be in touch." He put his cigarette out in the saucer. "For the record, I did not kill Heather and neither did the scum I front for. And, a final word to the superb mimic—go back into the show as soon as you've observed a respectable period of mourning. Again, my sympathies, and good day."

With a wave to Bick and the few stragglers at the bar, Avery was out the door.

Job tossed back the few drops of whiskey remaining in his shot glass and wiped his mouth with his forearm. "Is it true what he said?" he asked Bill.

"I don't know what he said."

"About him being at the play when it happened," Job made himself clear.

"It must be," Bill said. "He's too smart to lie about something like that and I'm sure someone in the audience would have seen him there. He might even have spoken to Mr. Aldridge that night."

Job nodded thoughtfully, then said, "Makes no difference. I'm gonna kill him anyway."

Returning to the lodge, Bill made a pot of coffee and served himself and Job in the kitchen. To keep his sanity he willed himself immune to the memories the room evoked, as well as to Avery's jabbering and Job's threats.

When Job had been questioned by the police he told them the story of Bill's leaving home exactly as Bill had instructed him to. They at least had got that right. But it seemed to Bill that that was all they had got right. Now Avery was giving them orders and Job was talking crazy.

And why was Avery so eager to have Bill go back into the show? To get Bill away from the lodge and Job, so Avery could continue to run the operation without Bill's interference? Heather was out of the way and Avery didn't want anyone taking her place. Could be. But then anything could be. And if Avery didn't kill Heather, either with his own hands or by proxy, who did? And why with a jockstrap? Why the ultimate degradation? Why everything.

The coffee was tasteless but hot, and the fact that he could register the sensation was heartening. So were the familiar sounds that came in through the kitchen windows and screen door: the gulls, screeching as they soared; the tenants chattering in rapid, singsong Spanish as they scrambled up and down the driveway; and the railroad's early evening cannonball signaling its departure from Montauk for points west. All of them spoke to Bill and what they said was that he had come home and he would stay there. The private runs must end, as must his so-called stage career and, if necessary, his relationship with Lisa, which he considered bogus because she was in love with what the mimic had claimed to be and not with who he was.

"I'm going to the police and tell them everything, like Heather wanted to do. We owe it to her." Bill made his thoughts known.

"Avery's mob will kill you," Job said, unaware of how commonplace the idea of murder had become since selling his soul and losing his daughter and son.

"Did you ever hear of being put in protective custody?"

"You mean they'll arrest you—and me," Job told him.

"I don't care, Job. If you want to run I'll give you time to get out before I do it."

"Sure, kid. I'll get on the boat and head for the South Seas. You wanna come? I never saw a woman in a sarong except in the movies."

"I'm serious, Job."

"So am I, kid. Only all I want to do now is put Heather to rest the way we got to, and I don't want you doing anything foolish until we do. You hear? The funeral is tomorrow. Ian and me talked about it this morning. He's making the arrangements at Williams in East Hampton. Tomorrow at noon. Then a cremation. After, we're taking Heather out on *Job's Patience* for her last run and I'm gonna put her ashes . . ." He broke off abruptly, overcome with emotion he expressed by turning his face from his listener.

Either unable or unwilling to stop the tears that burned his eyes before overflowing the dam, Bill put a firm hand on Job's trembling shoulder. Neither spoke for some minutes and when the torrent ebbed they appeared unwilling to relinquish the moment, their mutual offer of comfort a balm for their misery.

"You got anything in this house for dinner?" Bill asked, breaking the spell.

"No need. The Edwardses are fixing dinner for us, at their place."

"Are we going to have a wake?" Bill speculated.

"We're going to do what we do," Job asserted with pride.

Giving this a moment's thought, Bill got out of his chair and said, "And I know what I'm going to do."

"Nothing foolish," Job warned.

"Just the opposite, Job. I'm going to do something very, very smart."

When Bill reached for the telephone in the front room he wondered how large an audience his call would garner. The one he had made to Heather might as well have been a full page ad in the *Star*. He punched out the number from memory and after one ring a voice answered, "Reo residence."

"Is Paul there? Paul Monroe."

"May I ask who's calling, sir?"

"Tell him it's Bill."

When Paul came on the line, Bill asked, "Was that a butler?"

"Sure. I couldn't get through the day without one. Is the funeral set?"

"Tomorrow at noon, in East Hampton. But that's not why I'm calling. Can you get a car?"

"I guess Michael would lend me one of his. Maybe the Rolls."

"Good. Call Lisa and tell her I'm inviting both of you to dinner tonight. I'll give you directions."

"What's this all about?" Paul wanted to know.

"I want to show you and Lisa something."

"Like what?" Paul persisted.

"Like what we do, that's what."

When Paul and Lisa arrived at the lodge, in the Land Rover not the Rolls, they expressed their sympathies to Job, who expressed his pleasure at meeting Bill's friends, especially the beautiful young lady, after which there was an embarrassing silence. Bill took his guests on a tour of the lodge, including the exterior of the run-down cabins and the utility room that now had all the charm of a used-parts depot for large appliances. Bill's room still contained the original shower curtain that served as his closet door.

"It's like a resort version of *The Grapes of Wrath*," Paul announced after the tour, then saved the association from being too offensive by adding, "but quaint." Lisa offered no opinion.

On to the Edwardses'—a large, rambling, shingled house with a widow's walk looking east to Gosman's Dock, Long Island Sound and a good portion of Star Island in Lake Montauk. Ian still lived with his parents, as did his younger, unmarried sister. His married siblings, brother and sister, arrived with their families, which consisted of five children, ages six weeks to six years. Also arriving, in a steady stream, were friends and neighbors, all bearing a covered dish to add to the array on the banquet table.

Mr. Edwards opened clams taken from an ice-filled hamper. There was corn on the cob, potato salad, macaroni salad, mussels in a wine sauce, no less than three versions of the famous Old Stone Highway Fish Stew and boiled lobsters as abundant as hot dogs at a backyard barbecue. Desserts ranged from homemade apple and blueberry pies to brownies, strawberries and cream and Mrs. Edwards's renowned chocolate layer cake with her own special chocolate icing whose recipe she vowed she would take to the grave.

Everyone had a quiet word with Job and Bill but they did not dwell on the tragedy. A good sailor keeps a weathered eye fore, not aft. Nor did they ask Bill where he had been the past year because they already knew—and those who had seen him perform at the John Drew kept their opinions to themselves because they were a people who wasted nothing, not even words.

Lisa, in a neat cap-sleeved wrap she favored, managed to look overdressed when compared to the girls in their shorts, jeans and ankle-length wraparound skirts that embellished their generous proportions and, by contrast, Lisa's lithe figure. "I feel like a Barbie doll," she whispered to Paul, although with the din in the crowded room there was really no need to whisper.

"Which makes me a Ken doll," Paul said, only he seemed pleased by the comparison.

The boys stared at Lisa and the girls stared at Paul, but after a polite hello or a timid handshake, Barbie and Ken were ignored with only Bill, Job and a nervous Ian to see to their needs and keep them company. Everyone was polite and kind to a fault, but never was *them* and *us* more apparent.

When Ian brought out his guitar and began to strum, a small group gathered around him until his music rose above the noise and everyone turned their attention to the tall, blond young man. As he played, he sang what were obviously his own compositions and were, surprisingly, mostly love ballads. "And this one," he told his listeners at the end of the impromptu concert, "me and Heather composed together and it was going to be our wedding song." With that, Ian delivered his musical eulogy to the woman he loved for which even the toddlers stood still and silent in the room full of bowed heads.

"That was lovely," Lisa said to Bill.

"It's what we do," he answered with immodesty. Taking Lisa by the hand, he led her upstairs and out onto the widow's walk.

Dark clouds were moving in from the west, carried on a steady, humid breeze that kept their hair and clothing in motion as they gazed down at the brilliantly lit Gosman's Dock. "It's going to rain," Lisa observed.

"Maybe. Maybe not. Sometimes it goes on like this for days without a drop of rain falling—especially when the farmers are praying for rain."

Finally alone with Bill, Lisa used the moment to confront him with what had occupied her thoughts since she and Paul arrived at the lodge. "Why did you invite Paul and me here tonight?"

"I wanted you to see where I came from," he answered.

She laughed. "Paul called you a clam digger and he was right, but you brought me here hoping I would flee in horror and never speak to you again. Correct?"

"The thought crossed my mind."

"Or did you secretly imagine a tear-jerker ending where I embrace Mrs. Edwards, beg her for her chocolate icing recipe, and we live happily ever after in quaint Montauk. Well, Mr. Ryan, I'm not going to do either because I don't care where you came from but where you're going—with me.

"I don't like or dislike these people," Lisa continued honestly, "and I'm sure they feel the same way about me. We could be from different planets for all I care. I make them uncomfortable but no more so than they make me feel like a department store mannequin."

"Did you see the way the men are looking at you?" Bill offered. "They think I'm the luckiest son of a bitch since Casanova."

"And what do you think, Bill?"

"I'm from this planet, that's what I think."

"Why did you leave it?" Lisa quickly responded.

The question made his discomfort discernible even in the walk's shadowy light. "I can't tell you that."

"Has it got anything to do with Heather's murder—or something horrible that might happen to you?"

"I can't tell you now, but I will when the time is right."

"Please tell me now," she pressed.

"I don't like being questioned, Lisa."

"And I don't like being lied to and brought here to be put on exhibition."

"That's not why I brought you here," he uttered, making a sincere effort to keep from shouting.

"Then why did you bring me here?"

"To show you who I am."

"I know who you are," Lisa argued, "and I love who you are. And I know who I am but you refuse to extend me the same courtesy."

"I adore you," Bill implored as if it were a painful admission.

"Then don't ask me to change who I am. Please don't ask me to do that. You left here once and we found each other. You can do it again, and we can go on from there."

He encircled her with his arms and the fire he never failed to spark within her began to glow in spite of the sharp wind and ominous clouds scudding above them. With his lips an inch from hers he pleaded, "Don't make my leaving a condition of your love." Then he closed the gap.

MICHAEL ANTHONY REO

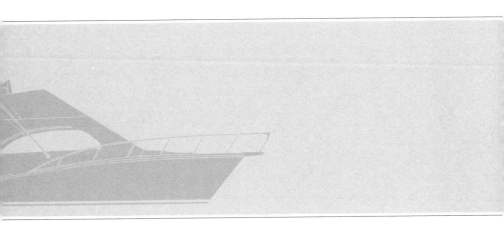

CHAPTER TWENTY

The Jockstrap Murder was how the tabloids described the homicide in the Amagansett cottage. Michael thought this only fair if one considered the ecdysiast Gypsy Rose Lee and her sensational mystery thriller of yore, *The G-String Murders*. In this age of sexual equality, it was only right that the G-string's male counterpart be given equal time and billing.

In the sensational press, all murdered young ladies are described as "beautiful." Heather was no exception. Add to this hook the fact that the "beautiful" young girl was found dead with a *Freddy Parc jockstrap* tied around her throat in a cottage in the *Hamptons* by a *male supermodel,* and you have the kind of story that heretofore existed only in pulp fiction and tabloid heaven—and they didn't omit a single, startling fact.

There was a photo of Paul in Freddy's briefs. A photo of a Freddy Parc jockstrap, presumably for those who had never seen one, and a photo of Freddy taking a bow after the showing in New York of his spring line. Bill and Lisa were mentioned as sharing the cottage with Paul, but there was, as yet, no mention of Bill's relationship to the victim. That connection, when it surfaced, would prompt another bold headline, no doubt with coverage of Heather's funeral. Bill and

Lisa's show was noted briefly, but its producer, Joshua Aldridge, was ignored. All in all, Freddy got the most coverage and if this translated into sales, Freddy Parc Enterprises would have a banner day on Wall Street.

Thanks to the media's obsession with the Jockstrap Murder, the Fates that had denied fame to Heather Ryan in her lifetime overcompensated at her funeral in a way that bordered on the obscene. The East Hampton Town police, as is their wont, cordoned off Newtown Lane for a good hundred yards north and south of Williams Funeral Home. This resulted in a traffic jam far greater than would have occurred had vehicles been allowed to flow, unimpeded, along the thoroughfare so popular with shoppers and sightseers.

The police did keep the sidewalk in front of the funeral home clear of the uninvited, but seemingly multitudes congregated across the street. Here, the usual gawkers were joined by the press covering the Jockstrap Murder, a television crew from the county's local network, a group carrying posters denouncing Freddy Parc products in general and Paul Monroe's scantily clad image in particular, and a larger group shouting their support of Freddy and Paul. The lunch crowd deserted Babettes (where you can actually get a gift-wrapped burrito), the Grand Cafe and the Barefoot Contessa, and became part of the throng.

Anticipating just such a scene, Michael had John drop Vicky and him off at the railroad station, which was a short walk from their destination.

"It's a circus," Vicky pronounced with disdain.

Michael surmised that she was recalling her father's funeral a year earlier, which had also drawn the press and television coverage, albeit national as well as local. Thankfully, they had been spared the hooters and rooters so in abundance today.

"And why are we here?" Vicky added.

"We're here in support of Paul and his friends. We promised his parents we would keep an eye on him."

"Judging from this mob and those signs, the last thing Paul needs is more people ogling him," Vicky observed.

"And Josh Aldridge invited us to attend," Michael said.

"Why?"

"I think for a New York show of hands in support of Bill Ryan. Aldridge, remember, is trying to change his discovery's image."

"At a funeral?" Vicky was dismayed.

"Hey, you work with what you got," Michael spoofed.

"Don't be crude, Michael. Think of that poor girl."

Michael searched the mob for a familiar face and focused in on an efficient-looking young woman in horn-rimmed glasses, carrying a clipboard and pencil. She spotted Michael at the same time and waved him to her post behind the yellow tape labeled POLICE LINE, DO NOT CROSS.

"Mr. and Mrs. Reo," she recited in her best Katharine Hepburn voice. "I'm Jan Solinsky with the Aldridge Agency."

"Hello, Ms. Solinsky," Vicky acknowledged the greeting.

Knowing that she was a friend of Eddy Evans, and suspecting that their relationship may have been more than platonic at one time, Michael viewed Jan Solinsky with more interest than she otherwise would have commanded. Advancing from a secretary with aspirations to the former bed partner of a handsome, young detective had boosted Jan Solinsky's career socially, if not professionally.

"Mr. Aldridge asked me to facilitate his guests. You are on the list, of course," Jan said without consulting her clipboard. With a gesture she motioned for a uniformed policeman to raise the tape for Mr. and Mrs. Reo as if it were a velvet rope.

"A circus," Vicky repeated.

"If it is, my dear, we're the clowns."

The silence inside the funeral parlor was in sharp contrast to the tumult they had just escaped. The aroma of freshly cut flowers competing with each other for dominance was as staggering as the number of wreaths and bouquets that filled the room. The Montauk clans were as generous in their send-offs as the extended family of a departing mafioso. Due to the number of attendees a dividing wall had been removed to combine two viewing rooms into one, with folding chairs arranged in semicircular rows around the closed casket.

The New Yorkers were gathered in a group to the left of the closed coffin. To its right, Bill Ryan, shifting nervously from foot to foot, stood between an older man Michael guessed was Heather's father, Job Ryan, and Paul Monroe. Michael was instantly reminded of the opening night party where Bill had been similarly positioned between two stalwarts—his agent/producer and his girlfriend. Would Bill Ryan ever be able to stand alone?

Accompanying Bill, Job and Paul were an assortment of men and women, all looking grossly uncomfortable in their suits and dark print dresses. Their familial resemblance made Michael certain the blond young man in the foreground was Heather's fiancé, whose name Paul had told him but now escaped Michael, accompanied by his immediate family. Other local families made up most of the people seated on the folding chairs.

"That must be Heather's father standing next to Bill," Vicky said, also assaying the mourners.

The New Yorkers consisted of Lisa Kennedy, Joshua Aldridge, Amanda Richards, Freddy Parc and his most current wife and, to Michael's surprise, Tony Vasquez. The two groups eyeing each other warily from opposite ends of the coffin seemed to ridicule the tenet that heralded death as the great equalizer.

"I'm so proud of Paul, choosing to be with Bill and the girl's father rather than appearing chummy with the marquee names," Michael said.

"But why isn't Lisa with Bill?" Vicky noted. "Or is she making a statement?"

"How observant you are," Michael complimented his wife. "And what do you think of Amanda in such close proximity to her nemesis, director Vasquez?"

"If thoughts could kill," Vicky rejoined.

Michael thought Job a once handsome man gone to seed. Being prey to the elements and lean times, fishermen and farmers lost the bloom of youth far sooner than the sheltered and the pampered. If Joshua Aldridge had his way, Bill Ryan would escape that destiny.

"I'm not standing up there," Vicky said.

"Nor am I." Michael spotted two empty chairs at the end of one of the rows and taking Vicky's arm he headed for them. Once seated, Michael spotted Lieutenant Christopher Oliveri and Eddy Evans in the crowd. If Oliveri's intent was to keep a low profile, he succeeded admirably. Given the venue, and Oliveri's perfectly pressed blue suit, he could have been mistaken for a pallbearer. Seeing Eddy, Michael was reminded that he wanted to speak to the detective to inform him of what Paul had to say after his visit with Bill and Lisa Kennedy yesterday afternoon.

Nodding discreetly toward the two men, Michael informed Vicky, "That's Lieutenant Oliveri with Eddy."

Assaying the man, Vicky whispered back, "You didn't tell me he was so good-looking."

"You didn't ask."

Then Michael spotted the photographer, Avery, in the crowd. He wondered if Eddy knew the man by sight and, if so, what Eddy thought of Avery's presence at Heather Ryan's funeral.

Waiting for the service to begin, Michael contemplated Heather's family and friends. Trying to decide who they resembled in their somber finery, he hit upon the perfect correlation: amateur theater company players who had forgotten their lines the moment the curtain went up. Why do old acquaintances always appear embarrassed in each other's company on solemn occasions? Was it because Yankee constraint frowned upon public displays, regardless of the circumstances?

Paul and Bill had elected to wear navy blue blazer jackets and gray flannels. Or, more likely, that's what Paul chose to wear and he had probably advised Bill to do the same. Looking at the two, Michael concluded that they were handsome enough to get away with murder. He mentally shuddered at the metaphor, remembering Oliveri's presence. Thoughts, it was said, have wings.

Heather's kin, Bill and Job Ryan, looked more apprehensive than sad and Michael attributed this to their particular way of expressing grief.

Seeing Bill standing with Job and the Montauk family, and not with Aldridge and Lisa, made it clear where Bill Ryan belonged and where he wanted to be. If, as Vicky had pointed out, Lisa's position bespoke a similar stance, Michael didn't see much hope in their budding romance or in the future of *Pale Sun, Bright Moon*. Was Aldridge aware of this, too?

Turning to the other group, Michael noted that Lisa Kennedy looked stunning in an expensive black sheath while Joshua Aldridge's countenance would have one believe that Heather Ryan had been his nearest and dearest. Amanda, also in black, appeared more pensive than bereaved, an expression any good director would have recommended for the funeral close-up. Holding fast to Aldridge's arm, actress and agent could have been any well-preserved, middle-aged couple burying a child and wondering what went wrong along the way. Bringing up the rear were Tony Vasquez in his expensive suit and Freddy Parc and his latest wife, resplendent in Freddy's original creations.

Michael suddenly saw this sad occasion as that moment in a drama when the entire company is assembled for the sole purpose of giving the clever leading man a chance to verbally pull together all the plot pieces, climaxing with a finger-pointing cry of *j'accuse* at the villain.

Thankfully, such a scene wasn't going to happen here, but the thought did have Michael speculating on the riddle of Heather's death. After Paul's disclosures of last night, Michael concluded that he could indeed point an accusing finger if he knew the answer to several questions.

Did Heather want to meet with Bill solely to discuss her pregnancy?

Was she silenced before that meeting could take place? (For, unless the murderer was a nutcase and she a random victim, Heather Ryan was clearly silenced.)

Who else knew Heather was going to meet with Bill that night, and where and when the meeting would take place?

Finally, who possessed a fourth key to the cottage? (That another key existed was vital to Paul's defense.)

After his talk with Paul, Michael believed he could answer almost all of the above if he knew why Bill Ryan had left Montauk to go chasing rainbows in New York—and Michael couldn't wait to liaise with Eddy Evans.

Those paying their final respects to Heather Ryan were that volatile combination of East Hampton's human infrastructure—sophisticated New Yorkers and the locals who served them. Michael was convinced that when the two had clashed, Heather Ryan took the fall.

The hum of conversation in the room ebbed when a man wearing a clerical collar made his way to what might be called center stage. After shaking hands with Job and Bill he faced the mourners and, with a practiced hand motion, brought the room to its feet.

Opening the Bible he carried, he adjusted his glasses and began to recite the inevitable. "The Lord is my shepherd, I shall not want . . ."

The principal players bowed their heads and donned the mask of tragedy. Did one conceal the face of a murderer?

Michael and Vicky moved with the crowd headed for the rear and the exit onto Newtown Lane. However, just as they stepped outside, they once again came face-to-face with the efficient Jan Solinsky.

"Mr. and Mrs. Reo," she said, "Mr. Aldridge's car is in the parking lot in the rear. He would like you to join Ms. Richards and him for lunch. If you would just wait a moment until the crowd clears, I can take you right to the car. Mr. Aldridge will just be a few moments."

Vicky looked unhappy and Michael shrugged hopelessly. "We could tender our regrets," Vicky insisted.

"We could, but we won't," Michael answered.

CHAPTER TWENTY-ONE

While waiting for Aldridge and deliberately avoiding Vicky's pouting gaze, Michael mentally ticked off what he knew about the life and times of Joshua Aldridge. Melding fact and gossip with conjecture based on firsthand knowledge of show business as practiced in New York and Hollywood, he came up with a portrait of the man that was remarkably accurate.

Joshua Aldridge was an independent agent in a town lousy with independent agents. He came from a show business family that spanned the genre from legitimate theater to vaudeville to the silver screen. His father, Chester Aldridge, had been a moderately successful child actor in films before making it big on Broadway. Chester enrolled his only son in professional schools from an early age, confident that the boy would follow family tradition and keep the Aldridge name in lights for yet another generation.

Joshua was ambivalent about the acting profession but, to please a father he worshiped, the boy allowed himself to be groomed for a vocation to which he was not suited and one in which supply far exceeded demand. Trading on his father's fame, the younger Aldridge managed to get several small parts in unmemorable offerings both on and off Broadway. The senior Aldridge won the lead in a Broadway production that had all the earmarks of a roaring success, and a script that called for a young actor to play the lead's son in what was touted as a pivotal role.

In true show business fashion, Chester was able to fulfill a lifetime ambition when he secured the part for his son. Chester sincerely believed that here was a chance for the Aldridge family to assume the positions vacated by the Barrymores and Skinners. This scenario would not have a happy ending.

Joshua suffered through the audition, suffered through rehearsals and, the final embarrassment, suffered through his humiliating notices from the out-of-town critics. As the date for the New York opening neared, even Chester realized that for the good of the show, Joshua would have to be replaced.

Chester refused to be present when, in Boston, the director gave Joshua his notice. Nor could Chester find the time to offer a consoling word to his son or even see him before Joshua left for New York. The young man departed Boston believing that he had failed in the role of beloved son both on and off the stage.

The story should end in a reconciliation scene between *père et fils* on opening night, with the show a smash and Joshua on his way to medical school. However, this is show business, and as they say, funny things happen between Boston and New York. What happened was the actor who replaced Joshua as Chester's stage son. In this talented and attractive young man, Chester's dream of seeing his son win the hearts and applause of audiences and critics came to fruition. Sadly, it was this stage son, not his kin, who took the bows on opening night.

So infatuated with the young man was Chester Aldridge that rumors originating in Boston rode the rails to New York and settled in along with the run of the show.

Ironically, Chester's most successful show and the one that was to emblazon the Aldridge name in theatrical history served only to estrange the star from both his wife and his son. Although the rumors surrounding Chester and his stage son were never proved, Mrs.

Aldridge elected to retire to their country home in Vermont and begged Joshua to join her. But he had other plans.

Joshua could not act and he could not direct, but thanks to his training, and life with father, he was as aware of his shortcomings as he was aware of those who possessed what he lacked. This expertise and Chester's only legacy—the family name and a few good connections—was the foundation upon which the *Aldridge Theatrical Agency* was founded.

As an agent Joshua could not only control the talent upon whom the industry was dependent, but he would also have the opportunity to discover and groom a talent that would make Chester remembered solely as the father of Joshua Aldridge.

Thanks to what might or might not have been his father's proclivity for a certain young man, Joshua came out of that experience as a closet homophobic. Closeted because, in show business, being homophobic is tantamount to an avid atheist entertaining hopes of becoming the next pope. Joshua subtly reminded gay producers, casting directors and actors of the rumors surrounding his father, while establishing himself as the foremost agent of pretty young actresses who were not averse to trading their charms for a bit part.

Hence, his passport was valid in both countries, but he had few genuine friends. To be sure, theatrical agents don't need friends to stay in business; they need to find jobs for their clients, and this Joshua Aldridge did often enough to pay the rent and keep a roof over his head.

By the time he had turned gray, which enhanced his good looks, he had become the kind of wheeler-dealer who earned the respect, if not the admiration, of those he represented and served. However, in all those intervening years his search for a superstar in the rough proved futile, but he did manage to snag one in her prime one night at a party in the home of a producer whose Broadway hits were legendary.

Amanda Richards, her brown hair falling in a cascade of soft waves to her shoulders, smiled across the room at Joshua Aldridge in a pose that had graced dozens of *Playbills*. Reading the gesture as an invitation, Aldridge approached the actress. "Ms. Richards, how nice to see you again. We met at a party very much like this one a few months ago."

"If you've been to one party in this town, you've been to them all," Amanda replied, then she told him precisely where and when their first encounter had taken place.

Flattered, Aldridge answered, "I remembered, but I didn't think you would."

"I never forget a handsome man, Mr. Aldridge. A real man, that is. They're a dying breed."

"I thought you had an endless supply, Ms. Richards."

"If gossip were fact, I wouldn't be here alone."

Naming a politician Amanda had been romantically linked with in recent months, Aldridge said, "I understand he's all male and a yard long."

It was crude, but like many who reside on a pedestal, Amanda Richards enjoyed being treated like one of the crowd, especially by her male companions.

"Are you jealous or confident, Mr. Aldridge?" She placed a cigarette between her lips as Aldridge removed a book of matches from his jacket pocket and lit it for her.

"Confident, Ms. Richards. Confident in the fact that the next man in your life should be your new agent. Joshua Aldridge at your service."

Amanda almost choked as she drew on her cigarette. "You're kidding."

"As a matter of fact, Ms. Richards, I'm not. I hear your current associates, who shall be nameless, failed to get you the screen role when your play was optioned for a film."

"I didn't want the screen role, Mr. Aldridge."

"Bull. All actresses want screen roles, even those who were handed an Academy Award and a boot in the ass back-to-back."

"How picturesque," Amanda exhaled along with a stream of smoke.

"A brash and randy young man I know has written a play titled *Outrageous Fortune*. It's next season's hit, if I can talk a producer into reading it, and I can do that if I can deliver Amanda Richards in the lead."

"Thank you," Amanda cooed, but there was no mistaking the fact that she was intrigued by the brazen agent.

"You're at the top of your career, Ms. Richards, and bored to tears. What you need is a challenge."

"And what you need is Amanda Richards to keep you solvent."

Aldridge lit his own cigarette and blew smoke into the air. "At least we understand each other, and that's as good a basis as any for forming an alliance. Now tell me you're not interested."

"But I am interested, Mr. Aldridge. And when I read your script I may even be interested in that," Amanda flirted. Handing him her glass she asked, "Would you color this for me, Joshua? I may call you Joshua?"

The Maidstone Arms Inn is an East Hampton landmark. Facing the town pond, it stands among the grand homes on Main Street, west of the business district, in as quaint a setting as one is likely to find on all of Long Island.

Aldridge had reserved a table in the bar room—the seating favored by the cognoscenti, especially in winter, when a comforting wood fire crackled in the brick fireplace. But this not being winter, a huge arrangement of flowers replaced the burning logs on the hearth, and a lunch crowd that gaped at the arrival of Amanda Richards replaced the cognoscenti.

Aldridge had explained on the short ride to the restaurant that there was to be a cremation, not an interment, for Heather Ryan, and that Lisa had gone back to Montauk with Bill.

"And Paul?" Michael asked.

"Paul?" Aldridge seemed surprised. "Yes, I suppose he's with them, too."

No sooner were they seated when, at a signal from Aldridge, the bartender left his post and hurried to their table bearing the familiar ice bucket on a tripod in which a bottle of champagne—very good champagne—was being chilled. "I know it's customary for the mourners to take food and drink after the final tribute, but isn't this a bit much?" Michael protested.

"Blame it on me," Amanda spoke up. "I know it seems almost ghoulish but we show people are very superstitious and I insist on a champagne toast, for luck, when I agree to do a show."

"A show?" Vicky said, unable to mask her disappointment. "What show?"

A waitress placed a champagne flute before each of them as the bartender stood by to pour.

"What she means," Aldridge explained, "is your film."

Overjoyed, Michael bent toward Amanda and kissed her cheek. "For a moment I thought you were about to renege on us. Thank you, Amanda. Thank you. My first production and your return to films. The signs are auspicious." Michael was overtly excited and beaming with pleasure.

"From your lips to the ears of the god of box office receipts," Amanda said. "Who's directing?"

"With you on board, Amanda," Vicky told her, looking as relieved as Michael, "we'll have our choice of director. They'll be lining up for the chance to work with you. I'm thrilled, Amanda, I really am."

The D word having been spoken gave Michael the opening he had been waiting for. "Speaking of directors, can we know what Tony Vasquez was doing at the funeral?"

"I asked him to attend," Aldridge said. "He's been sober for years now, as you may have heard, and he's written a film script. In fact, Michael, you're not the only one getting his feet wet in the film business. I'm going to produce Tony's brainchild."

"How did you and Vasquez get together?" Michael asked.

"Mutual friends," was all Aldridge had to say on the subject and Michael knew better than to ask him to name names. In the film business secrecy is both expected and respected.

"Do you have backing?" Michael tried again, anticipating the same result, and he was not disappointed.

"Are you making an offer?" was how Aldridge dodged the question.

"Are you doing this for Bill and Lisa?" Vicky got in on the questioning.

"I'm doing it for myself," Aldridge told her, "but they are the reasons I'm interested in Tony's script. It could have been tailor-made for them."

All this for Bill Ryan, whose talent, at best, showed promise? was Michael's take on the venture. But then Michael reminded himself that he was taking a gamble with the untried Paul Monroe.

"I actually gave Tony a hug and a peck," Amanda admitted, "so all is forgiven, if not forgotten."

When the bartender popped the cork, the celebrants had the undivided attention of every person lunching in the room. The onlookers would be the forerunners of the rumor of the week that stated Amanda Richards had become engaged to a distinguished gentleman with gray hair at lunch at the Maidstone Arms Inn.

After filling each glass, the bartender retreated to his post as Amanda raised hers and toasted, "To us, *just as we're together and here, for the rest of our beautiful days.*"

They all drank as Michael made a mental note of the lyricist Amanda had stolen the line from, as Vicky was sure to ask.

"Of course we haven't talked money," Aldridge reminded them.

"Spoken like a true agent," Amanda cried. "I'm sure we'll come to an agreement. Michael and Vicky are not cheap."

"We're not Daddy Warbucks, either," Vicky quickly got in.

"No, my dear, but your father was," Amanda said.

"My father worked for Kirk in the early days of television," Aldridge said. "I think he drove a hard bargain."

"Who? Your father or mine?" They all laughed at Vicky's little joke as the waitress passed out the menus.

Michael thought it typical of Joshua Aldridge to use the familiar "Kirk" rather than Joseph Kirkpatrick or Mr. Kirkpatrick when referring to Vicky's father. Aldridge couldn't resist dropping a name even in the company of the "name's" daughter and son-in-law. Cheeky, was Joshua Aldridge. And just how far would he go to get on the A-list of Hollywood producers? Michael didn't like the idea of being used as a stepping-stone.

"Thank you for coming to the service today." Aldridge addressed Michael and Vicky.

"Actually we did it as a show of support for Paul," Michael said.

"How good of you," Amanda said, signaling for the waitress to refill her glass.

"So Paul Monroe will play the culprit in Amanda's film," Aldridge stated.

The contract was not yet signed and it was already "Amanda's film." Michael would have to set the record straight but now was neither the time nor the place. "He is," Michael said.

"I'm only doing this so I can run around in my birthday suit with Paul," Amanda announced loud enough for the entire room to hear.

"Amanda," Vicky chided, "it's a serious film, not sexploitation."

"How can you tell the difference these days?" Amanda shot back.

"You have a point, Amanda." Michael did not wish to get into any discussions of how certain scenes in *The Hampton Affair* would be shot when Amanda was apparently feeling the effects of her second glass of champagne. He knew there were many hurdles to get over before they all got down to the nitty-gritty of actual filming.

"Too bad you didn't sign on Paul." Michael could not help needling Aldridge.

"I'll admit I was sore at him for beating my boy out of the Freddy Parc contract."

"Ancient history," Amanda declared. "If I'm to work with Paul I insist that we all be friends, Joshua. I kissed Tony Vasquez because you're going to work with him." Thanks to Amanda's practiced delivery it would have been redundant to add "Better you than me" to her final line.

As everyone glanced at their menus, Michael said to no one in particular, "I was surprised to see Freddy Parc at the funeral."

"Like you, he was there to support Paul," Aldridge quickly answered. "Paul is in an awkward position and it would cost Freddy a fortune to jettison the ad campaign."

Cheeky? Josh Aldridge was insolent. Michael opened his mouth to protest but he caught Vicky's glance that seemed to beg restraint, and he said instead, "As it turns out both Bill and Lisa were at the theater at the time the murder was committed. How fortunate for them."

"We were all at the theater," Aldridge said. "And my concern is keeping Bill in the show. He considered Heather his sister and feels he's to blame for what happened to her."

"The party," Michael stated.

Aldridge nodded. "I guess Paul has apprised you of the situation. Bill thinks that if we hadn't dragged him to the party, he would have got back to the cottage in time to meet with Heather. The fact is, the show ran late and I believe the poor girl was dead before we rang down the final curtain, so the party wasn't a factor, but try to tell Bill that."

"Who's to say who's to blame?" Amanda spoke up, removing the glasses she used for reading with a theatrical flourish. "No one knew he had a date to meet that poor child."

"Someone knew," Michael said.

"Paul and Bill are very close," Aldridge intimated.

Riled, Michael no longer saw any reason for restraint. "Paul swears he didn't know about Bill's date with Heather and I believe him."

"So do I," Amanda said, "and so does Joshua. Now, is anyone interested in eating?"

Again, everyone consulted their menus. "Is Avery part of your film package?" Michael asked his menu.

"Avery?" Aldridge cried, clearly surprised at the question.

"Yes," Michael answered. "He was at your opening the other night and today he was at the funeral. I was just wondering what his interest was in both events."

"Bill, I imagine," Aldridge claimed. "I hired Avery to do the photos of Bill for Freddy's contest. You see, Avery worked for Freddy and I thought it would give me an edge."

"Joshua played his ace in the hole and Paul trumped him," Amanda said, laughing.

"I got burned," Aldridge confessed.

"And Avery is no longer with Freddy Parc, is he?" Michael observed.

"No. He left Freddy after the contest," Aldridge said.

"Why?" Michael grilled.

Annoyed, Aldridge snapped back, "How would I know?"

"We heard Avery was taking photos in Montauk last year for an art book," Vicky informed the table. "Maybe he found himself a publisher."

"Bill is from Montauk," Michael ruminated just as Tony Vasquez appeared in the doorway.

"That dreadful man," Amanda uttered as she blew Vasquez a kiss. "What's he doing here?"

"He's staying at the inn," Aldridge informed them. "Now let's see—I'm for the filet of sole and a salad. You order the wine, Michael. You're the connoisseur."

EDDY EVANS

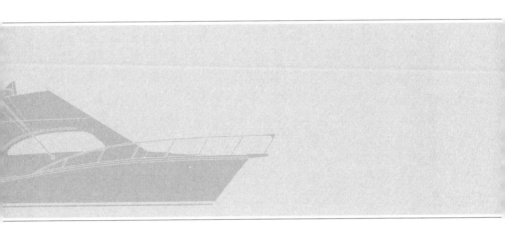

CHAPTER TWENTY-TWO

Christopher Oliveri lived on Bluff Road in Amagansett, in an area once sardonically referred to as Little Italy. This unlikely epithet owed its genesis to the Long Island Railroad when, a hundred years ago, it had hired Italian immigrants as laborers to lay track from New York to Montauk. At the end of the line these men discovered an area very much like the country they had left—abutting an ocean rather than a sea. Instead of riding back on the rails they had laid, they used their pay to buy land at ten bucks an acre and settled down to farm Amagansett's fertile soil.

Today, a building lot in Little Italy would demand half a million dollars an acre, minimum. Italians love the good earth and the Oliveri family and their brethren prospered and bought, bought and prospered. Carrying on yet another Italian tradition, they were fruitful and multiplied.

It was a modest house that had been in the Oliveri family for three generations, sitting on a generous acre. The front lawn was, as one would expect, meticulously cut and Eddy knew that the backyard garden was a favorite of the sponsors of East Hampton's annual Garden Tour. Christopher Oliveri had designed the garden and his wife maintained it under her husband's critical eye and helpful hand. Their only child, a daughter, was working in Maine this summer as a camp counselor after completing her first year at a prestigious Boston college.

Lydia Oliveri greeted Eddy with a hug and a kiss. "His Nibs is on the back porch," she informed Eddy with a playful wink.

She was a handsome woman, with dark hair and eyes and a generous figure that happily proclaimed her love for cooking and for the fruits of her labor. She had gone to East Hampton High, as had her husband, and attended Suffolk Community College. Christopher had gone from high school to the New York Police Academy, certain of his vocation from birth, or so his wife claimed. The high school sweethearts had married shortly after Christopher joined the town police and Lydia had commenced teaching the first grade at the Amagansett elementary school.

"You know the way, Eddy," Lydia said. "I'll get you a beer, unless you want a proper drink."

"What's the lieutenant drinking?"

"Beer," she said.

"I'll have the same."

"You can have what you want, Eddy," Lydia counseled.

"I want a beer, Lydia."

Laughing, she left him and headed for her kitchen.

It was always startling to see Christopher Oliveri at home in jeans and a sweatshirt, so much were his suits and starched collars a part of his persona. He was sitting in a wicker chair on his screen-enclosed back porch, puffing on an expensive cigar and admiring his garden, which at this hour was awash in the golden glow of the early evening summer sunlight.

"Come in, Eddy, come in," Oliveri said with a welcoming gesture of the hand that held his cigar. "Is Lydia getting you a drink?"

"Yes, sir." Eddy came onto the porch and settled in a similar wicker chair separated from Oliveri's by a matching coffee table.

"A cigar?" Oliveri offered. He was a genial host as well as an honest and fair supervisor. He had read Eddy the riot act over the incident involving Michael Reo's visit to Paul Monroe and then let it go. Christopher Oliveri did not hold grudges, especially with his men and more so with a man as good at the job as Eddy Evans.

"No thanks," Eddy declined the offer.

"It's my only vice," Oliveri said with a shrug that made Eddy wonder if the lieutenant was bragging or complaining.

"And a vice you had better confine to the screen porch," his wife said, entering with Eddy's bottle of beer and a pilsner glass. "The screen porch and the backyard are the only places he can smoke those dreadful stogies."

Eddy smiled diffidently. He wasn't used to hearing people reprimanding the lieutenant and giving him orders. Not even the Chief. It was rumored around the station house that the rigid and stern Lieutenant Oliveri was a pussycat in his own home.

Placing Eddy's beer and glass on the wicker table, Lydia retreated with a wave and a smile for Eddy.

"You sure you want to get married, Eddy?" Oliveri asked before his wife was out of hearing range.

"Of course he does," Lydia called back and then was gone.

"Cheers," Oliveri toasted, lifting his glass.

Eddy filled his own glass, topping it with an inch of foam, and returned the salute.

"I spent the day with the county narcotics people," Oliveri stated, placing his glass on the table.

The simple statement caused Eddy's stomach to go queasy on him. "The drug raid last year," Eddy guessed.

"You were assigned to interview Bill Ryan regarding his pickup truck being parked practically in front of the raided premises." Oliveri took another pull on his cigar.

"I told you that," Eddy answered. "And Job Ryan said—"

"I know what Job Ryan said, Eddy. I read your report."

"I didn't connect the incident to the dead girl because nothing ever came of it," Eddy defended his negligence.

"Can't say as I blame you," Oliveri answered. The statement was music to Eddy's ears and antacid to his stomach. "Thanks to poor Heather's death I got a call from the county boys and they have condescended to put us in the picture. Generous, eh?"

"There's a connection between Heather Ryan's murder and the drug raid in Sag Harbor last year?" Eddy spoke as if Oliveri had hinted that Heather's death was a prelude to a terrorist attack on East Hampton.

"I think Heather's death was a direct result of that raid, Eddy."

"I don't get it, sir."

"You will when I tell you what I learned in Riverhead today." Oliveri finished his beer and tapped the ash off his cigar into a large crystal ashtray before beginning. "A year ago last spring, Job and Bill Ryan began making weekly runs on *Job's Patience* to a destination off Block Island where they would rendezvous with another boat and exchange packages. In short, Job and Bill were probably trading cash for drugs, most likely cocaine."

Amazed, Eddy began, "So Bill left town . . ."

"Because you scared the shit out of him, Eddy. The kid was delivering to that house in Sag Harbor but somehow managed to get out before the police moved in.

"Job's movements have been under surveillance by the narcotics people since the first time Job met up with a vessel called the *Billy Budd*. Literary crowd, eh, Eddy? They didn't move in on Job for two reasons. One, they didn't know who Job was working for and, two, they didn't know who was supplying the *Billy Budd*. The only hope of finding out was to keep the operation going. They did cut off the street supply whenever possible, like closing down the Sag Harbor house, but Job and the people distributing from the house are penny-ante. It was the big boys they wanted.

"In fact, they were very pleased that Bill had managed to get out of the house before the raid. The fact that he was delivering at the time of the raid was a not unusual snafu on the part of the narc squad. When our men spotted Bill's truck, the narc boys had to pretend to investigate its presence there and you got the job."

"Job continued doing the runs?" Eddy asked, still bewildered by what he was hearing.

Oliveri nodded. "It ended last September, just like the tourist season. Curious? And began again this summer. They've traced the *Billy Budd* connection to Canada and are close to moving in on that end of it with the help of the Canadian authorities, and they believe they know who gives Job Ryan orders on the East End, but they ain't giving us a name until they have solid proof. Trusting souls, the narc boys."

"Job Ryan is a good man, Chris. A third- or fourth-generation Montauk fisherman. This is hard to believe. And Bill really did get scouted by that agent. I mean, he's in a show now."

"Job was a fisherman in need of ready cash, like most of them, I'm sure. Temptation, Eddy. There are big bucks floating around our little villages and everyone wants their share and they don't seem to care how they get it. We've even managed to get ourselves editorialized in the *New York Times*." Oliveri rummaged through a stack of books and magazines piled on the lower shelf of the wicker table. "Here it is. Last Sunday's editorial."

Opening the paper he began to read, " 'The South Fork of Long Island, once a potato patch, is now a land of tycoons and movie stars and models and the kind of people who attend publicity parties for perfumes and wristwatches.' " Looking at Eddy he offered the aside, "That covers your Mr. Reo's crowd to perfection."

Continuing, Oliveri quoted, " '. . . in the Hamptons these days, where every house is a mansion and every mansion is a fiefdom. To most of us, there is something soporific in the sound of millionaires whining at the edge of the ocean. It is a sound of summer, a sound as characteristic of the season as crickets keening in the high grass.' " Folding the newspaper, Oliveri commented, "And that, Eddy, is the state of our union. It's what keeps us in business. As for Bill Ryan, he simply lucked out with that Aldridge guy inviting him to New

York. It gave him the perfect excuse to run and leave Job holding down the fort."

Eddy was puzzled. "If the narc people are uncertain of who Job gets his orders from, how did they get wise to Job?"

"Thanks to a tip from Canada, they had been trailing the *Billy Budd*. That led them to the Ryans from the first night Job linked up with that trawler."

"Are we going to pick up Bill—and Job?"

"Not yet," Oliveri told him. "If we show our hand too soon we'll queer the narc operation. They keep making little raids like the one in Sag Harbor and that cuts the supply for a short time. If we come down on the Ryans it will scare off their East Hampton connection and the narc boys want him and who he may lead to."

"Do they know who killed Heather?"

"No, but they'd like us to find out."

"And does this let Paul Monroe off the hook?" Eddy wanted to know.

"Absolutely not. The narcotics people checked him out and he's clean, but they also told me Paul Monroe and Bill Ryan are very chummy and maybe Paul was doing his friend a favor. It's thin, I know, but motive has been our stumbling block from the start, and our friends in Riverhead have supplied us with a strong contender for the blue ribbon."

"I can't believe that, sir. Heather was Bill's sister in all but actual fact and she was pregnant. Bill might have gotten mixed up with drugs, a lot of young people out here do, but that doesn't make him a murderer."

"You never know with drugs, Eddy. You start with a social sniff and you end up hooked. Or, you make a buck selling a few ounces of pot and you end up married to the mob. That's an expensive girl the Ryan boy got for himself—and maybe Paul Monroe on the side. Christ knows, the underwear model is pretty enough. Heather Ryan certainly knew what Job was up to. She had to. Suppose she wanted more of the kitty and threatened to talk if she didn't get it."

Eddy drank his beer and recalled Michael Reo's statement—*Someone only wanted to silence her*—and he had to concede that maybe Mr. Reo was more of a detective than Oliveri and himself combined. He did not make his assumption known to his host but he did tell him, "Sorry, Chris, but I'm not buying it. Helen knew Heather Ryan and liked her. She just wasn't that kind of person. She was wild about Ian Edwards and looking forward to marrying him."

"Did Helen have any idea of Job Ryan's financial situation?" Oliveri asked.

Eddy shook his head. "Not a clue. Did you learn anything from the narc people?"

"No change in his bank balance, but he's doing very little fishing or chartering in the summer and zip all winter, but he's not starving. Those cabin rentals don't even cover his tax rate, so he must be putting it under the mattress. The old codger is no fool. And if his daughter was Snow White, as you say, perhaps she was going to blow the whistle on her father and Bill and had to be put out of the way."

Michael's words once again echoed in Eddy's head. "And you think Bill got Paul Monroe to do the job? No way, Chris."

"Remember Leopold and Loeb?" Oliveri reminded Eddy.

"I want to forget them and so should you." It wasn't often Eddy openly criticized his boss but when he did the lieutenant took it with grace if not gratitude.

"Should we also forget the locked cottage and the key in Paul's possession?" Oliveri asked, discernibly skirting the fact that Paul Monroe was related to Michael Reo. "Bill told us Heather wanted to see him about breaking the news of her pregnancy to Job. In all your years out here, Eddy, did you ever hear of a local getting riled over a daughter getting in the family way before her wedding?"

Eddy was forced to shake his head in answer as he tried to imagine what Helen's father would have had to say on the subject.

Oliveri went on, "Paul told us he didn't know Bill was going to meet Heather that night but Bill practically told us Paul did know, and tried to cover his error. We both agreed that Bill was lying and that Paul was in on it."

Eddy picked up his glass as he nodded grudgingly.

Oliveri went in for the kill. "Paul told you he knew about that party after the show, so he was aware of the fact that Bill wasn't going to be able to meet Heather at the appointed time."

"But Bill didn't know about the party," Eddy pointed out.

"So he says, and so his buddy Paul says. They lied about everything else, so why not about that? I think Heather Ryan was set up," Oliveri summed up.

"Then why did Bill tear ass out of that party like a bat out of hell?" Eddy protested.

"After the fact, Eddy. He bolted after the fact. Heather was already dead and maybe he knew it."

"And Paul implicated himself by telling us the cottage was sealed when he arrived?" Eddy tried again.

"They all make mistakes, Eddy. Especially the amateurs. The locked cottage was theirs."

The sun had left the sky and twilight now blanketed the garden. Oliveri switched on the table lamp and Eddy blinked at its artificial glow. "I just can't believe it," was his assessment of Oliveri's theory. "And it's not just because Paul is related to Michael Reo," he finally admitted.

"I'm not saying that's how it happened," Oliveri asserted. "I'm saying that's how it could have happened. Our job is to prove or disprove all the possibilities, and my scenario is a very distinct possibility. Paul's guilt or innocence has nothing to do with his relations."

All possibilities? Looking at the darkening sky, Eddy said, "Helen did tell me something interesting."

"Like what?"

"Heather came to see Helen last summer to ask her what she knew about a guy named Avery. You know Helen is our celebrity guru."

"I give up," Oliveri answered. "Who's Avery?"

"A photographer. He was taking pictures in Montauk last year for a book."

Impatient, Oliveri asked, "So what's the connection?"

"Avery works for, or used to work for, Freddy Parc. He was the guy who shot the infamous underwear ads a few years back."

Like a bloodhound on to a new scent, introspection gave way to animated excitement as Oliveri stirred in his chair and remarked, "Paul Monroe works for Freddy Parc."

"Paul is Freddy Parc's supermodel," Eddy corrected.

"If I ask you something, Eddy, would you promise never to repeat it?"

"Sure. What is it?"

"What the hell is a supermodel?" Oliveri pleaded.

Laughing, Eddy said, "I have no idea, Chris, but if I ever get the nerve to ask Helen, I'll pass it on."

The mood lightened considerably. Oliveri offered, "You want another beer, Eddy?"

"Sure. But only if you get up and get it without bothering Lydia."

Standing, Oliveri threatened, "I'll tell that one at your bachelor party." With a shrug of resignation, he picked up Eddy's empty beer bottle and went to fetch their drinks. While he was out of the room, Eddy thought about the man called Avery and made a momentous decision. When Oliveri returned with the beers and a bag of pretzels, Eddy announced as he refilled his glass, "I told Michael Reo about Heather's interest in the man called Avery."

"Why the hell did you do that?" Oliveri cried.

Having made the decision to level with Oliveri, Eddy refused to cower under the lieutenant's menacing gaze. "Because Avery moves in circles Mr. Reo is very familiar with. Don't worry, I didn't tell Mr. Reo to investigate Avery for us. I just put a bug in his ear to rouse his curiosity. He'll make some inquiries and pass on to me what he learns. Believe me, when it comes to dish, those people leave no stone unturned."

"Dish? Christ, Eddy, you're starting to sound like them, and all Reo will tell us is who this Avery is screwing. That's all those people talk about."

"There are times when I think it's all the men on the force talk about," Eddy noted, and was rewarded with a frown instead of the hoped for smile. Feeling he couldn't get in any deeper, Eddy confided, "Mr. Reo offered to trade information with us in an effort to solve Heather Ryan's murder."

Oliveri almost jumped out of his chair. "Now if that doesn't take the prize," he shouted. "Do I have to remind you that everything we discussed here regarding the narc operation is strictly confidential?"

Looking hurt, Eddy responded, "No, Chris, you don't have to remind me."

Pointing with the cigar, Oliveri lectured, "The guy likes to play detective and he has the balls to think we'll play along with him. The rich are different than you and me, Eddy—they're crazy. What does he know that we don't, or can't learn for ourselves?"

"If you calm down, I'll tell you," Eddy answered. "He can tell us if this Avery is worth checking out. And, when I was there this morning he told me Paul was meeting with Bill and the girl, Lisa Kennedy, for the first time since the murder. I think Mr. Reo will get Paul to tell him what went on at that meeting. It may answer a lot of our questions."

"Reo will only try to protect the supermodel."

"I don't think so, Chris. He wants to prove Paul is innocent. There's a difference."

Oliveri once again tapped the ash off his cigar as he proclaimed, "Heather Ryan was killed because her family was involved in drug trafficking. Who put the jockstrap around her neck is the question."

"Why a jockstrap? Maybe that should be our question," Eddy proposed. "A Freddy Parc jockstrap, no less. You used the term 'East Hampton connection.' It seems to me there's a New York connection here, too. That's where Mr. Reo can be of help."

Finally getting the cigar lit and puffing on it to keep it that way, Oliveri replied, "What are you suggesting, Eddy?"

"That we sit down with Michael Reo and listen to what he has to say."

"I would rather sit down with a cobra," Oliveri growled.

CHAPTER TWENTY-THREE

When Eddy arrived at the Dunemere Lane house it was John who opened the door for him and the man immediately began to pump Eddy for information regarding Heather Ryan's murder. With Lieutenant Oliveri's warning in mind, Eddy told John everything that was in the New York and local papers, and as an extra added attraction, he whispered, "Our latest lead being confidential, that's all I can say for now, John." With an understanding nod, John led Eddy to the den, where Michael was seated in a swivel chair behind his executive desk. Vicky was out and this not being one of the days Ms. Johnson announced herself, the Kirkpatrick Foundation side of the huge room was bereft of personnel.

"Just the man I want to see," Michael greeted. "Have a seat. Would you like a drink? Coffee?"

"Nothing, thanks, Mr. Reo. I tried to see you after the funeral this afternoon but you were occupied."

"I went to lunch with Aldridge and Amanda Richards. He's the man who produced the show at the John Drew and, incidentally, the man who lured Bill Ryan from Montauk last year."

"I saw him," Eddy said. "Helen pointed him out to me." Thanks to Eddy's bragging, Michael was aware of Helen's reputation as East

Hampton's film critic, celebrity spotter and unofficial Hollywood gossip columnist. "I recognized Amanda Richards and I know Freddy Parc by sight." Eddy lowered himself into a leather visitor's chair.

"Did you see Avery?" Michael asked.

"Helen pointed him out, too. A tall drink of water," was Eddy's assessment of Avery.

"All bones and no meat," Michael said. "Can I ask you if you knew Heather and Bill Ryan, personally?"

Cautiously, Eddy answered, "I saw them around and may have spoken to them. Why do you ask?"

"I just wanted to know if you ever heard any talk of Bill Ryan wanting to become an actor," Michael answered.

Eddy nervously crossed an ankle over a knee. "Helen knew them. She was a few years ahead of Bill and Heather in high school but it's a small town and a small school. All the kids who overlap at the high school know each other at least by sight."

Michael had never met Helen Weaver, knowing only that her parents owned a video rental store in the Springs. Telling Michael that Helen was a few years older than the Ryan children was tantamount to telling him Helen's age. Before Michael could make the observation, Eddy stated, "I'm a few years older than Helen." It was an admission that always embarrassed him.

Sensing his discomfort, Michael offered, "I'll tell you something, Eddy. All the teenage girls who drool over a Paul Monroe will one day happily settle down with an Eddy Evans."

Flustered, Eddy quickly responded to Michael's query. "Didn't Paul tell you why Bill went to New York?" Eddy questioned.

"He told me what Bill Ryan told him—and I don't believe it." Michael watched Eddy fidget in his chair and the body language told him that that was all the answer he was going to get from the detective. Spreading his arms, Michael said, "Did you know the agent, Josh Aldridge, entered Bill Ryan in the Freddy Parc contest? The one that got Paul the modeling job."

"So Bill lost the contest?"

"Clever deduction," Michael said amiably, "but it's better than a *'no comment'*—or did you remember Freddy Parc's credo that a *'no comment'* is the most telling comment of all?" Michael teased and poor Eddy squirmed—but now the body language was accompanied by a broad grin.

"Okay," Michael said, "let me know, if you can, what you think of this one. You told me Avery was in Montauk last year taking photos for a proposed art book. I learned that Aldridge hired Avery to photograph Bill for the contest. Avery seems to be popping up all over."

This had Eddy uncrossing his legs and leaning forward in his chair. "Did Paul tell you what he discussed with Bill and Lisa Kennedy yesterday?"

"He did," was all Michael would impart.

"Are you willing to share it with us?"

With an exaggerated lift of his eyebrows, Michael exclaimed, "Us?"

"I told Lieutenant Oliveri that you offered to share information with us," Eddy explained.

"And what did your lieutenant say, Eddy?"

"He said he would rather sit down with a cobra."

Nodding thoughtfully, Michael observed, "You're honest, Eddy. I'll say that for you."

"So is Chris Oliveri, Mr. Reo. He can be contentious with our summer visitors but that's because he's nostalgic for the days when the potato fields yielded fodder for a pot of boiling water rather than grist for *Architectural Digest*."

"Nicely put," Michael complimented Eddy's colorful and apt insight into the convictions and gripes of many old-guard Hamptonites. Feigning a sigh, Michael agreed, "I'll meet with your lieutenant and sally down your one-way street, Eddy—to a point."

"Why not go all the way?" Eddy protested.

"Because until I know where all this is leading, I have the right to remain silent and have a lawyer present."

On the way out, it was Maddy who accosted Detective Evans. "Excuse me, Eddy," Maddy began, "I want to tell you how Ms. Johnson thinks you can identify the murderer."

"What happened to the trapdoor theory?"

This was dismissed with a wave of her hand. "That was yesterday. It's the murder weapon you should examine."

"The athletic supporter?" Eddy was intrigued.

"Yes, Eddy. That thing. What size is it?"

Unable to figure out where this was leading, Eddy could only take the plunge and ask, "Why do you want to know that, Maddy?"

"Don't you see? If the thing belongs to the murderer, and it must, you could eliminate all the suspects it doesn't fit and nab the guy it does fit—like Cinderella's glass slipper."

Amazed, Eddy answered, "Suppose the murderer is a woman, Maddy?"

"Where would a woman get such a thing?"

"From her husband or boyfriend, of course."

Maddy was shocked but had to admit it was a possibility. "I'll tell Ms. Johnson, Eddy."

"Let me know what she thinks."

"Oh, I will, Eddy. I will."

"We meet again, Lieutenant Oliveri." Michael extended his hand along with the salutation.

"But we were never formally introduced, Mr. Reo." Oliveri shook Michael's hand, almost crushing it in the process.

"That's right. Without a proper introduction you told me to get lost and threatened to arrest Paul for murder. Nice to know you."

In the role of Mother Hen, Eddy Evans appeared on the verge of cackling at his chicks' opening salvos. In lieu of that, he offered Michael a seat opposite the lieutenant, positioning the visitor with his back to the door. Eddy remained standing. "Coffee, Mr. Reo?" Eddy asked hopefully.

"No thanks, Eddy," Michael declined.

Eyeing Michael, Oliveri said, "Back in the ninth grade a girl in our class collected your pictures; cut 'em out of newspapers and magazines. We didn't know who you were because you weren't in the movies, and she told us you were a playboy. We thought that made you the owner of the magazine we used to pass around in the locker room."

Michael took this with a gracious nod and a smile. "I'll pass that around to Hugh."

"Give him my regards, Mr. Reo. And now that we've dropped the prerequisite name in true East Hampton fashion, would you tell me what you know about the death of Heather Ryan?"

Today, Christopher Oliveri wore a dark blue summer suit, white shirt and rep tie. Eddy believed that extra starch had been worked into the shirt's collar and cuffs. In contrast, the "playboy" had dressed down in jeans, polo shirt and cord jacket.

"I know Paul Monroe did not do it," Michael said emphatically.

Eddy had warned Michael against beginning the meeting by proclaiming Paul Monroe's innocence. This was not going well.

"Paul didn't know Bill was going to meet with Heather that night," Michael stated.

"We think he did know, Mr. Reo."

"Please hear me out, Lieutenant. Not knowing about the party, and believing Lisa Kennedy was going out after the show, Bill thought he could be home in time to meet with Heather at ten. Paul was at Freddy Parc's and Bill feared Paul would be home before him and run into Heather, so he told Paul that he was meeting an old girlfriend that night—not his sister, Heather Ryan. Paul did not lie to you when he said he didn't know Bill Ryan had a date with his sister."

"Semantics, Mr. Reo." Oliveri shrugged off Michael's defense of Paul Monroe. "He knew Bill was meeting a girl. Why didn't he tell us that?"

"Because he was afraid," Michael answered, "and confused. He thought it best to keep out of it until he talked to Bill. Christ, he found a dead girl on his bed and is told she's his friend's sister when he never knew his friend had a sister. Give the kid a break, Lieutenant."

Eddy extended an olive branch with the words, "We're not accusing Paul of anything."

"Not yet," Oliveri added, causing Eddy to wince. "Do you know why the girl was so eager to meet with Bill?"

Michael pulled a face as if evaluating the question and how it should be addressed. When he spoke his tone implied confidentiality. "According to Paul, Bill admitted telling Aldridge and Lisa one story and you another."

"I'll tell you that Bill Ryan said Heather wanted him to break the news of her pregnancy to her father, Job," Oliveri traded information.

"And he told Aldridge and Lisa that Heather was uncertain if she wanted to marry the father of her child. He implied there was another man in the picture," Michael stated. Oliveri turned his gaze on Eddy Evans. Seeing this, Michael quickly continued, "But Bill swears that was a lie. He said he doesn't know why he said it. He insisted he told you the truth."

"And I think he's lying out of both sides of his mouth," Oliveri barked. "Did Bill tell anyone else about Heather's supposed other man?"

That took Michael by surprise. "I don't know, but what difference does it make?"

Eddy waited for Oliveri's hesitant nod before telling Michael, "It's been rumored around town that there was another man in Heather Ryan's life."

"Jesus," Michael exclaimed. "Where did you hear that?"

"We can't say at the present time," Oliveri got in before Eddy could reply.

It was the first piece of shared information that seemed to shed new light on the case, and both the seasoned pros and Michael Reo struggled silently to find the hole in the puzzle that could accommodate it—seemingly without success. But it did act as an incentive to continue trading information in the manner of allies, and not leery adversaries. "How about that coffee, Eddy?" Michael asked.

"I'll have one, too," Oliveri joined in.

Grateful for the truce, Eddy, who had remained standing, happily complied but before leaving the room he tossed a poser into the pot. "Do you think Bill was telling the truth the first time and then decided to protect the other guy?"

"I don't think so," Michael answered. "I can't see Bill covering for Heather's murderer. Revenge—yes—but not complicity. Bill Ryan's grief is very real."

When Eddy left, Oliveri addressed Michael across the table. "You told Eddy that you don't believe Bill left home to become an actor. Why, Mr. Reo?"

"I'll tell you, Lieutenant. I've been around actors, both the working variety and the hopefuls, all my life, and none of them has ever carried on in the manner of our Bill Ryan. Paul told me Bill was reluctant to set foot on a stage, and when he did, the best he could do was ape an actor whose technique he mastered from watching old films on video. He is a natural mimic, I'll say that for the guy. Now, he doesn't want to go back into the show. I know genuinely bereaved actors to go from a funeral to an audition on the one percent chance they might get the role. Bill Ryan wants to be an actor like I want to be a policeman—no offense intended."

Oliveri's smile was an indication of his more amiable disposition toward Michael Reo. "Then why did he leave?"

Eddy was back, passing out cardboard containers of coffee. "I put milk in all of them. Sugar's on the side." With that he took a dozen paper packets of sugar and artificial sweeteners out of his jacket pocket and tossed them on the table.

Reaching for the coffee, Michael said, "I told you Paul said Bill was reluctant to appear in the show; however, Paul was even more specific on the subject. He thinks Bill was reluctant to go on the stage here, in East Hampton—meaning Bill Ryan did not want to return in triumph, or at all." Michael took a deep breath and stated, "I think, gentlemen, that when Bill Ryan left Montauk, he was running away from something—or someone."

Eddy, who had taken the chair next to Michael, began to stir his coffee vigorously with a multicolored striped swizzle stick although he had not added sugar to his container. Lieutenant Oliveri, avoiding his own container of coffee, watched Eddy stir. The pair could not have been more responsive to Michael's hypothesis if they had vocalized their thoughts.

"I've touched a live wire," Michael said with obvious joy.

Surprisingly, the lieutenant allowed Eddy to tackle the delicate situation. "When you agreed to this meeting, I said we would share with you anything that we didn't deem confidential."

"And that's all we can say." Oliveri closed the subject.

Eddy continued to stir his coffee thinking, *The cat is not out of the bag, but Mr. Reo now knows what's in the bag.* He was consoled by the fact that Christopher Oliveri was present when the cat roared and therefore could not pin the blame on his subordinate. Eddy was also grateful that Mr. Reo had the good sense not to pursue the point. But then why should he? He got what he came for. Eddy hoped Mr. Reo would give in kind.

"Avery." Oliveri laid another card on the table.

"One word says it all," Michael quoted and got two questioning gazes. "That's how he bills himself," Michael explained.

"And what does the one word say?" Oliveri asked.

"He worked for Freddy Parc as in-house photographer and general gofer. What he usually went for, so I heard, was a little coke and a little hash to liven up parties and put out-of-town buyers in a buying mood—and a little pimping on the side, I imagine."

When his listeners started at this, Michael shrugged. "Come on, gentlemen, we're all adults. You both know Marlboros aren't the only things that get passed around at posh parties in New York and Malibu East, as we're now called."

"Go on," Oliveri ordered.

"Avery takes pictures in Montauk last year for a proposed art book of seascapes. Did he meet Bill Ryan on his rounds? Bill Ryan is a perfect candidate for Avery's discriminating eye."

"He's gay?" Eddy surmised.

"For Avery, that would be a step up. I think he's asexual but be that as it may, the agent, Joshua Aldridge, spots Bill on a fishing boat and invites him to become a star." With a wry glance at Eddy, Michael said, "For reasons we do not know, Bill takes up Aldridge's offer."

Picking up the story, Eddy told his boss, "Aldridge entered Bill in the Freddy Parc contest. The one Freddy Parc ran to find a model for his jockey shorts. Avery took the photos of Bill for the contest—and Bill lost to Paul Monroe."

"It sounds like an item in *Dan's Papers*," Oliveri complained. "What the hell does it all mean?"

"How many coincidences does it take for the plot to be more calculated than happenstance?" Michael asked Oliveri. "I think Bill Ryan was shanghaied, if you'll excuse the B-movie dialogue."

"I thought you believed he ran scared," Oliveri noted.

"Semantics, Lieutenant," Michael retorted with a wink at Eddy. "Let's say he was forced to run. Do you know what a package deal is?"

"Enlighten us," Oliveri requested.

"An agent has a writer, a director and an actor and actress in his stable, as they say. The writer pens a script to fit the talents of both the performers and the director. The agent takes the so-called package to a producer, who finds the money to put on the show or make the film."

"Interesting," Oliveri observed, unimpressed.

"I bet Eddy can tell you what I'm thinking," Michael said.

With a show of confidence, Eddy did. "We have the agent, Joshua Aldridge. We have the actor and actress, Bill Ryan and Lisa Kennedy. And Helen told me the director, Tony Vasquez, is in town."

"Maybe we should have invited Helen," Michael said. "Yes, Tony Vasquez is here and he's a writer as well as a director. You see, Lieutenant, Josh Aldridge is putting together a package. I think choosing Bill Ryan as part of the deal was no accident."

"But why Bill Ryan?" Oliveri cried.

"Therein lies the rub. And why the jockstrap, come to think of it?" Michael reflected.

Eddy almost jumped out of his chair. "To point a finger," he exclaimed. "The murderer left behind someone else's calling card to take the heat off himself." Excited, Eddy babbled, "Maddy said we could identify the murderer by the size of the jockstrap."

"What?" Oliveri shouted. "And who in blazes is Maddy?"

"My housekeeper," Michael said calmly.

"This is too much, Eddy," Oliveri complained.

"No, Chris, listen. Maddy said the jockstrap must have belonged to the murderer, so we could eliminate all the suspects the damn thing didn't fit. I know that's nuts, but there is some rationale in it. I mean, the jockstrap was meant to identify the murderer, or so the murderer wants us to believe. It's a Freddy Parc jockstrap. Freddy was at home that night with all his dinner guests to vouch for him, so who does that leave us?"

Not convinced but giving the proposal serious thought, Oliveri said, "You may have something there. Paul Monroe and Avery are both associated with Freddy Parc, but only Paul had a key to the house."

"Avery was at the theater that night with a few hundred witnesses, including me, to vouch for him," Michael remarked. "In fact, all of the New York crowd and a good portion of Bill's old Montauk friends were at the theater the night of Heather Ryan's murder. It was someone who wasn't at the theater—which points to a local—and someone who had a key."

"Which points to Paul Monroe," Oliveri said.

Michael retaliated with, "Let's not forget Heather's mysterious other beau. The one who may or may not exist. It's beginning to look like he does exist."

"Helen never heard of him," Eddy joined in. "She says Heather was in love with Ian Edwards."

"But there has to be a fourth key," Michael said, hitting the table with the palm of his hand and threatening the containers of coffee that all three men had forgotten in the fervor of conversation.

"There is," Eddy said. Without waiting for a nod from Oliveri, he told Michael, "We checked with the real estate agent who handles the cottage. Originally, there were two keys plus the agent's master key. She gave keys to Bill and Lisa when they rented the cottage and had one made for Paul when he joined them. The master key went back in her desk drawer with all the other house keys she holds and it hasn't left there since."

"Paul didn't do it," Michael persevered.

"Someone did it," Oliveri said.

When Michael left the station house, Oliveri leaned back in his chair and put his hands together as if in prayer. "So, this Avery supplied the goodies for Freddy's parties."

"He must be the guy the narc boys are watching," Eddy said, "but he was at the theater that night."

"These bastards have long arms. He could have hired a hit man. Heather Ryan wanted something they didn't want to give her or she posed a threat to their operation. Either was her death notice. And, if Freddy Parc is a user and was giving them a hard time for any reason, the jockstrap might have been used to scare the hell out of him. You were right, Eddy. The weapon is a calling card, but not the murderer's."

"Too bad we couldn't tell Mr. Reo why Bill left Montauk," Eddy was thinking.

"He's no fool," Oliveri conceded. "You heard him. He suspects Bill was on the run, and thanks to Paul, he knows Bill was unhappy about returning here. For now, let him pursue his 'package' theory while we take a closer look at this Avery, and if there is no drug connection to the murder, Reo might come up with another motive for it."

"What about opportunity?" Eddy responded.

"The key. Always the key," Oliveri moaned. "And, Eddy, one more thing."

"Yeah, Chris."

"Don't gossip with housekeepers."

"Yes, sir."

MICHAEL ANTHONY REO

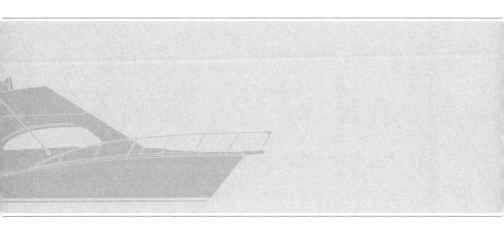

CHAPTER TWENTY-FOUR

"Don't give away all our money," Michael cautioned, entering the den.

Raising her blond head and removing her reading glasses Vicky assured her husband, "That would be impossible. It seems to come in faster than I can dole it out."

He kissed his wife before dropping into the chair usually occupied by Ms. Johnson. "Quiet, or people will think I married you for your money—which I didn't, but it helped." Looking about he asked, "Is Paul out?"

"As usual, he is. The young don't sit still for very long. He's either in Montauk holding his friend's hand or in Amagansett holding Lisa's hand, which gives him the opportunity to charm Amanda," Vicky told Michael.

"I'm glad Paul and Amanda have met informally, through Lisa, rather than being introduced by me in the line of duty. It gives them time to get to know each other before they start throwing things at each other."

Vicky was at her desk, wearing her philanthropist hat, as Michael liked to say when she administered to the family foundation. Knowing it would be impossible to get any work done with Michael at her elbow, Vicky rested her glasses and fountain pen on the desk and did what she had been doing since the day she met Michael Anthony Reo, over twenty years ago. She deferred to him by asking, "How did the meeting go with Eddy and the handsome Lieutenant Oliveri?"

"Smashingly. Oliveri's shirt collar is so starched, one wrong move and he could cut his own throat. I suspect his white boxers are also starched, accounting for the perpetual scowl on his handsome face."

Shaking her head woefully, Vicky said, "I'd love to know what he thinks of you."

Ignoring that, Michael recited the minutes of his meeting with East Hampton's finest. "I'd like to know when Aldridge approached Bill. What I mean is, how long did Bill wait before he took advantage of Aldridge's offer? My hunch is that Bill had no intention of following up with Aldridge until he had to get out of town, and you should have seen the look on their faces when I dropped that bomb. They know something, but they ain't talking."

"Neither is Paul," Vicky said.

"I think Paul has told us all he knows. To wit: Bill is not enamored of acting, nor did he want to return to East Hampton. Factor in the Aldridge/Avery connection and if you believe it's all coincidental, you believe in Santa Claus."

Vicky laughed. "But I do believe in Santa Claus. Who else puts all those lovely things under my tree?"

"Your old man's legacy, that's who," Michael answered. "And be serious. Oliveri is leaning on Paul and we have to see that he doesn't pounce."

The mention of taking care of Paul Monroe immediately put Vicky in a reflective mood. "He's the boy we never had, isn't he, Michael?" Long resigned to the fact that they were childless, Vicky's question was not intended to open old wounds. Vicky and Michael had been examined by renowned physicians on both sides of the Atlantic, none of whom could give a medical reason why their marriage was not fruitful. Their sex life being a paragon of marital bliss, Michael stoically shrugged off their barren state with the disclaimer, "We're the children of our own union."

"And he's the actor you always wanted to be," Vicky went on.

"Thank you, Doctor Freud. I also think he's perfect for our film, so my concern is practical as well as psychological. Not to mention the fact that he is my blood kin."

"Thank you, Doctor Feelgood," Vicky countered.

Looking out the glass sliders to the back lawn, Michael spotted John pulling weeds from among the pachysandra surrounding a majestic and ancient elm tree that had provided a shady respite from the summer sun for as many years as Michael could remember. For John it was more a labor of love than a chore as the Reos did employ a professional lawn care service. Seeing John brought to mind the trapdoor theory and Michael was thinking Heather's murderer could have hidden in the cottage and fled while Paul was calling the police. But how did the murderer, and Heather Ryan, get in the cottage? With a key, of course. Paul's key? Whose but Paul's?

"I told them about Josh Aldridge's package deal but they didn't seem too impressed. And where does Avery fit in, I wonder?"

"Certainly not the producer," Vicky protested. "He has neither the experience nor the money."

"Aldridge is the producer, but Avery's ex-employer, Freddy Parc, has the loot."

"Freddy would want Paul, not Bill, in a film he was backing, with Paul pulling up his pants over guess what at the start of every scene. And in case you've forgotten, Josh has the first lady of the American theater under contract. So why is he giving her to us in favor of two unknowns?"

Watching John get laboriously to his feet clutching a handful of weeds, Michael again conjured up a picture of the murderer hiding in a closet, awaiting his escape. Those who hide do so because they want to remain unknown. "I think you just asked the most profound question of the season. Like I always say, it's the questions, not the answers, that matter."

"I never heard you say that, dear, but explain yourself anyway."

"Unknowns." Michael paused for effect. "Amanda is famous and wise to the minutiae of her trade. Then we have Tony Vasquez, a has-been who would sell his soul, if he has one, for the chance at a come-back; a young actress awaiting the big break and a shy actor Paul lovingly calls a clam digger who doesn't know his arse from his elbow."

"You mean Josh went out of his way to put together a cast of characters who don't know the right questions to ask?"

"Or who won't ask questions," Michael said. "Curious, isn't it?"

"It's more than curious, Michael, but what has it to do with Heather Ryan?"

"That's what I'm going to find out."

"Let it go, Michael," Vicky pleaded. "Heather certainly has nothing to do with Josh's weird package deal so it can't have anything to do with her death."

"Two out of the three keys to that cottage belong to members in good standing of Aldridge's cast, and why the Freddy Parc jockstrap? I knew that damn garment practically had Paul's name on it from day one—a fact our friend Eddy also now realizes and said as much to Oliveri. Why was Bill meeting with Heather the night of his show's opening? To discuss her condition? They had nine months to ponder that issue. And who started the rumor about Heather's other boyfriend? If Bill told this only to Lisa and Aldridge before denying it, then Lisa or Aldridge mentioned it to someone else. Why?"

"People talk, Michael," Vicky protested. "Lisa or Josh may have mentioned it to anyone else in all innocence. Lisa is staying with Amanda, for heaven's sake. Can you imagine the gossip going on there?"

Either not hearing, or not wanting to hear, Michael raced on, "Did you notice Job and Bill Ryan at the funeral? At the time I thought they looked apprehensive rather than sad. Now I think they looked scared, not anxious, and I want to know why."

Having no answer to Michael's question, or certain no response would suffice, Vicky picked up her fountain pen and laid it down again. "When you told Eddy and Oliveri that Avery supplied the drugs for Freddy's parties you thought the two were naive to the drug scene here and in New York. That seems strange for a couple of savvy cops." Michael nodded thoughtfully but said nothing. After a long pause, Vicky remembered, "Wasn't Tony Vasquez's downfall due to drugs?"

Leaning toward his wife, Michael ran his finger across her cheek before bending to kiss it. "Keep asking questions and you may solve this case for the police."

"Skip the rhetoric," Vicky said irritably, "and tell me what you mean."

"I think you hit on the thread that may connect all our players."

"Drugs?" Vicky exclaimed.

"Avery, Vasquez, a disinclined actor on the run and a cast of unknowns. Do you know anything about laundering money?"

"No, Michael. Father used to talk about it, but I never understood it."

"Neither do I," he admitted, "but it goes something like this: After literally passing the buck in a series of convoluted exchanges that leaves no paper trail, money gotten illegally, or dirty money, finds its way into legitimate businesses where it becomes clean money. Hence, laundering. Theatrical enterprises are most susceptible to this loot because producers are always desperately in need of backers and therefore are willing to get into bed with anyone who has megabucks to spare.

"The night I escorted Amanda to the theater we talked about Aldridge meeting Bill Ryan on a fishing boat. I asked Amanda what Aldridge was doing on a fishing boat and she said Aldridge was courting angels and if they wanted to go fishing, the producer goes where the money goes—or words to that effect."

"Observant," Vicky said.

"Indeed. You can see why Aldridge doesn't want Amanda looking over his shoulder. Also note, it was in Montauk where Aldridge and his cronies went fishing."

Picking up her fountain pen and holding it between her fingers as one would a cigarette, Vicky was not fully convinced. "It's all guesswork, Michael, and no fact."

"Perhaps. But there is someone the proverbial stone's throw from here who may be able to enlighten us."

"Why not discuss it with Eddy and Lieutenant Oliveri first?" Vicky counseled, trying to stem the inevitable.

"I will when I know more. For now, let them go chasing after Heather Ryan's mysterious other beau while I try to learn how Avery fits into the picture."

"Don't meddle, Michael," Vicky said, vehemently. "If you are right, these people won't be amused."

Getting out of his chair, he forewarned, "We're in too deep, my love."

"Oh, Michael," she moaned, shaking her fountain pen at her husband's retreating back.

Michael decided to bicycle up Dunemere Lane to the Maidstone Arms Inn, located on Route 27. On the short ride he mentally reviewed everything he knew, or had ever heard, about Tony Vasquez.

Several decades ago, Tony Vasquez, a self-styled poet residing in San Francisco, was spokesperson for the young of the land, hailed as flower children. Having mounted a political and sexual revolution, the victorious rebels began extracting their spoils in the form of mass takeovers. As if overnight, they became the spokesperson for American businesses from Madison Avenue to Wall Street. Hollywood studios, in keeping with the times, turned over the reigns of producing films to anyone with a glimmer of talent who was born after the big war.

Surprisingly, the gimmick worked and a good number of innovative films, as well as films that questioned the socially acceptable norms of most Americans, were made and met with great success. At the age of twenty-five, Tony Vasquez was the writer/director of three of the biggest artistic and financial successes of that decade.

Having experimented with marijuana in his lean years, Tony advanced to the more expensive, more sophisticated mind enhancers when he prospered. Long before the country turned to the right and put a minor movie star in the oval office, Tony Vasquez had surrendered his talent to his addiction.

Because of his past record the studio ignored erratic shooting schedules, inflated budgets and prestigious stars, including Amanda Richards, being treated like extras. They even turned their heads when Tony married his daughter-in-law in Las Vegas the day after she divorced Tony's son in Mexico. But anyone who could count knew that the child she bore Tony was conceived before she went south of the border. The studio was, in fact, willing to forgive Tony Vasquez anything but the sluggish box office and poor reviews that plagued his fourth and fifth efforts. As the decade and long hair slipped into obscurity, so did Tony Vasquez.

The young man in the small office just off the entrance foyer of the Maidstone Arms Inn called up to Tony Vasquez's room and announced Michael to their guest. Putting the house phone down, he turned to Michael and politely asked him to wait in the lounge. "Mr. Vasquez will be down shortly, Mr. Reo. I hope your lunch yesterday was satisfactory."

"It was, thank you."

"And how exciting to have Amanda Richards with us. And, of course, Mrs. Reo."

"I will convey the compliment to Ms. Richards—and to Mrs. Reo," Michael said.

The lounge was actually the inn's front porch, furnished with couches and comfortable chairs covered in a bright print fabric. A row of screened windows faced the pond and the old town cemetery. The

James Lane Cafe, where the events that led to Michael's calling on Tony Vasquez started, was just on the opposite side of the pond.

The cemetery's tombstones contained the names and dates of many early East Hampton settlers, including the town's founder, Lion Gardiner. It must have been the recent death of Heather Ryan coupled with Michael's ruminations on the life and times of Tony Vasquez and the flower children of a previous generation that reminded him of one of the many legends concerning East Hampton's founding father.

When Heather Flower, daughter of Wyandanch, one of the most powerful chiefs of the Long Island Indians, was abducted by a rival tribe, it was Lion Gardiner who secured her rescue. In gratitude, Wyandanch gave Lion a good portion of what is now central Long Island. This was one of the reasons it was said that Lion Gardiner could have his coachman drive him from East Hampton to New York City without ever leaving his own property. Michael's reaction to this was, "Who cut his lawn?"

Michael now wondered if Heather Ryan had been named after the Indian chief's daughter.

Tony Vasquez entered the lounge wearing his good suit, which confirmed Michael's guess that it was the only suit he owned. Michael imagined the poor guy sitting in his room upstairs all day, clad only in his underwear, lest he wrinkle the suit.

"I hope I'm not intruding," Michael said, taking the hand Vasquez had extended.

"It's kind of you to think you might be," Vasquez answered. "Actually, I sit in my room most of the day taking in the view and hoping it's not a harbinger of things to come—but then sooner or later it's where we'll all end up, isn't it?"

They sat in chairs separated by a table holding a lamp and an ashtray that was purely decorative since the new Suffolk County law forbade smoking in public places.

"You won't end up across the street," Michael told him, "nor will I. Like our motels in July and August, there are no vacancies."

"Standing room only," Vasquez kidded. "A director's three favorite words." Adjusting the razor-sharp crease in his suit pants, Vasquez added, "I would offer you a drink but I don't know if the bar is open between meals."

"No thanks," Michael assured him. "It's a bit early for me."

"It's always a bit early for me," Vasquez answered. "As I'm sure you've heard, I've been on the wagon for nine years. Nary a nip nor a sniff in all that time."

"Congratulations," Michael offered.

"What for? I haven't been able to get it up since I joined the living dead."

"Really? I always thought booze and drugs were a downer, no pun intended."

"They are, but when you're on them you don't know it." Vasquez laughed. "I understand your champagne lunch yesterday was in honor of Amanda committing herself to doing your film."

"That's correct, Tony."

"Then I doubt your visit today is to ask me to direct. The lady holds a humongous grudge in her silken talons. Did you see the film we did together?" When Michael nodded, Vasquez asked, "What's your opinion? Be honest, Michael, it's all in the past."

After reflecting for a moment, Michael told him, "I've always thought she performed as if she were imitating a drag queen imitating Amanda Richards."

Now it was Vasquez who seemed to be weighing Michael's response before answering. "I've always heard that Michael Reo was a very perceptive and knowledgeable judge of the performing arts, and you have just validated your own notices. I told Amanda to cut the drag queen routine the first day of shooting and she responded by not speaking to me from that day to the present."

"I understand she gave you a reconciliatory hug and I saw her blow you a kiss yesterday," Michael reminded him.

"And I can imagine what she said while doing it."

Michael thought it best not to tell him. He also thought it best not to tell the director that the script he had written for Amanda contained a plot and dialogue that was material for a drag queen's takeoff on Amanda Richards, hence Amanda had played it the only way it could be played.

"So what can I do for you, Michael?"

"I'd like to know about the package Aldridge has put together."

"Ask Aldridge. You lunch with him. I don't."

"I did ask him but he's not talking."

"What makes you think I will?"

"Because you're not an agent, and I'm a viable producer who's always on the lookout for talent—writers, directors and the like."

"You don't fuck around, do you?"

"Perceptive and knowledgeable, that's me. Remember?"

"Cute. Why do you want to know?" Vasquez asked with noticeably less rancor in his tone.

"I expect to start shooting in a few months and I'm interested in some of the people you seem to be interested in. What's your time frame?"

Vasquez laughed in Michael's face. "I hope you're a better producer than actor. What are you after?"

Seeing no reason to continue the charade, Michael stated, "Information."

"Such as?"

"Tell me about Aldridge's package."

Opening his arms in a gesture of despair, Vasquez said, "I don't know if we have one. Or even if I have a deal. This girl's murder has fucked up the works royally."

"Because Ryan wants out?"

"That's part of it. The money men don't like the idea of their star being involved in a murder. His sister's murder, no less. It makes them antsy."

With a hint of irony, Michael mumbled, "I wonder why?" Louder, he asked, "So why not get a new star? Mimics are easy to come by."

Vasquez began stirring restlessly in his chair. "So you noticed?"

"Only the deaf wouldn't notice," Michael assured him.

Vasquez stared out the window and spoke not a word for so long Michael thought the interview had been terminated. He was about to rise when Vasquez began, "Last year Avery was on the coast and he came to me with pictures of the guy I now know is Bill Ryan. He asked me if I would be interested in doing a film script to go with the face." Michael's astounded gaze had Vasquez assuring him, "Not unusual. Believe me, scripts have been developed around everything from song titles to the producer's girlfriend's bust line.

"He also said that if his people liked the script, I might get to direct—and was I interested? No one has offered me a job in nine years and he asks me if I'm interested."

"Avery? 'His people'?" Michael quoted, not hiding his interest. "Avery is fronting for the money people?"

"I understand he's getting credit as executive producer, whatever the hell that means."

Trying to make sense of what he was hearing, Michael asked, "And why Bill Ryan?"

"Aldridge spotted Ryan and told Avery the boy had potential. He's a looker, you have to say that for him."

"Had you seen Bill act before you saw him on stage last week?"

Looking sheepish, Vasquez shook his head. "You mean because I told you he was hot stuff? That was pure hype, Michael. You know Bill was doing Tony Perkins. Remember him? The crazy thing is, when Avery showed me Bill's photos, I dusted off an old script Paramount asked me to do for a kid they were touting as the new Tony Perkins. Is that serendipity, or what?"

Serendipity, or what? seemed to be the very basis of Joshua Aldridge's package, Michael thought. "Aldridge's bank is beginning to take on the aroma of an outhouse in August. What's your take on it, Tony?"

"Can you offer me a job?" Vasquez queried. "Any crumb will do. Even second-unit director."

"Sorry, Tony. Not possible."

"Then I strongly recommend you fuck off, Reo, and keep your lily-white nose out of the latrine."

CHAPTER TWENTY-FIVE

"Amanda Richards called," Maddy told Michael when he entered the house, "and Miss Vicky has gone to visit with her."

This, unfortunately, was to be expected. Amanda had committed to do the film and now she would want the undivided attention of her producers. Michael would have to caution Vicky and lay down the law to Amanda. They would not jump whenever the actress snapped her fingers.

"And Mr. Aldridge called," Maddy said. "He would like you to call him as soon as you can."

"Did he leave a number?"

"He did. It's on your desk in the den."

Bicycling back home, Michael had speculated as to who Tony Vasquez would call first—Avery or Aldridge. It appeared to be Joshua Aldridge. "I'm returning your call," Michael said when he got Aldridge on the line.

"Thanks." Aldridge sounded his usual composed self, which no doubt came with a lot of practice. "If it's not an imposition, could you come to my place for a chat? It shouldn't take long."

Michael glanced at his desk clock. It was almost five and he remembered that he hadn't had a thing to eat or drink since taking a few sips of the dreadful coffee Eddy had served at the police station that morning. However, he couldn't resist hearing what Aldridge had to say now that Michael's interest in the agent's film deal was out in the open.

"Give me directions and I'll come right over," Michael agreed.

When he had the information, Michael rang off and ran upstairs where he splashed water on his face, changed his jeans for a pair of chinos but stuck with the polo shirt and cord jacket. Vicky had taken the Land Rover, which left Michael no choice but to take the Rolls. It was a choice he was only too happy to have thrust upon him as he especially enjoyed driving the Rolls when dressing down, in contrast to the car's opulence.

Heading west toward Wainscott, he passed the Poxabogue driving range and nine-hole golf course. The Poxabogue coffee shop boasted the fact, via a sign over its entrance, that it served breakfast all day. It also served a fine no-nonsense sandwich and a good cup of coffee. It was a place Michael and Vicky frequented when in need of an old-fashioned New York coffee shop fix. Poxabogue offered a tuna on rye, presented on a dish devoid of a mound of dubious greens and sans the bean sprout garnish.

The atmosphere was strictly country kitchen, and weather permitting, one could dine on the patio overlooking the course. It was still virgin territory to the tourists and the Reos hoped it would keep its chastity.

Aldridge's home was an oversized, shingled saltbox built on a potato field that had been parceled into two-acre building lots, making the former owner a passive farmer and an active millionaire. Aldridge's acreage was just down the road from a cosmetic king's mansion that included a steepled church (alas, a small steepled church) carted in from New England to serve as a library for the household.

There was a silver Mercedes convertible parked in the driveway that Michael knew to be MJ Barrett's. Well! And a black Ferrari that

Michael knew to be Freddy Parc's. Michael's Rolls completed the picture of East Hampton's typical midsummer driveway population.

Aldridge himself opened the door to a gracious living space, with glass sliders looking out to a tiled patio and a generous amount of field and sky. The agent offered Michael a broad smile and a firm handshake. "You know Freddy and, of course, MJ," Aldridge said.

Both men, seated on a couch and holding drinks, nodded at Michael. They looked as uncomfortable as Michael was beginning to feel. Freddy Parc appeared to be a contemporary of young MJ Barrett although he made no secret of having a son in college—the boy being a product of Parc's first wife. Parc's current wife was his third or fourth—Michael had lost count. It was said that Parc married every time it was rumored he was getting it off with one of his male models.

Tonight he wore his own designer jeans and a ruffled formal shirt that was all the rage last year and Michael feared was making a comeback. Parc was fashionably thin, fashionably tanned and fashionably *lifted.* He was a successful couturier, putting out a line for both men and women while his perfume and men's cologne commanded their own counters in the better department stores. It had been rumored that Freddy Parc was going to put out a line of condoms, in designer tones, with an ad campaign that boasted, "Freddy is into everything." Thankfully, this remained a rumor.

MJ, as befits a lawyer, was in tie and jacket, which accentuated his discomfort.

"I suppose you're wondering what this is all about," Aldridge stated with a wave of his hand to encompass his three guests.

"Could it have anything to do with my visit to Tony Vasquez a few hours ago?" Michael responded.

"Why don't you help yourself to a drink," Aldridge invited, "and then we'll talk."

There was a bar set up on a sideboard where Michael helped himself to a glass of white wine, not daring anything stronger on an empty stomach. Spotting a bowl of peanuts, he grabbed a handful before joining the party and taking a chair opposite the couch. Catching MJ's eye, Michael winked. MJ responded with a hopeless shrug of his suited shoulders.

In an effort to shorten the suspense and MJ's agony, Michael plunged right in with, "I'm not butting into your business, Josh. I'm trying to help clear Paul, who's in a lousy position thanks to his house key."

"We're all concerned for Paul," Parc said.

"Really?" Michael questioned. "You haven't been near him since this thing happened."

"You must understand my position, Michael," Parc exploded. "I don't know what the outcome of this affair will be and I've been advised to take a wait-and-see stance. Paul represents my company and I have an obligation to a higher power—my stockholders. That's why I wanted Paul's lawyer present at this meeting, to hear firsthand what Josh and I have to say."

Pleased to know why he had been summoned, MJ delivered his opening lawyer line, "Paul Monroe has not been accused of anything."

"I'm not saying he has, but I want it made clear that the business deal I entered into with Josh has nothing to do with Paul Monroe or the death of that unfortunate girl," Parc announced.

Aldridge raised his hand in the air in the manner of a student seeking permission to speak. Not waiting to be called upon, he said, "We're not here to argue but to state some facts for Michael's clarification."

Sampling the wine—it was a very good wine—Michael said, "I'm listening."

"About a year ago," Aldridge began, "Freddy came to me with a proposition. He wanted to put money into a film for the purpose of diversification."

"It makes good business sense," Parc injected.

With a nod at Parc, Aldridge continued, "Avery, the photographer who worked for Freddy, was taking photos in Montauk with an eye to producing an art book. He thought the area a perfect location for a film. I took a group of men—"

"Business associates of mine," Parc again interrupted. "Men interested in investing in our project."

Aldridge picked up where he left off. "I took the group on a fishing jaunt out of Montauk the way public relations people take the press on junkets—to arouse their interest. It's no secret that I met Bill Ryan on that fishing boat. I thought him a diamond in the rough and gave him my card. Surprisingly enough, he turned up in my office a few months later. Freddy was putting on a contest for a model to tout his line of men's briefs—"

"We were going to rig the contest." Obviously unable to keep his mouth shut, Parc took the floor. "First Avery left my employ so it wouldn't look too suspicious when Bill won. After, Avery took Bill's composite for the contest. We had ten finalists. Eight of them were also-rans. We put Paul in to make it look like a real contest and get royally screwed. The judges insisted on interviewing the finalists. Some crap about choosing the total man and not just a handsome face. That did it. Up against Paul's natural charisma Bill came off like a retard."

Michael was thinking that Vicky had not been off the mark when she said Freddy Parc would back a picture featuring his model showing off Freddy Parc's complete line. In effect, an advertisement for Freddy Parc Enterprises that people paid to see. As much as Michael loathed the idea he had to admit it was one hell of a gimmick.

Aldridge took up the story. "Avery flew to the coast on business and ran into Tony Vasquez. He showed Tony the photos he'd taken of Bill and asked Tony to come up with a scenario to go with the image Bill's photos projected. Tony did, and we liked it. Having lost the contest, I put together the showcase for Bill and Lisa, hoping to launch Bill from Broadway rather than billboard and magazine ads." Aldridge spread his arms. "Finis."

Like hell it is, Michael almost shouted but managed to keep his cool. "Who are the men interested in the project?" he asked Parc.

"Just businessmen who prefer to remain in the background like most venture capitalists," Parc answered. "But as you can see, none of this has anything to do with that girl's murder. She was meeting Bill for personal family reasons and some madman got her. The bastard used one of my products for his own perverted reasons."

"How did the murderer get into and out of the house?" MJ asked, saving Michael the trouble.

"That's for the police to figure out, not us," Adridge said. "All we wanted to do today was clear the air as to our interest in Bill Ryan." When no one answered, he elaborated, "And if Bill refuses to go back into the show our interest may by terminated."

"Why?" Michael argued. "As you must know, Bill is a mimic, not an actor, and good actors, especially young and handsome actors, are begging for roles."

"There's a time factor." Parc spoke for Aldridge. "We would have to find someone, groom him and then present him to our backers. These men are gamblers who move fast and have already waited a year for this deal to come to fruition. They won't wait another year."

"But we haven't given up on Bill," Aldridge quickly got in. "We might still be able to talk him into staying with the show and with us."

Here, Parc rose. Assuming the air of a CEO on the run, he glanced at his designer wristwatch and announced his departure. "It was good seeing you, Michael, and you, MJ. I hope this meeting cleared the air." The latter was directed solely at Michael.

Michael and MJ also got up to shake Parc's hand. "It doesn't help Paul's cause," Michael said.

"No, I'm afraid it doesn't. And don't forget, I've a vested interest in Paul, too. If necessary I'll supply all the legal help he may need."

Bastard, Michael fumed as his eyes followed Parc to the front door and watched as Parc spoke quietly to Aldridge before taking his leave. Michael and MJ refused Aldridge's offer of another drink and without even an attempt at making small talk they headed for the door.

Aldridge thanked them both for coming and politely cautioned,

"Everything we discussed is confidential." On this final note the meeting ended.

Once outside, Michael said to MJ, "Did you enjoy your stroll down the garden path?"

"What the hell was that all about?" MJ demanded.

"It's a long story and I've had a long day and nothing to eat since breakfast. I'll tell you everything I know tomorrow."

"Great. I come in on the middle of the movie and now you tell me I have to leave before it ends. Why was I invited?"

"To bear witness to their innocence."

"I imagine that will make sense when you fill me in?"

"Promise," Michael said.

"One question?"

"One, and make it short," Michael answered.

"Can I invite Paul to dinner?"

"As his lawyer or—"

"Objection," MJ challenged.

"Overruled." Michael got into his Rolls and backed out of the driveway.

Having no intention of doing anything that evening except enjoying one of Maddy's delectable dinners, discussing the day's events with Vicky and going to bed early, Michael skirted the circular driveway that would leave him at his front door and drove the Rolls directly into the garage at the rear of the house. Tomorrow he would, or would not, tell Eddy Evans what he now believed was fact. Aldridge's package was being financed by dirty money. Most likely because he owed his suppliers big, Freddy Parc was acting as their beard and Avery, in his usual role, was the gofer.

What could Eddy and his boss, Oliveri, do about this not so remarkable discovery? Zilch—that's what. If the United States government was unable to cut off the drug cartels and their numerous tentacles, what could the EHPD do about them? Besides, it seemed clear from his meeting with Aldridge and Parc that their wheeling and dealing, however bogus, had nothing to do with Heather Ryan's murder.

Coming in the back door, Michael followed his nose to the kitchen and peeked in. A rib roast surrounded by potatoes, quartered, awaited the oven, and several aromatic pots bubbled on the range. Michael sniffed the air in blissful anticipation. "Ambrosia," he sighed.

Maddy turned from her stove and barked, "They're in the drawing room."

Michael's stomach did a nosedive. When Joseph Kirkpatrick was alive, Maddy's verbal delivery had been a reliable barometer of the old man's mood. Were he alive, Michael would guess from the house-keeper's tone that Kirk was on a rampage. Being dead, that left only Vicky and Paul to cause such anxiety.

"What's wrong, Maddy?"

"I don't know for sure. You best get in there." Translation: *I wasn't able to hear everything but from what I did hear it sounds like a lulu.*

Since converting the den into their summer offices, Michael and Vicky avoided that room when not working and gathered in the more formal drawing room for cocktails before dinner. When Michael walked into the room Paul leaped out of his chair, spilling a good bit of the drink in his hand, and shouted, "Heather Ryan was killed by the mob!"

"Good grief," Michael moaned, "what now?"

"Paul," Vicky scolded like an irate mother at her wits' end, "sit down and calm down."

"What are you talking about?" Michael cried.

"If I didn't light a cigarette today," Vicky proclaimed, "I never will. First Amanda and now Paul's revelation."

"Let's all stop talking at once," Michael ordered, "and tell me what's happened."

Paul, his blue eyes febrile, regained his seat and told Michael, "Bill and his father were drug runners for the mob."

Michael sank into a chair. "Jesus! Who told you that?"

"You look awful, Michael," Vicky remarked.

John entered with a tray supporting one very dry martini in a crystal stem glass. "Not now, John," Michael said with a wave of his hand.

"Better take it," Vicky advised. "You're going to need it."

Vicky had her martini and Paul was drinking a concoction he called a Seven and Seven. A combination of 7UP and a shot of Seagram's 7 Crown whiskey, the sight of which turned Michael's stomach when he had something in it to turn. Michael took the drink from John's tray and John departed—but not very far.

The excitement Michael's entrance had created seemed to ebb with John's arrival and departure, affording Michael the opportunity to ask, "Now, Paul, what is this all about?"

Now more composed and perhaps embarrassed by his outburst, Paul answered, "Bill confessed everything to me. He's going to the police tomorrow. That's what Heather was going to do. That's why Avery killed her."

"Don't say that, Paul," Vicky reprimanded. "We don't know who murdered Heather Ryan."

Once more calling for quiet, Michael said to Paul, "Take a deep breath and tell me what Bill confessed to—and start from the beginning."

Given the spotlight, the excited boy became the suave storyteller, keeping his audience spellbound in the process. In spite of what he was hearing, Michael reveled in Paul's ability to command an audience. Paul Monroe would have won the Freddy Parc contest even if he wasn't so exceedingly attractive.

Michael listened without saying a word until Paul got to the part where Eddy Evans paid a call on the Ryan household.

"Eddy!" Michael roared.

"Eddy," Vicky said. "That's what he knows that you don't."

Michael drank his martini.

"Heather called Bill the day of the play's opening," Paul ended, "and told him that she was going to the police. Bill arranged to meet her and—Well, the rest you know."

Michael was shaking his head. The drug connection had everything to do with Heather Ryan's death. "But Avery didn't do it," he said aloud. "He was at the theater that night."

"So was Josh Aldridge," Vicky reminded him.

"And Freddy Parc was at home," Michael said, "with a houseful of company."

"And I was at the cottage with a key in my pocket," Paul murmured.

"Don't worry, Paul. When the police hear this they'll get off your case," Michael said, sounding relieved.

"But how did they get into the cottage?" Paul griped.

"Now that the police know why Heather was murdered, it will make it easier for them to figure out how it was done. When did you say Bill was going to the police?"

"In the morning," Paul answered.

"Good. We can have a nice meal and get a good night's rest before the ship hits the sand. The police are aware of Avery's presence in Montauk and his link to Bill Ryan. They'll pick him up as soon as they hear what Bill has to tell them." There being nothing more he could do at present, Michael began to enjoy his martini and wondered vocally, "Was Lisa with you when Bill opened up?"

"No. He wants me to tell her," Paul said. "I'll call her after dinner. This just might be the end of that romance. He wanted her to give up everything and share a fishing boat with him in Montauk—the crazy clam digger. Wait till she hears this."

"Wait till Aldridge hears this," Michael said with a smile of pure satisfaction.

"He probably already knows," Paul stated.

"What?" Now it was Michael leaping out of his chair. "What did you say?"

Looking startled, Paul said, "Mr. Aldridge must already know. Bill was going to call him after he talked to me. I mean, it's only fair that Mr. Aldridge should hear it before Bill goes public. Bill owes him that much."

"When did you leave Bill?" Michael asked Paul.

"About an hour ago," Paul said. "I got here just before you. What's the matter?"

An hour ago. Just when the meeting at Aldridge's had broken up. If Bill got through to Aldridge as soon as Michael and MJ left the house, that gave Aldridge about one hour to act. Going for the phone, Michael yelled, "I've got to speak to Eddy."

"What's wrong?" Paul tried again.

Ashen, Vicky was now on her feet. "Michael, do you think Josh will call Avery and Avery will go after Bill? Good lord—like Heather?"

"It's too late for that. They'll know Bill talked to Paul and one leak is fatal for that crowd. All Avery can do now is run."

"They'll pick him up on the expressway," Vicky speculated, not hiding her joy at the thought.

Joining the others, Paul was up and pleading, "Would someone tell me what's going on? Is Bill in danger?"

Michael dialed the operator and asked her to connect him to the East Hampton police. Waiting, he called over his shoulder, "Bill is safe and Avery is in cahoots with Aldridge . . ." Breaking off abruptly he spoke to the desk sergeant who had picked up after one ring. "This is Michael Reo. Is Detective Evans there or Lieutenant Oliveri? . . . Is there a way of contacting them? . . . Take my number and have either of them call me as soon as possible. It's in connection with the murder of Heather Ryan. Thank you."

"Mr. Aldridge is a drug runner?" Paul sank back in his chair.

"No, Paul," Vicky answered. "It's more complicated than that. Just sit tight for now and have another Seven and Seven."

Michael was rummaging through his wallet. "Got it. Eddy's home phone number, and his cell phone number."

Vicky noticed Maddy and John standing in the doorway. How long they had been there was questionable. "The roast is in the oven, Miss Vicky. Dinner will be ready in twenty minutes—if you're having dinner."

Everyone turned their attention to Michael as he spoke to Eddy Evans's voice mail. "Eddy? Michael Reo. It's about seven. P.M., that is. Call me as soon as you get this message. I left a message at the station house, too. It's important." Punching out more numbers, then waiting impatiently, Michael told his listeners, "He's not answering his cell phone." With that, he left Eddy another message.

"Are we having dinner, Michael?" Vicky asked.

"You bet we are. Medium rare, Maddy, and the potatoes crispy." The phone rang and they all started, then froze as Michael rushed to answer it. "Michael Reo here. . . . MJ?" He listened, not speaking a word as Vicky, Paul, John and Maddy held their breath. Seconds later he told the caller, "I'm on my way," then broke the connection.

Michael turned to his audience. "That was MJ. He got word that something is happening in Montauk. The police are all over West Lake Drive, converging on Job's Fishing Lodge."

"I'm coming with you," Vicky said.

"So am I." Paul was again on his feet.

"The roast will be well done by the time you get back," Maddy warned the fleeing trio.

BILL RYAN

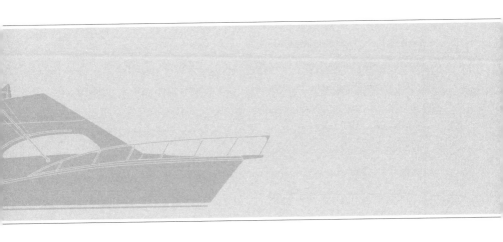

CHAPTER TWENTY-SIX

The cabin dwellers who congregated day and night on their doorsteps, gossiping and drinking Coca-Cola, were awed into silence and abstinence by the black Mercedes speeding up the driveway and coming to an abrupt halt at the door over which the letters I-C-E were prominently, if misleadingly, displayed. In their native land those who drove expensive black cars were to be respected and shunned. This reaction to the car's sudden appearance on their turf proved that their language was not the only thing they had carried over the border.

Standing at the kitchen window, Job ordered, "Let me handle this, you hear?"

Coming up beside Job, Bill watched Avery get out of the car and head for the door. "What does he want?"

"He don't look too happy. Maybe he heard that you're planning on tossing him into jail first thing tomorrow."

"He couldn't," Bill answered, not sounding as certain as his words implied.

Avery came into the house without bothering to knock, an impudence that riled Bill, and marched straight into the kitchen but, in spite of this insolence, his insufferable swagger had been reduced to a furtive strut and his usually mocking stare replaced with what could only be fear. Bill thought that if he were responsible for this dramatic change in the Ryan family's nemesis, he could die happy.

"So," Avery lashed out at Bill as he came through the doorway, "what happened to your sister wasn't enough for you. No, you have to pick up where she left off, you stupid bastard."

Bill went for Avery, his arms raised, but Job grabbed him by the waist and pulled him back with an amazing show of strength. "I don't know what you're talking about," Bill shouted at Avery, "but get the fuck out of here before I kill you."

Job pushed Bill back against the refrigerator and held him there, again exhibiting the fact that the vigor of his youth had not gone the way of his looks. "I told you to let me handle this," he barked into Bill's face. With their eyes locked on each other in a hypnotic gaze, Job mouthed the words, "You understand?"

Taking courage from Job's stance between Bill and himself, Avery responded, "You don't know what I'm talking about? Spare me the bullshit, you crazy fool." Avery's pallid skin seemed to have broken out in strawberry-colored patches. "You go blabbing to everyone you know that you're going to the police in the morning and you have the balls to tell me you don't know what I'm talking about?" Making sure that Job was keeping Bill pinned against the refrigerator door, Avery kicked a chair away from the kitchen table and ranted, "You are a fuck-ing misfit—an idiot—a goddamned prick and screwing machine."

Bill kept his eyes glued on Job but the man's expression was inscrutable. "You understand," Job kept mouthing into Bill's face with his head turned from the rabid photographer. All Bill understood was that a few moments ago he and Job had been seated at the kitchen table, discussing what tomorrow might bring when Bill went to the police—and now they were involved in a brawl with the man Bill hoped he would never see again outside a court of law. Job had raised no objec-tions to Bill's resolve to turn himself in to the cop Eddy Evans. As Heather had tried to communicate her plans to Bill before going to the police, so now Bill was giving Job the opportunity to join him or run.

Bill told Job he could take the nest egg (most of it in cash and hidden in the house) they had amassed while on Avery's payroll and disappear or he could take his chances, along with Bill, on being granted immunity for turning informer. Bill found a certain justice in using the money to shield Job while Avery took the fall. Job had said that he had no intention of leaving Montauk but he did not say that he would go to the police with Bill, nor what he might do if he didn't.

And Job wasn't drinking, which upset Bill more than if he were downing a six-pack per hour. The man was strangely sullen and focused on something only he could see, reminding Bill of the day he had found Job sitting in Bick's with Avery. The day Job had vowed to kill Avery.

Besides Job, Bill had confided his plans to Paul Monroe and Mr. Aldridge. He immediately dismissed any thought of Paul talking to Avery. Paul hardly knew Avery, but Mr. Aldridge knew him. He had hired Avery to take Bill's composite. Bill's mind raced back to last summer when Mr. Aldridge and his business associates had charted *Job's Patience* and a week later Avery had turned up at their front door. At the time, Bill had thought that a theatrical agent and a fashion photographer were in the same fraternity. "Mr. Aldridge knows everything," he said, not realizing that he had spoken aloud.

Taking his fury out once more on the chair he had toppled, Avery now kicked it across the room. "Fool. Damn fool," Avery repeated. "How many times do I have to tell you that you don't know dick and if you don't know dick you should keep your mouth shut and do as you're told. Look what happened to Heather."

With that, Job's fingers pressed painfully into Bill's chest as he held him fast to the refrigerator door. "What do you want from us?" Job asked, turning to look at Avery.

"You," Avery pointed. "I want you to get me the fuck out of here—now—on your damn boat."

Bill felt Job's hand relax, then drop to his side. He was released, but he kept his back glued to the refrigerator door, never taking his eyes off Job. "Where are we going?" Job asked.

"The usual meeting place. They'll be waiting for us."

"What about the boy?"

"Job . . ." Bill shouted.

"He stays," Avery said. "He has a date with the police, remember? Only by the time he gets there he'll be the only one left to arrest."

Taking hold of Job's arm, Bill implored, "Don't do it, Job."

With a wink, Job chuckled, "What don't you want me to do, kid?"

Bill tugged on the arm he was holding. "Stay with me, Job."

"Suppose I don't go without the boy?" Job challenged.

Avery removed a revolver from his jacket pocket. "If you think I don't know how to use this, you're right. I'm also in a rush and nervous."

At the sight of the weapon, Job stiffened. He had often told Bill that weekend yachtsmen—Job's term for the pilots of pleasure crafts—were more dangerous at sea than hurricanes and tidal waves. On dry land, trying to reason with a frightened man holding a loaded gun that seemed to scare him more than the person he was threatening was suicide.

With a shrug, Job touched Bill's cheek. "I changed my mind, kid. I'm gonna beat it." Then he did something he had never done before. He placed his hands on Bill's shoulders and kissed him on the mouth.

Standing tall and proud as he always did when bringing *Job's Patience* out of its slip and into Lake Montauk, Job tooted his horn playfully and raised his cap to the few people strolling the pier. His passenger was seated on the wooden bench that was affixed to both sides of the cabin, looking askance at the attention Job was drawing to their departure. From the moment he had arrived at the lodge, Avery had not once exhibited the pompous and effeminate pose he enjoyed using with the Ryan men, confronting them instead with the man behind the mask. A man of great ambition, little talent and no scruples.

An hour or less before sunset, the boat headed toward the inlet that would take it into Long Island Sound. Job could see the late afternoon crowd departing Gosman's Dock mingling for a time with the arrival of the early diners. Starboard was Gin Beach, beginning to empty save for a few youngsters who waved when Job tooted once again.

"Can't you keep your hand off that fucking cord?" Avery called out.

"Aboard this craft I give the orders, not take them. If you're unhappy it's just a ten-minute swim to the beach."

Silence. Then Avery was at the helm, next to Job. "Don't be a wiseass. I can't swim. Which reminds me—where are the life pre-servers?"

"Lift the bench seat and you'll find a few dozen of them."

Avery extracted a cigarette from his pack. Striking a match he cupped it to hold the flame and succeeded in igniting the tobacco. Wiping his forehead with the back of his hand he asked, "Is it always this choppy?"

His eyes straight ahead, Job answered, "Choppy? It's a piece of glass."

Puffing nervously, Avery watched the boats passing them, on their way back to port, and looked as if he wished they were headed in the same direction. Suddenly he began haranguing Job. "You got yourself into this mess—you and your kids. No one twisted your arm. You could have said no."

"I blame no one but myself," Job told him. "I got in on my own, but when I wanted out you wouldn't let me go."

"Out?" Avery sneered. "There is no way out of this business. It's a lifetime commitment." For good measure he added, "And I didn't kill your girl."

"But you ordered it."

"Think what you will."

"I think," Job said, "that if I never met you Heather would be alive today."

With a wave of disgust, Avery turned away. "You have anything to drink on this tub?"

"If you're not feeling well a drink won't make it better."

"Anyplace to lie down?"

"Try the bench; it's the best we've got."

As they progressed there were fewer and fewer boats in the immediate vicinity until, just halfway to Block Island, they were alone on the water except for a few ships outlined on the horizon beneath a red sky. Heather often referred to the spot as "the point of no return," giving the position a sense of impending doom and adding a little spice to the trip for their more gullible fares.

Job cut the engine and spoke to the darkening sky, his blue eyes clouded with tears. "The point of no return, girl. The point of no return."

Avery was not on the bench but hanging over the rail. The man was so tall he appeared to be bent in two with only the bottom half visible. Job Ryan tossed back his head and laughed as he marched purposely toward the pant legs that looked to contain stilts. With one clean sweep he took hold of Avery's ankles as if they were the handles of a wheelbarrow and heaved the man with one name headfirst into the sea.

There was a cry—or was it the wind?—and then nothing.

Job Ryan raised his face to the sky now drained of all color and drank in the scent of sea air, enjoying for a few minutes the feel of *Job's Patience* bobbing eagerly, as if in a hurry to move on.

Job had always said he wanted to be buried at sea, off the deck of *Job's Patience*—and he never did give an inchworm's ass for an audience.

MICHAEL ANTHONY REO

CHAPTER TWENTY-SEVEN

The four men sat at a table in Fierro's Restaurant & Pizza off Newtown Lane in East Hampton, where they had agreed to share two large pies. It wasn't Maddy's rib roast and roasted potatoes but for Michael it was a feast fit for an Italian/American king.

Paul and Vicky had stayed in Montauk with Bill Ryan, hoping to convince Bill to return to the Dunemere Lane house with them, if just for that evening. To Michael's surprise, Oliveri had invited him and MJ to share one of Mr. Fierro's pies. It was Michael who had insisted on ordering two.

Leaving Vicky the Rolls, Michael got a ride back to East Hampton with MJ, giving him the opportunity to brief MJ on all the facts, as he had promised he would do, before they rejoined the policemen.

Once seated, Oliveri and Eddy told their story, giving Michael time to devour two slices without having to stop to make polite sounds. Reaching for a third, but far from sated, Michael said, "Aldridge tipped off Avery as soon as he got Bill's call. His picture deal is being financed with drug money and Freddy Parc is fronting for them. Avery was the bag man."

"Try and prove it," Eddy responded.

"The narcotics boys knew about Job's trips from day one," Oliveri said. "They didn't stop him because they were after bigger fish—namely, Job's East Hampton connection. Avery's cover was so perfect they failed to connect him with Job until Bill Ryan left Montauk. A photographer taking pictures for an art book. What could be more natural? After the raid in Sag Harbor, they kept their eyes on Bill all the way to New York. There they discovered Bill's benefactor was a friend of Avery's. The link was too good to ignore. From then on they included Avery in their surveillance but he was very clever. By that I mean he never got his hands dirty. They would have had a hard time putting together a case against him.

"Of course, we never knew about Avery until Eddy's girl, Helen, told us Heather was asking questions about him."

Keeping pace with Michael slice for slice, Eddy smiled with unabashed pride. Oliveri, of course, ate modestly, dabbing at his mouth with a paper napkin after each bite. MJ gave up after his second slice, concentrating on the conversation instead.

Eddy said to Michael, "I asked you who Avery was, hoping you would take the hint and work up a dossier on him—which you did."

Oliveri continued, "I blame the narcotics people for playing this so close to the vest until the very last minute. They believed Heather's murder was drug related but when they learned the details, they balked. Her secret meeting with Bill and the fact that she was pregnant made it look like a domestic case. Only Bill, Lisa and Paul had keys to the cottage and their chief suspect, Avery, was at the theater that night."

"Job couldn't care less about the locked cottage or Avery's airtight alibi," Eddy stated. "He held Avery responsible for Heather's death, ignoring the fact that his greed opened the door to Avery and his friends. When Avery arrived at the lodge today and ordered Job to take him out on the boat, Job couldn't have been happier. Bill thinks Job was trying to put together a scheme to lure Avery onto *Job's Patience* and Avery played right into his hands. Job had a plan, all right. He even wrote out a will days before, leaving everything to Bill.

"Avery refused to take Bill, which was fine with Job, and Bill called us as soon as they left. We contacted the Shore Patrol but they were too far to get there in time to intercept them."

"Why was Bill so important to Aldridge's movie?" MJ asked.

"For control," Michael answered. "Oh, I'm sure Aldridge thought he had a diamond in the rough, as he called Bill—and he's been looking for a personality he could turn into a star for years. If Bill did make it big, which I personally doubt would have happened, Aldridge and his associates could keep Bill in bondage because of the boy's involvement with the drug trade. They also had Job Ryan in a straitjacket for the same reason. Only poor Heather upset the apple cart."

"Will this be the end of the film deal?" was MJ's next question.

"No doubt," Michael said. "With their bag man exposed, Job's and Bill's involvement made public and Job's daughter murdered, the police are too close for comfort. They'll dump Aldridge and, for now, Freddy Parc, but never fear, if they want to put money into a film there are no end of hopeful producers waiting in line."

Abandoning his second slice of pizza after a few nibbles, Oliveri touched his napkin to his lips and told MJ, "But their operation on the East End has been seriously crippled, thanks to Avery's SOS to the *Billy Budd*. When the Shore Patrol boarded it they found a half dozen big shots as well as the crew waiting to rescue Avery. They've all been taken into custody."

MJ listened, nodded solemnly and wondered, "But what has all this got to do with Heather's murder?"

This astute question put a moratorium on the chatter and the chewing. Michael broke the spell. "I wonder if Avery knew Heather was meeting with Bill that night."

Without waiting for a cue from Oliveri, Eddy told Michael, "We knew because Bill left a message on Heather's answering machine, which we confiscated when we searched her room. But Job's phone was being tapped—not by the police—so Avery must have got the same message."

"And if he suspected what Heather was up to . . ." MJ let his thought go unfinished.

Eddy articulated what they were all thinking. "Avery was at the theater that night."

Reluctantly, Michael said, "Everyone was at the theater that night."

"Everyone except Paul," Oliveri announced ominously.

"You have no case against Paul," MJ countered. "He didn't even know the girl, and even if he did, Paul had nothing to lose if she was going to blab to the police. Her murder was drug-related."

As if talking to himself, Michael said, "That's it, MJ—who had the most to lose if Heather went to the police? Avery, naturally. He would have been arrested on the spot. She didn't know one person Avery was fronting for and neither did her father or Bill. Heather Ryan's confession would have placed only Avery in jeopardy."

"Avery was at the theater that night," Oliveri repeated the mantra, "and I doubt if his colleagues would chance a murder to save his skin, even if they did have a key to that cottage." His tone made it clear that the last word on the subject had just been spoken. The congenial atmosphere that had prevailed when the four had entered Fierro's was suddenly as cold as the untouched pizza slices on their tin trays.

"I invited you and Mr. Barrett here to bring closure to our association." Oliveri spoke to Michael as Eddy examined the huge map of Long Island on the pizza parlor's wall. "It's no secret that I'm not overjoyed at your hiring Eddy to moonlight on your film project, and I don't particularly like discussing police business with civilians. However, Mr. Reo, I did ask for your input the other day and I'm grateful for what you had to tell us. Now that one aspect of this case has come to an end—a tragic end at that—I suggest you keep your counsel and we'll keep ours."

"You mean the party is over," Michael joked in an attempt at levity.

"I mean leave Heather Ryan's murder to us, Mr. Reo." With that, Oliveri rose. "We had better get back to the station, Eddy. They'll be waiting for us. Good evening, Mr. Reo. Mr. Barrett."

Tearing himself away from the map of Long Island and with an apologetic shrug of his shoulders, Eddy followed his boss out of the restaurant.

"My stomach hurts," Michael complained when the pair were gone.

"It should," MJ said without sympathy. "You ate like a peasant."

"And Lieutenant Oliveri ate like a bird."

"The man has class, Michael. The man has great class."

CHAPTER TWENTY-EIGHT

"Carrot juice," Amanda Richards boasted to the group assembled on the Reos' back patio the day after the shocking events in Montauk. "From now until the moment they film my last close-up I am on a regimen that would tax a Trappist monk. Diet, exercise and meditation under the supervision of the latest guru who claims to have the secret of perpetual youth."

"Or," Paul suggested, "you could be filmed through cotton gauze as all the older . . ." He stopped, but not in the dramatic nick of time. In the thunderous silence, a golfer, on the other side of the tall privet hedge that separates the Dunemere Lane house from the Maidstone Club's green, let out a cry of either joy or anguish.

MJ Barrett looked deeply into his Bloody Mary, Lisa Kennedy looked at her fingernails, Vicky and Michael looked at each other— and Amanda burst into laughter. "He's adorable," the actress proclaimed, alleviating the tension but not Paul's scarlet face. "But we may have to stuff his mouth with gauze before the director calls it a wrap."

Fearing Paul would apologize and prolong the moment, Michael steered the conversation to a more somber theme. "I wish Bill had come this afternoon," he said. "You know I never did get a chance to meet him."

"He's at his home," Lisa said, "and I think it's comforting for him to be there. Paul and I met his friends and neighbors so I know he won't starve or want for company. They rally around in times like these and don't pry."

Turning to MJ, Paul asked, "Will he be arrested?"

"No. But the police will question him endlessly and to no avail. He doesn't know anything the narcotics people don't know. Michael has retained me to represent him."

"That's very generous of you, Michael," Amanda said, lighting a cigarette—a vice her regimen obviously did not curtail. "And thank you for saying you would consider Lisa for our film. Joshua will be thrilled, and the young people can use a little good news after all that's happened." In spite of her earlier acerbic harping on Lisa's beauty and lack of talent, Amanda was ready to give her fellow artist a break in true show business fashion with not a trace of envy or jealousy. It was the gesture of a dedicated performer.

"I'm overwhelmed, Mr. Reo," Lisa joined in.

"Please remember, I said I would test you," Michael warned. "How you test will determine the outcome. And I do have other actresses in mind."

"I'm grateful for the consideration," Lisa said.

"We'll be filming in East Hampton," Vicky reminded Lisa. "If you do make the cut you'll be near Bill. Who knows, you may even get to like it here so much you won't want to leave."

"Paul and I will both be able to watch over our Bill," Lisa answered, making it clear that friendship, not romance, prompted the offering. "Ian Edwards is interested in going into partnership with Bill to develop the lodge property, so he'll be busy with something he loves, not prancing around a stage."

"And Ian has an unmarried kid sister," Paul again spoke his mind.

With a threatening look at Paul, Michael predicted, "I take it Aldridge will post closing notices for the showcase."

"I knew that play was ill-fated from the night it opened," Amanda told the group. "I told Joshua it was bad luck for the producer to go backstage on opening night. It's just not done."

"A pity," Vicky said. "It's a nice little show, and we thought you were wonderful, Lisa."

"Excuse me," Michael interrupted, "but what did you say, Amanda?"

"About what?"

"About Aldridge being backstage. Wasn't he sitting with you?"

Puffing happily, Amanda elaborated, "He was as nervous as a cat because they were having technical problems which delayed the curtain. The minute the house lights went out, Joshua flew backstage to make sure everything was in working order—and he stayed there until a few minutes before the play ended."

"Did you see him backstage, Lisa?" Michael questioned.

"I was on stage more than off, but I did see him back there and I remember him going out the stage door for a smoke. Why?"

"Michael . . ." Vicky uttered, but was silenced by a wave of her husband's hand.

Putting down his drink, Michael went on questioning Lisa, "And where was your house key?"

"In my purse."

"And your purse was in your dressing room." Michael did not ask but stated. "And Bill's street clothes were in the men's dressing room." Without waiting for an answer, Michael was out of his seat and heading into the house.

"Michael, what are you up to?" Vicky called after him.

Without turning, he shouted, "Excuse me," and was gone. In the den he dialed Eddy's cell phone number. When the detective identified himself Michael dispensed with a polite greeting and gushed, "What are you doing?"

"I'm home, cleaning out the basement. I just unearthed a Valentine card a girl put on my desk in the sixth grade."

"Cute," Michael said. "I'm going to ask you two questions, Eddy, and I want answers."

"I hope it's not about Heather's murder, Mr. Reo."

"It is, Eddy. And if Oliveri gives you the sack I'll make you my assistant producer."

"I don't want to be an assistant producer," Eddy assured Michael. "I want to be a policeman."

Strange. None of the East Hampton locals wanted to be a star—and who could blame them? "How long would it take you to get from the John Drew to Amagansett in the evening, remembering the light and the traffic going through East Hampton?"

After a pause, Eddy said, "I wouldn't go along Main Street. The theater's parking lot opens to Pond View Lane. I would go south on Pond View to Further Lane and straight to Bluff Road in Amagansett. Then I could take any of the Amagansett lanes into the town—no lights, and very little traffic. I could do it in five minutes."

"And who told you that there might be another man in Heather Ryan's life—other than Ian Edwards?"

With undisguised anguish, Eddy begged, "I can't."

"Was it your friend Jan? Aldridge's secretary."

Eddy's audible sigh told Michael what he wanted to know. "Put down your Valentine, call Lieutenant Oliveri and both of you meet me at the home of Joshua Aldridge. He's in Wainscott."

Frustrated, Eddy whined, "Why, Mr. Reo?"

"To arrest him for the murder of Heather Ryan."

When Michael put down the phone and turned he found Vicky, Amanda, MJ, Paul, Lisa, John, Maddy and Ms. Johnson bunched together in the doorway, staring at him.

With an accusing finger Michael pointed and shouted, "*J'accuse!*"

Ms. Johnson clutched her bosom and screamed.

Michael pulled up to the house on the former potato field and before he was out of his car Aldridge appeared at the front door. "Amanda is driving you crazy and you've come to register a formal complaint with her agent." Aldridge spoke as Michael walked up the path to the door.

"No. Amanda told me you spent more time backstage than in the seat next to her the night your play opened."

Aldridge's hospitable smile became a frown, but other than that he showed no sign of surprise or disquiet at Michael's statement. Stepping aside he invited, "Please come in?"

Michael followed the agent into the house. "Would you like a drink?" Aldridge offered.

"This isn't a social call."

"I gathered it wasn't but if you don't mind, I'll have one." Aldridge went to the bar and poured whiskey into a glass. He drank without diluting it.

"I could forgive you anything," Michael said, "but trying to frame an innocent boy."

"I don't know what you're talking about," Aldridge said.

"You were backstage that night. Not in your seat."

"Is there a law against that?"

As if Aldridge had not spoken, Michael proceeded, "You had your choice of keys. Lisa's or Bill's, both with their street clothes in their dressing rooms. You went out the back door as if you were going for a cigarette and drove to the cottage to meet Heather Ryan. When you returned to the theater you replaced the key. Did you also arrange for the lighting failure to delay the opening curtain, making certain the play would still be running when Heather Ryan got to the cottage?

"Five minutes there and back and ten to do the job. Twenty minutes in all and no one would miss you. Backstage they would think you had gone to your seat, and Amanda believed you were backstage throughout the performance."

Aldridge sat and pointed to a chair for Michael's use. When

Michael continued to stand, Aldridge said, "What are you doing here?" One had to admire Aldridge's composure in light of Michael's accusations, and Michael now understood how such a man could commit a murder and host a party all in the same night.

"Avery told you that Heather Ryan was going to blow his cover and where and when she was going to meet Bill to discuss her move. I imagine he also told you how you could stop her and get away with it. Avery had that kind of a mind. If you didn't take his suggestion, he would have been history before the sun rose the next day. The operation here would have been stopped, temporarily, and only poor Job and Bill would have been taken into custody.

"I wondered who had the most to lose if Heather had gone to the police. Avery was the logical candidate, but I was wrong. Knowing in advance what Heather was up to, Avery had time to run and his friends had time to withdraw and regroup. But if Avery disappeared so would Freddy Parc and his bankers. Your dream of a lifetime—the chance to produce a film and create a star—shattered because of Heather Ryan. I think the only coincidence in all this was your taking an interest in the son of the man Avery had hired to fetch his dope on the high seas, but how nicely that, too, fit in with your scheme."

Raising his glass Aldridge said, "You sound like a writer hawking a story to a disinterested producer."

Shrugging off the comment, Michael shouted, "You hated Paul's guts from the moment he won the contest, in spite of all you and Parc did to rig it in Bill's favor."

Aldridge applauded silently. "You have that right."

"You used the Freddy Parc jockstrap to point a finger at Paul but I think the locked cottage was pure luck. When Bill told you there was another man in Heather's life, you passed it on to your secretary even though Bill later denied it. I'm sure she told you she was a friend of the detective Eddy Evans, and you knew she would blab it to him. It was just another red herring for the police, in case they didn't get the point of the murder weapon."

Aldridge got up to pour himself another whiskey, asking Michael, "Are you sure you don't want a drink?" When he had refilled his glass, Aldridge said calmly, "You can't prove a thing."

"Circumstantial, I know, but the prosecution could make some case against you," Michael told him. "Your involvement with Freddy Parc and Avery and the company they keep would all come out in the wash."

Aldridge drank his neat whiskey and looked out the glass doors to the open field and the late afternoon sky. "Have you ever wanted anything so bad you would kill for it?"

"No," Michael said. "I never have and I hope I never will."

"Then I pity you. It's the passion that separates the winners from the bums." Aldridge opened the drawer of the sideboard that held the bar setup and removed a pistol. "Don't worry, I have a permit for this. It's very dark and lonely out here in the winter."

"Put that thing down," Michael ordered.

As if he were lecturing a class, Aldridge continued to speak, waving the pistol like a baton. "I think the jockstrap implied kinky sex—which only the tabloids hinted at—and, of course, the police would associate it with Freddy's pretty-boy model."

Faking a bit of bravado, Michael said, "You don't think I was foolish enough to come here on my own. Vicky, MJ, Amanda and Lisa know I'm here, and why. So do the police."

"Really? I guess I should believe you. But I'm not going to use this on you, Michael. Give me some credit for prudence." Aldridge pointed the pistol at his head. "How about this?"

"You won't."

"Why not?"

"Because you're a showman, Aldridge, and you can't resist the drama of a trial. Don't tell me you haven't thought of it? Thanks to you it already has a catchy name—the Jockstrap Murder. And what a lineup of witnesses. A casting director's dream. The beloved actress, Amanda Richards; the celebrated underwear maven, Freddy Parc; the infamous Hollywood director who married his son's wife, Tony Vasquez; the daughter of Joseph Kirkpatrick and her husband, Michael and Victoria Reo.

"For youth and beauty we have Lisa Kennedy, Paul Monroe and Bill Ryan." Michael endowed the finale with a flourish that was more pretense than heartfelt. "The trial of the century that will secure a place for the name of Joshua Aldridge in the annals of show business well into the new millennium." His forehead glistening, Michael took an uncertain step toward Aldridge just as a car came tearing up the driveway.

Joshua Aldridge smiled at something only he could see and lowered his hand, dropping the pistol.

EPILOGUE

The two couples occupied a booth at Meghan's, enjoying each other's company and the pub's congenial atmosphere. Only a bottle of rather good wine on their table indicated that this evening was different from other nights they had spent in their favorite local bistro.

"Tell us, Helen," Lydia Oliveri said, "why did you pick November twenty-fifth for your wedding day?"

"I wanted a late fall wedding," Helen explained, "and the twenty-fifth is the night of the new moon. A new moon, a new life, a new everything."

"How romantic," Lydia exclaimed.

Picking up his wineglass, Chris Oliveri proposed, "Here's to the happy couple and the best man, yours truly. I'm honored you asked me, Eddy. Was I your first choice?"

Eddy looked as if he were about to burst with pride, joy and embarrassment, all at the same time. "First and only choice, Chris. Who else would I have wanted?"

The lieutenant was dressed in a pair of summer slacks and a designer polo shirt, a comfortable outfit he would concede to be seen in only at Meghan's. With an impish smile he answered Eddy, "Michael Reo, for one."

"Eddy told me he was going to ask you back when we became engaged," Helen said. "Michael Reo was never considered."

Nonplussed, Eddy said, "I like Michael Reo, but he's more a business associate than a friend."

Lydia Oliveri declared, "We're here to celebrate the wedding date, not talk business."

"I know why we're here," Oliveri asserted, "but I want to say that I'm willing to eat crow along with my fried chicken. Your business associate did solve our case, thanks to his actress chum. And it was you, Eddy, who told me Reo's pals could be of help to us—and they were. The bridegroom gets the blue ribbon." Oliveri drank his wine and then topped all their glasses.

"Do you think we have a case?" Eddy asked.

"The DA didn't want to touch it until we questioned the stage crew who worked that night and one of them, outside for a smoke, remembered seeing Aldridge get into his car and drive off. He's willing to swear to it in the witness box."

"So the defense will have to come up with a reason for him leaving the theater," Helen commented, "and try to prove he didn't go to the cottage to meet Heather. If Aldridge can't come up with a witness to account for his time, he's finished."

Eddy looked at his future bride as if she had just tried the prosecution's case, and won. "Helen heard that Bill Ryan has applied to the bank for a big loan to upgrade his property and Michael Reo is going to be his guarantor."

"With the Reo money backing him," Lydia said, "they'll give Bill a blank check and tell him to fill it in."

"He wants to restore the lodge to a first-class motel and fishing paradise, as it once was," Helen told them. "Ian Edwards is going in on it with Bill."

"As it once was," Oliveri reflected. "Maybe there's hope for us after all. With men like Bill and Ian sticking to the old ways and values, and Helen and Eddy getting set to raise a family here, and a guy like

Michael Reo willing to give the locals a boost instead of a shove, we may just survive our celebrated affluence and have a lot to be thankful for."

"Like Meghan's," Eddy proclaimed as their burgers, chicken and fries were being placed before them.

"Haven't you heard?" the waitress asked anxiously. "We're closing."

"What?" Eddy cried.

"After twenty-one years, we're out of here," she disclosed. "Burgers can't pay the rent they're now asking, so this is going to become an upscale Japanese restaurant."

Dumbfounded, the foursome looked as if they had just lost their best friend, and in a sense, they had.

"Sushi, anyone?" Helen jested.

"I would rather commit hara-kiri," Lieutenant Oliveri swore.